The Bear and the Wolf

Book 4 in the New World Series
By
Griff Hosker

Contents

The Bear and the Wolf...i
Prologue 2
Chapter 1 Erik.. 4
Chapter 2 Fótr 25
Chapter 3 Fótr 36
Chapter 4 Fótr 48
Chapter 5 Fótr 60
Chapter 6 Fótr 72
Chapter 7 Fótr 84
Chapter 8 Fótr 96
Chapter 9 Fótr 107
Chapter 10 Fótr 121
Chapter 11 Fótr 133
Chapter 12 Erik... 146
Chapter 13 Erik... 160
Chapter 14 Erik... 170
Chapter 15 Erik... 184
Chapter 16 Erik... 194
Chapter 17 Erik... 205
Fótr.. 219
Erik 221
The End... 222
Norse Calendar 223
Glossary.. 224
Historical Note... 228
Other books by Griff Hosker 231

Published by Sword Books Ltd 2020

Copyright © Griff Hosker First Edition 2020

The Bear and the Wolf

The author has asserted their moral right under the Copyright, Designs and Patents Act, 1988, to be identified as the author of this work. All Rights reserved. No part of this publication may be reproduced, copied, stored in a retrieval system, or transmitted, in any form or by any means, without the prior written consent of the copyright holder, nor be otherwise circulated in any form of binding or cover other than that in which it is published and without a similar condition being imposed on the subsequent purchaser.

A CIP catalogue record for this title is available from the British Library.

Cover by Design for Writers

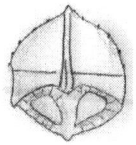

Prologue

In Valhalla the two brothers, Lars and Snorri, watched as the newly dead warriors walked with eyes filled with wonder into the Allfather's mead hall. They saw their sons, Siggi and Arne, along with Arne's son, Lars, as they approached them followed by the other men of their clan who had died in the battle with the Skraeling, the Penobscot. As with all newly dead warriors, they entered Valhalla with eyes wide as they took in the tables heaving with meats, cheese, mead and ale and warriors long dead. Snorri had but recently joined his brother, yet both shared the same mixed feelings as they neared their eldest sons. They were glad to see them but sad for it meant they had died.

Snorri turned to his brother, "It is but a little time since I came here. I thought that the clan would have returned across the seas by now."

Lars shook his head, "You know the Three Sisters, Snorri Long Fingers, they weave and they spin. Let us hear the tale of our sons and let us enjoy the moment."

It was just then that Siggi saw his father and rushed over, "This is Valhalla!"

Odin's commanding voice boomed out, "Clan of the Fox, you are welcome. There is mead and ale! Tell your brothers, here, of your glorious death!"

Arne sounded disappointed as he said, "I thought there would have been more warriors!"

Lars smiled, "Odin has many halls. This is the hall of our clans. We spend eternity with family and brothers in arms. Welcome, Arne and Lars, your son!"

As he grasped his son's arm Arne shook his head, "I have failed you, father! I have led the clan to disaster. Erik did all that he could to save us but…" he suddenly looked around, as did

Siggi. The others who had died were with them but not Erik. "Where is he, where is my brother?"

"Your brother?"

"Aye, Erik the Navigator! He was the one who came to help us back to the ship. The last I saw of him, he was alone on the top of the waterfall, defending Siggi here and then…"

Lars looked sad, "Then he has died without his sword." He shook his head, "I would have liked to have seen him again for Snorri here has told me of all that he did. He was a real Viking and a hero."

Arne nodded, "And I am not; I know that now. It was my vanity and my wife which led me to ignore the words of Snorri, Erik and my brother Fótr. I am ashamed now of the way I treated Fótr. He will be left to lead the clan."

Snorri waved a hand at the warriors with his son and nephew, "If there is a clan to lead. I see here the greatest warriors of the clan. Siggi, I thought you were going back to the east?"

Siggi's face showed the regret at listening to the wrong brother, "We might have been although Erik negotiated a peace with the Skraeling, the Mi'kmaq', and we could have stayed."

Arne nodded, miserably, "Which I ignored. The wrong brother led the clan."

"This was meant to be. We can curse the Norns all we like, here in the safety of Valhalla, but it will do little good. Fótr has had a great weight thrust upon his shoulders but the Norns spin for a purpose."

Snorri nodded, "And the volvas of the clan, Helga, Ada and the others, whilst not as powerful as my wife can hold the clan together while Fótr grows." He looked at his son, "They will go back to the east?"

He nodded, "I believe that they will for the warriors who died were the ones who wished to carve out a home in this savage wilderness. The ones who remain wish to go east and they seek a home in the Land of the Wolf."

Lars put his arm around his son, "Then let us drink some ale and toast the son who will never join us and whose spirit will forever fly as a seabird above the seas he loved so much. Let us drink to Erik the Navigator."

Chapter 1 Erik

Despair is the wrong word to use but it was close to despair that I felt as I was reborn in a new world with Laughing Deer and Stands Alone. The others had left me to return to Bear Island, and we were surrounded by the Penobscot who would hunt us down, kill me and enslave Laughing Deer and her sister once more. Yet even in the depths of despair, I felt hope for my dream had become reality. Gytha had promised me that it would, and I also had the hope that, on Bear Island, the clan would be waiting for me. The first thing we had to do was get as far north as we could as quickly as possible. Crossing the river had been difficult for Stands Alone would not come near to me but we had managed it. I hoped that we would now be able to lose the Penobscot. What lay ahead I had no idea for we had come south by sea. Laughing Deer had not passed this way either and so I would have to use my skills as a navigator, but on land. The sun showed me where north was and so I led us north along the first animal trail I found. I would shun the trails used by the Skraeling as the Penobscot would use those. I now saw that the coming of Bear Tooth into our lives had been important for without it I would not have been able to speak to Laughing Deer. Did her tribe know about the Norns too or was this thread mine alone?

I had my bow slung across my back and I had my seax in my hand. I had my ale skin and we had a little dried deer meat, but it would not last and I knew that we had many miles to walk. My other belongings were wrapped in my oiled cloak which I had tied across my back. The nights were still icily cold at times but

The Bear and the Wolf

each day brought more warmth. The march through the forest would keep us warm. In my head, I estimated a hundred or so miles, possibly more, as I knew the coast was riven with gullies, ravines and rivers. We might have to backtrack to find our way. I did not know what Laughing Deer would make of our clan but the Norns had bound us together. I kept glancing over my shoulder as we moved ever north. Laughing Deer held her sister's hand. She carried their belongings over her back as did I and I rued that we did not have a boat. I wondered if I could have risked stealing one. I dismissed the thought immediately for the Penobscot would have caught us. We now had a chance to escape; it was a slim one, but I would take it.

The animal trail descended to a narrow stream and, looking at the sun, I realised that we had been walking for some hours. I could continue but the younger girl would be tiring. I pointed to the stream, "We will rest there and eat. I will go back down the trail."

Laughing Deer nodded, "Do not hurry back for we need to make water and my sister fears you."

I could do little about that. I dropped my gear except for my sword and bow and headed back down the trail. I saw our footprints. They were distinctive and would lead the Penobscot directly to us. We would have to walk in the stream for a while and hope to throw them from our trail. I heard noises in the deep and dark forest, but I knew that they were the noises of animals and not hunters. I backtracked for half a mile but heard no noise which suggested danger. I headed for the stream.

When I reached the beck, I saw that Laughing Deer and her sister had collected some crustaceans. She smiled at me, "These are good eating. They are better cooked, but they will have to do this way."

I took the two she offered me gratefully and, using my seax, ripped them open and sucked out the succulent flesh. "They are good. Has your sister eaten?"

"She has." As the little girl still eyed me suspiciously, Laughing Deer said, "It will take time for her to grow used to you; the Penobscot hurt her. She will be like this with all men for a while." I nodded for after their experience then it was understandable. "Where do we go?"

I pointed north and west, "We head for the coast. My clan has settled on an island and they have a ship. If we can reach there then we will be safe."

"How many days is it?"

"I do not know but Bear Tooth said it was the land the people of the Mi'kmaq tribe occupied when you were taken."

Her face fell. "Then it will take at least seven days of walking. We will have to head towards the setting sun for a while as there are deep ravines ahead and my sister cannot swim."

"Should we walk up this piece of water?" It meant travelling in the opposite direction and take us closer to our enemies, but I trusted Laughing Deer.

She nodded, "It will turn and eventually take us in the right direction and the water will hide our trail." She turned to her sister, "Take off your mockasin; we do not wish to ruin them." As her sister obeyed, Laughing Deer turned to me, "What about your mockasin?"

I shook my head, "These are made of sealskin and they are tough. I will lead. You must tell me when we are to leave the water and if you need to stop."

"I will. We are tougher than we look and despite my sister's silence, we are both grateful for you have saved us. If it was not for my sister, then I would have taken my own life. The Penobscot are a cruel and evil people."

With that sobering thought in my head, I picked up my gear and headed upstream. The water did not come over my boots and I knew that it would become shallower. I was able to hop occasionally from rock to rock, but Stands Alone could not and our progress was not as swift as I would have wished.

Laughing Deer said after we had travelled perhaps half a mile, "We need to leave the stream for the sides will be too steep for Stands Alone to climb."

I looked ahead and saw that Laughing Deer was right. I might have scaled the sides and possibly Laughing Deer, but the child would have struggled. I nodded and we crossed to the right bank. The sun was getting lower in the sky and we would need to find somewhere to shelter. I remembered the sound of the large cats Ebbe and I had heard as we had sailed the snekke. I did not wish

The Bear and the Wolf

to fall foul of those. The going was harder than I had expected, and I had to help both Laughing Deer and her sister up some of the more difficult stretches. It would have been easier had Stands Alone allowed me to hold her hand or touch her back, but she recoiled when my hand went near her and I had to pull the two of them up with Laughing Deer holding Stands Alone's hand.

When we reached the top, I found another animal trail and recognised the prints of the small deer I had hunted. Laughing Deer pointed to the right and I followed the trail which wound through the trees. I had not seen any berries nor fruits and wondered what we would eat. The crustaceans we had eaten at the stream seemed a distant memory. I almost despaired of finding a place to camp for the sun was setting when we came upon a small clearing in the trees. Laughing Deer said, "We will stop here. I will make a shelter while you find food."

That would be easier said than done but I dropped my gear and nocked an arrow. I headed through the woods, avoiding the trail. I think had it been earlier, or later then I would have had no success but the large grey squirrel which appeared just above me timed his foray into the forest badly. At ten paces I could not miss, and the animal was pinned to the tree. I retrieved the arrow and squirrel and headed back. I saw the unmistakeable pellets from the long-eared animals on the ground, and I decided that I would set some traps. To my surprise, Laughing Deer had fashioned a shelter from a pliant bush and was now covering the top with fronds of fir which she had gathered. I learned that every Mi'kmaq had this skill and they could make a good shelter within a short time.

She beamed when she saw the squirrel, "Give me your knife and I will prepare it. Light a fire."

"Are you certain? The smell of the smoke will carry."

"I do not think any Penobscot are close. They may find our trail but we need to cook this meat. I will make a fire with little smoke."

I know that Bear Tooth was impressed by the flint I used as it made a fire far quicker than his method. I saw Stands Alone watching me with wonder as I sparked the flint into the dried leaves and grass. Blowing on it I soon had flames and Laughing Deer carefully placed dead wood upon it. She poured water from her skin into the pot and then began to skilfully skin the squirrel. Leaving her to it I went to set some traps for the long-eared animals. Darkness fell quickly and the small fire was comforting.

She came to hand me the seax, "Stands Alone is weary. I will feed her first." Her eyes pleaded with me. "If you could stay away from the fire it will be easier. She fears men and I would have her calm while she eats."

"Of course." I went a little way from the fire and the shelter and took out my whetstone. I put an edge on the seax. My sword was still sharp and who knew when I would need a weapon again? When it was sharp, I sheathed it and sat on a fallen tree. The navigator in me wanted to know precisely where I was. I felt lost without my maps. When we reached Bear Island, I would make another.

A little while later Laughing Deer found me. "Thank you, she is asleep. You are kind and unlike any man I have ever met."

"You were sent to my dreams and the volva of our clan told me that you would change my life."

The little girl was in a deep sleep, and Laughing Deer handed me a bowl of food. "Volva?"

I used the word Bear Tooth had used, "Witch!"

"Ah." She did not seem upset by the concept. "The food is good?"

"The food is good."

"I bring great danger to you, Erik."

"How so?"

"The son of the chief of the Penobscot wants me for his woman."

"He would marry you?"

"No, for he has a wife. He wants me for his bed; by taking me each night he shows the power of his tribe over mine. He is a cruel man and he is the reason Stands Alone is as she is. He hurt her. He will hunt us down and try to capture us. If you were alone then you would be able to reach your island."

"Our threads are bound, and I am content."

She nodded and after cleaning the bowls she took the skin of the squirrel into the woods so that she could make water upon it. When she returned, she lay down and she patted the ground next to her. "Come, lie here with me." I lay down and she pressed her body into my back and put her arms around me. Our warmth would make Stands Alone and the two of us warmer. It was the Mi'kmaq way of sleeping. "If we reach your island, we can lie together properly but for now, this is all that there can be." She kissed the nape of my neck and I was content.

When I woke and checked the traps, I found that I had caught just one animal, but it would make a meal. I skinned it after we ate the last of the squirrel then we headed north. Perhaps it was my imagination but Stands Alone did not recoil as much when I passed her. When I woke, I saw her smiling at me, shyly, from behind Laughing Deer. It was a start. The march that day was easier because we were heading, for the most part, downhill. The trail we followed was also wider and I worried about that. When the rain came, I was pleased because that would help disguise our tracks. I had my sealskin cape, but Laughing Deer and her sister did not. I gave the cape to them so that they could be dry. I had stood many a watch and been soaked; it would do me no harm. The rain stopped during the afternoon and we made a camp by a small stream. I had no accurate way of recording how far we had travelled but I knew that we were roughly twenty miles from the falls. Had Stands Alone allowed it, I would have carried her upon my shoulders and we would have made better time.

I set more traps while Laughing Deer cooked the long-eared animal. This time Stands Alone allowed me to eat with them and it was the start of a slight change in her. Laughing Deer spoke in my ear as we lay down to sleep. "I think we come to a large body of water soon."

"The sea?"

"No. The Penobscot sometimes travel to these waters. They carry their boats and they fish there. We will have to be careful for they could have got ahead of us."

I had not thought of that. I had expected them to follow us and I had hoped that the rain would have washed away our sign. The thought that we might have to pass through a warband of Penobscot did not fill me with optimism. I touched the hammer around my neck. I prayed that Gytha was still watching over me although I had not heard her voice in my head since Laughing Deer had found me.

The Bear and the Wolf

The next day we found a small river and I followed it south for it might lead to the sea. It led, as Laughing Deer had predicted, to a large body of fresh water. We refilled the water skin and the now-empty ale skin from the river before making our way to somewhere we could cross. We backtracked up the river until we found some rocks. I hated the detour for we could have crossed the river when we had first seen it. I kept thinking I had Ebbe and Fótr with me. It was not her fault but Stands Alone was a burden. Once we crossed, I led us due east for the water was too big an obstacle and we could not get around it easily any other way. I decided that I would follow the next river we found directly to the sea.

As we walked, I said, "Laughing Deer, do you know how to make a birch bark boat?"

"How? Yes. Could I make one? No. I have not the skill in peeling the bark from the birch. Why do you ask?"

"I feel lost in this forest and if we could fashion a boat then I would be happier for we could use the rivers. We will need one in any case if we are to get to Bear Island."

"I cannot see that we will be able to build one for I have seen them made but never made one. That is the work of a warrior." I was depressed at her words for I knew not how we could make one.

We had no food left when we camped and so I sought a stream. I took my bow and I hunted fish. I managed to take two and I left some lines in the water with bone hooks. We ate the fish raw for having heard that the Penobscot used these waters I was loath to light a fire and draw them to us. We adopted the same positions that night as we slept. I was at the fore of the shelter, Laughing Deer behind me and Stands Alone behind her. The next morning Stands Alone even smiled at me although I still had not heard her utter a sound!

The next day, as we set off, I was convinced that I could smell the sea. As we were surrounded by woods that was impossible, but I think it was a yearning in me to be closer to that which I knew the best, the ocean. I wondered how the clan was doing. Had they got over the battle and who was their leader now that Arne and Siggi were dead? Fótr and Ada were ever in my mind as I still felt responsible for both of them and for my

The Bear and the Wolf

son and daughter. We had travelled, perhaps a mile, when we spied the river. It was too wide to ford for there were rocks and it was rough and wild. That was reassuring for it meant that the Penobscot could not use it.

The slopes on which the trees grew were steep and we were forced to walk closer to the river. That proved to be our undoing. We had just turned a bend and the river had quietened from the tumultuous roar when I spied the birch bark boat on the bank and the three Penobscot who were eating there. I held up my hand and Laughing Deer, seeing them too, stopped. Stands Alone did not and when she bumped into Laughing Deer she looked ahead and saw the Penobscot. It was then that she uttered her first sound and it was a scream. Even as the three Skraeling looked up and saw us I had dropped my gear and nocked an arrow, "Get up the slope! I will hold them off as long as I can!"

"No, we stand with you!" Laughing Deer's hand drew my seax from my scabbard as I took aim at the nearest warrior who was fifty paces from me. Laughing Deer would not go back willingly to her captors and would fight for her freedom. The warrior who raced at me had a bone vest on, and his shaven head had yellow and white feathers hanging down. In his hand, he carried a long spear and a club.

I released my first arrow and nocked another. The warrior looked down in horror as the metal tipped arrow drove through his bone vest. It drove him back and I heard his head crack as his skull smashed into a river rock. His death made the other two slow and I was able to send a second arrow, this time flint tipped, into the shoulder of a second warrior. They both screamed in anger and, with stone clubs and bone daggers they ran at me. One of them was bleeding heavily from my arrow. My third arrow hit not the one I aimed at, the one who was closing with me, but the wounded one. The unwounded warrior jinked to the side and my arrow hit the wounded one in the eye. I hurled my bow to the ground and drew my sword.

The last warrior was fast and agile. He hurled his stone club at me and it hit my shoulder. It was only the fact that I had the sword in two hands that saved me. I swept the sword up as he slashed his bone knife at me. My sword tore through his bone vest and into his chest. That was what saved me for his knife did

The Bear and the Wolf

not rip across my throat as he had intended but my forehead. Even so, blood briefly blinded me. The Skraeling was like a berserker and although badly wounded he raised his knife to end my life. Laughing Deer slashed with my seax and cut his arm to the bone. The bone knife fell to the ground and I back swung, and my sword almost severed his head.

I turned, "Are you hurt?"

Laughing Deer shook her head and said, "But you are!"

"We will deal with the wound later. Stay here while I see if there are more of them."

I sheathed my sword and wiped some river water across my face. I picked up my bow and, using the trees for cover, hurried down to the birch bark boat. I could see no sign of any more of them. The boat had paddles and they had left food. The Norns had spun and I would not spurn the opportunity the boat provided. I ran back to the other two and said, "Come, we will take their boat and sail down this river."

She shook her head, "No, first I see to the wound!" She knelt and scooped some water from the river, "Stands Alone, tear Yellow Feather's bone vest and give me the hide thongs which bind it together."

As she did so I said, "You know him?"

"He is Angry Voice's friend." Angry Voice was the warrior who wished Laughing Deer as his woman. She bathed my head and then Stands Alone handed her the thongs. She fastened them tightly about my forehead and the flow of blood slowed. I had honey and some vinegar left with the gear I had brought from the camp. When we had the chance then I would heal the wound myself.

"Come, let us go while we can." I shaded my eyes and saw that the sun would soon set, and I wished to be on the water when that happened. They picked up their belongings and then Stands Alone did something which surprised me. She picked up Yellow Feather's bone knife and, pulling down his breeks, she took his manhood, spat on it and hurled it into the river.

Laughing Deer looked sad and she put her arm around her sister, "Yellow Feather was one of those who hurt her!"

I nodded, the Norns threads appeared to have bound Stands Alone too.

The Bear and the Wolf

I put my belongings in the bottom of the boat where I saw some bags of food and two stone-tipped spears along with the fur of an animal; I did not recognise what kind of animal it was. It was more than big enough for us and with a chilly night on the river ahead of us it might prove useful. Laughing Deer placed Stands Alone in the middle, covering her with the fur, and then she sat in the bow. I lifted the stern and walked the boat into the river. I did not wish to risk ripping out her hull. I clambered aboard and the river took us. "Do not paddle. I will use this one to steer. Watch for rocks and tell me if you see white water."

I needed to learn to steer this strange vessel quickly. I found that it responded well to the paddle. A wide movement made an exaggerated turn and I was soon confident that I could navigate around larger rocks. The three Skraeling had been looking for us. Perhaps Angry Voice had sent out many of his warriors in small bands to try to capture us. We had been lucky. Now we had to use that luck. I tossed my cloak to Laughing Deer. "Take the two spears and fasten them with leather thongs to make a cross. When that is done see if you can fasten the cloak to them."

"Why?"

"If we have a wind then we can use it to become a sail and if we have rain it will provide a shelter."

"A sail?"

"Like the one on my ship, the one which sailed away."

"Where will you fix it?"

That was the problem for it would not be secured. "It will have to be held but if we have a strong enough wind then it will move us faster than paddles alone." I was really doing all that I could to affect an escape. I knew that the three bodies would be found and, even if there was a delay, Angry Voice would have others out looking for us and the wild water upstream would tell the Penobscot which direction we had taken. I had been lucky with Yellow Feathers and his companions. I could not count on such luck again. When she had finished, I said, "Now fold it up so that it will fit along the side of the boat. Laughing Deer, do the Penobscot fight at night?"

"Not unless they have to, and they do not like to travel at night."

"Then we can keep on down the river."

"We could but is that not dangerous?"

"Is it not more dangerous to make a camp and then find ourselves captured? Trust me, Laughing Deer, I am happier in a boat, any boat!" I could see that Stands Alone was afraid for she clung to the sides of the boat. "Fear not, little one, for these are well-made vessels and I know the water. I sailed a ship for more than thirty days without sight of land. I can sail along a river."

It was arrogant, of course, and I meant only to make the child less fearful but the Norns heard my words, perhaps the Allfather decided that I had grown too big for my boots but, as the sun set, the river spilt into a water which was a like a small sea and I was forced to stop.

Laughing Deer turned, "There are many such pools of water. Some are so large that they can take a day to cross."

I nodded, "And we cannot hide, can we?" I put my hand in the water and I felt a current. "This one must have an outlet. We will let the current take us there, but I will not leave this sea until I know there is neither a waterfall nor a shoal of rocks at the far end. You can both sleep for a while and I will wake you if I need you."

"I can stay awake!"

"Sleep. There is a full moon tonight and I will know when we near the outlet." She said nothing but soon I heard the gentle sound of her sleeping. I was content for I was on the water once more. This was neither *'Jötnar'* nor *'Njörðr'* but it would do. I put my steering paddle over so that we could close with one bank. If there was sudden danger, I wished to be close enough to land to escape it. It was cold and my breath appeared before me but Laughing Deer and Stands Alone would be warm beneath the fur. I saw the trees looming up and straightened her up. I had something to guide me in the absence of a compass. I kept the moon to larboard and knew that the water ran north to south. The current was not strong, and the motion was a gentle one. My passengers would be comfortable. Indeed, I was comfortable. This was even easier than sailing the snekke. The moon was the only indication of the passage of time. It rose and then dipped as it began to set. It was then I heard the sound of water ahead and felt the birch bark boat pick up speed.

"Laughing Deer, it is time to watch. Laughing Deer!"

"I am awake. Have I slept long?"

"I have not needed you before, but I do now. If you see bubbling water, then tell me for there may be rocks. Use your hands, along with your voice if you see any."

I watched her lean over the bow, and I prepared for a rough ride. In the event, the rough water only lasted for forty paces and although it was white tipped there were no rocks. I saw her beaming face turn to me and knew that we were through. I was in familiar territory and I had done this before. I was able to watch dawn from its first lightening to the warm glow from the east and then the bright light as it climbed over the trees to our left. I saw the river as it twisted and turned. I was able to gauge its size. It had grown and was now forty paces wide. I was desperate to make water but did not wish to risk landing.

Laughing Deer must have had the same need for she asked, "Can we not land for Stands Alone will need to make water?"

Reluctantly I put the paddle over and headed for the larboard bank. The river had a curve and where it had slowed it had deposited sand; it would do. I jumped out of the water and, lifting the stern, pulled the boat up. I held out my hand and, to my amazement, Stands Alone took it almost without thinking. Laughing Deer beamed as she climbed out too. They disappeared into the trees and I just dropped my breeks and used the river. I went to the improvised sail. The two spears were little bigger than Laughing Deer and it was not much of a sail. I saw that where Stands Alone had slept was a thwart made of a cross piece of timber. While I waited, I used my seax to make a hole in it. It took me until Laughing Deer and her sister returned to break through the wood and complete the task.

"I am going to try to make a hole for the spear to go through and to make a sail. You will need to place Stands Alone in the bow for when I ask you will need to fit the sail. Go into the woods and find berries to eat and climbers." I handed her my seax. "Cut them. They will need to be twice as long as me." I took out my sword. It was still sharp, and I used it to twist and turn. It bored through the wood. When I was satisfied, I tried the spear. It was a tight fit, but it held. I shouted, "Laughing Deer."

They returned and I held the boat pointing downstream so that they could board. I took the climbers and placed them by my

The Bear and the Wolf

feet. Stands Alone smiled as she placed a large leaf with a selection of berries on the thwart next to the stern. She was warming to me. This would be a clement day with a hot sun and I was grateful for the breeze which helped to move us along. I might have considered trying out my improvised sail except that the river still twisted and turned. I had decided that I would only use it once we reached the sea and had to contend with waves. I remembered how Bear Tooth's people had suffered when they had tried their boats in the open sea.

It was when I began to hear the sea birds that my hopes were raised. Laughing Deer looked up as they screeched in the sky above us and then her look of happiness was replaced by terror. She pointed upstream and, turning, I saw five birch bark boats and they were manned by the Penobscot. Angry Voice had found us!

"Paddle! Stands Alone get beneath the fur!"

I now had to paddle and to steer. Even as I dug in with the paddle, I knew that it was a race I could not win. The sea might be close but, as I glanced behind, I saw that they had five Skraeling in each boat and they were gaining. We were lighter but they had twice the power of Laughing Deer and me. We had to risk the sail.

"Laughing Deer put up the sail!"

She nodded and made her way back to the sail. I used the river to help us. I steered to the banks where the current was swifter and the river shallower. It was only a slight risk for us but it slowed down the progress that the Penobscot made. I had to watch ahead and behind. I saw that they were still inexorably gaining. Had they wished to kill us they could have used their bows, but they wanted us alive and that gave us a chance.

Laughing Deer struggled but she eventually managed to put the spear in the hole. As soon as she did, we leapt forward but the sail was not secured and I knew that the hole would soon be worn wider and the sail rendered useless.

"Tie the climbers to the bottom of the cloak and fasten them to the thwart." I did not know if she would be able to manage to tie them to the top corners of the cloak, but the bottom would have to do. Looking back, I saw that although we had made a gap the Penobscot were now working harder to close the gap and

The Bear and the Wolf

then I saw the sea. At least, I saw the islands in the middle of the estuary and saw the waves so that I knew the sea was close. It would be dangerous to risk it with my two passengers, but that danger was less than the risk of being captured.

My slight inattention almost brought us disaster as I hit an oncoming wave, not head-on but at an angle and Stands Alone screamed. "Go to your sister, Laughing Deer, and keep her close to the sail! Pray to your gods."

She nodded and shouted, "I trust you, Erik, and I trust this magic!" She pointed at the sail. It was only a cloak, but it billowed and pushed us on. I was not certain how long it would last but if it could take us away from the Penobscot then it would have served its purpose.

The wind was from the north and west. If this was the snekke then I could have used the sheets and stays to help me steer the boat. I peered under the sail and saw, far ahead, the open sea. There were still islands dotted in the distance and I vaguely recollected where we were. When we had sailed to the River of Peace, I had seen some rivers with similar islands. Which one were we in? I had to concentrate on steering us so that we hit the waves straight on and not at an angle. The fact that the weight of the boat was in the middle and stern helped us as the bow naturally rose. I glanced behind just as one of the Penobscot boats hit a wave badly and the boat and crew disappeared. We were now extending our lead but if Angry Voice truly wanted Laughing Deer then he would keep going as long as he could. I risked taking us to the south and east a little. It was only a minor adjustment of the paddle, but it meant we used the full power of the wind and we leapt forward. The next time I turned back the Penobscot had given up. I held the same course until we had left the river. I saw nothing behind and so I headed for the last island which lay ahead. It was a good half-mile from the nearest piece of land, and I would risk landing. The air was cold for it was still relatively early in the year and the sea had yet to warm up. We needed the fur more than ever. I needed to secure the top of the sail. I sailed until we had passed the island and, when I turned the paddle and we lost the wind, we stopped dead. I jumped into the icy sea and lifted the boat onto the beach. We had escaped the Penobscot, now we had to battle the sea! This would be a true test of Erik the Navigator.

After I had helped the other two from my boat I ran to the highest point on the tiny island. There were no trees and just a couple of hardy shrubs. Lying flat I peered north towards the river mouth. I saw nothing. I watched for what seemed like an age for I needed to know if we were being pursued. We were not and I returned to the boat.

"We will eat and then I will try to make the sail work better. See if there are shellfish. I do not think that there is wood for a fire but if you can find some then I will light one."

I went to the boat. I had work to do. I really needed nails but the nearest ones were on Bear Island. Instead, I used the stone heads of four arrows. I broke the shaft off and then used the hilt of my seax to hammer them into the sides of the boat; the barbs helped to dig them in. I then took four leather thongs from around my sealskin boots and made loops. I passed the honeysuckle climbers through the loops. It would allow me to move the sail to steerboard or larboard. I could use the wind rather than the paddle to steer. Here, we were in the lee of the small island but as soon as we left it then the wind would take my improvised sail and make us fly

Laughing Deer handed me some shellfish and I used my seax to take the meat. I still had some fishing lines and hooks. I would trail them from the stern. "We will not stop again until we find an island or a safe beach and that may not be for a day or so. I would stay here but the Penobscot are still close and they may seek us out. Make water now and do whatever else you need to. When we are at sea you either hold it in or go over the side."

Laughing Deer nodded, "And what of you? You need to sleep."

"If I can find an island between here and Bear Island then I will but do not worry about me. I am a navigator." As soon as we were aboard Laughing Deer and I paddled. We did not have to do it for long as the wind caught us, and we sped across the water. I had Laughing Deer and her sister move along the boat until we were well balanced. It had not mattered much in the river but now that was crucial. I looked at the sky and saw that it was clear. The Allfather favoured us. So long as the skies were clear, and we had the wind then we had a chance. If a storm blew up or we had heavy rain, then I would have to attempt to head to the coast and that would not be easy.

Within a short time, I saw another island in the distance and I contemplated stopping there for rest but, as we neared it, I saw another group of islands another five or so miles further away. It was still daylight and the weather held; I wanted as much distance between us and the enemy as possible. The islands were within sight of the coast and if a storm blew up, we could either sit it out on the island or try to get to the mainland. I saw, as we approached, that the island had some stumpy trees and I saw seabirds. We could light a fire and we might even have eggs to eat. By my calculation, we were fifteen or so miles from the island where we had eaten seafood and that was four miles from the last place we had seen the Penobscot. It was worth the risk.

I sailed us around into the lee of the island. We slowed and I let the cloak flap. I jumped into chest-deep water and pushed the boat towards the sand. Laughing Deer now understood what we had to do and she jumped out when the water was shallower. It lightened the load and she was able to help draw the boat up. The two of us drew the boat up on to the beach and I took the spear out of the hole I had made. Already it had worn looser, and I could see wear and tear on the spear. I hoped it would get us to Bear Island; after that, it would not matter for the clan would be there and we would be safe.

A climb to the top of the island confirmed that it was uninhabited. The danger from the smoke was minimal as the wind was blowing north and east and the many islands would make it hard for an enemy to identify its location. However, I was now convinced that the Penobscot, if they still hunted us, would have to use the land. Laughing Deer and Stands Alone had gathered more shellfish, some seaweed and dug up some edible tubers for our stew. There were pools of rainwater and she used those, with a little seawater for seasoning, to cook the food. After we had eaten, we cleaned my wound and I applied some of the vinegar and then smeared it with honey. Laughing Deer did not see any sign of badness and the wound smelled healthy. All was well. This time the shelter she made had the fur from the boat as a bed and, after we had eaten, I lay down on it and was asleep, instantly.

That night I dreamed, and it was a complicated one.

I heard Gytha's voice, but I did not see her. Instead, I saw many warriors, mainly Penobscot and they were fighting the Mi'kmaq. I saw Chief Wandering Moos and he was being assailed. Gytha's voice said, 'Aid them, Erik, for this is your destiny.' And then the image faded, and darkness enveloped me but Gytha continued. 'This is your land, and this is your duty. The fox will become a wolf and you will be the bear.' Then the light came, and I saw a mighty waterfall. It was bigger than the one where Arne had died, in fact, it looked as wide as a sea. Water crashed down and then I awoke.

It was raining and Laughing Deer was fetching the sail to lay against the entrance to our shelter. She was wet but she laughed in the dark. "It is good that we did not sail in the night, Erik. This was a wise decision." As she snuggled next to me, I wondered about the waterfall and what it meant. I did not go immediately back to sleep. I listened to the rain pounding on my oiled cloak. I had known when I had dreamed of Laughing Deer, that my future might be with her but I had thought I would take her east on *'Gytha'* and that we would begin a new life there. The battle with the Penobscot and the departure of my clan had forced me to think again about my future. It was no longer Laughing Deer and me, there was Stands Alone too. Was I to stay here? When I reached Bear Island would I have to say goodbye to Ada, Fótr, my son and daughter? When the rain ceased, I managed to fall asleep, but it was a fitful one and I did not rise refreshed.

I managed to extricate myself from Laughing Deer and I stepped out on to a damp and soggy island. I saw that the birch bark boat had filled with rain. I emptied the rainwater into the pot we used for cooking. A hot meal before we braved the sea would do us good and having lost our enemies there was not as much urgency. I could sail without taking quite as many risks. I took some dry wood which Laughing Deer had placed beneath our shelter and I lit the fire. I had just got it going when Laughing Deer appeared and, putting her arms around me she kissed me, hard.

The Bear and the Wolf

"What was that for?"

"I did not thank you for slaying Yellow Feather and the others." She gave me a chaste smile beneath hooded eyes, "And besides we both know that we are meant to be together. When we reach your Bear Island then Stands Alone can sleep with the other children there and we can lie together."

I had not explained yet, about Ada, and that would be tricky. Instead, I smiled. "I think my island is two or three days north of here. I vaguely recognise this island. If we have a benign wind, then we will sight it in two days. I will make some adjustments to the boat and you can cook food. The sea is chilly at this time of year and your sister looks frail."

I used the Mi'kmaq word weak as I did not know frail and Laughing Deer shook her head, "She is not weak but you are right, she needs to eat more and shellfish and tubers will not make her stronger."

I pointed to the sea, "One advantage of being at sea is that we can catch bigger fish. We do not have to eat them raw for there are many uninhabited islands between the mainland and Bear Island." I went to the boat and inverted it to drain the last of the water from it. I also checked the seams; they appeared to be holding but I wanted pine tar or seal oil to seal it. I smiled to myself as I righted it. When we reached Bear Island then we would not need the boat!

We left in the middle of the morning. The wind, which had veered in the night, now came from the south. It explained the rain. Had the wind been from the west it would have been a dry wind. Stands Alone smiled more now and I realised why. Each day took us further from the Penobscot. I wondered when she would speak again. Our progress was not as quick as I would have hoped, and I kept to the channel between the line of uninhabited islands and the mainland. The storm the night before had been a warning and I would heed it. If Stands Alone still did not talk at least she smiled occasionally. When the line I had baited with some animal guts from the long-eared animal caught a fish which was as long as my leg from my knee to my foot, she clapped her hands with delight. I used my seax to end its life and then gutted it while the wind took the sail and kept us on course. I threw the guts to the screaming sea birds above my head. That too made Stands Alone's eyes sparkle. I did not mind the birds. They were the spirits of sailors lost at sea. I might have known them, and their noise was just a language I could not speak.

As the afternoon approached evening, I sought the largest island I could see. This one had no undergrowth at all and that meant the sail would have to double as our home for the night. Thanks to the rain we had enough water, but I missed my mead and my ale. We still had a little kindling left and we used that to light a fire with the driftwood we found on the beach. I remembered that it had been a piece of driftwood I had found on Orkneyjar which had led me across the ocean. *Wyrd*. We sat beneath the shelter of the sail as clouds scudded from the south. The wind that brought them was slightly warmer than they had been, and I wondered what lands lay to the south. I shook my head; that voyage was for another. I had done with sailing on the Great Sea.

I turned the fish when I saw the skin on the bottom had blackened and the flesh had begun to flake. As I sat down and with Stands Alone nestling her head in her sister's lap, Laughing Deer asked, "What is your land like, Erik? I know that Bear Island is not your real home so, across the sea, where do you live and what are your homes like?"

"They are totally unlike yours. We stay in one place and we farm. We raise animals like sheep and cattle." I had to use the Norse words and her blank expressions showed me that she had no concept of them. I tried to explain them to her and then I realised that when we reached Bear Island, I could show them to her. "Our homes, you will also see on Bear Island for we used the earth to make walls and the trees to make the framework. We all live in large halls and we have a fire burning in the centre so that when the snow comes, we are warm." She nodded. "However, there are places which are bigger than our villages and there they build in stone. Some of the homes have an upstairs." That was the hardest concept of all to explain and I was grateful when the fish was ready, and we could eat it. I put large pieces on the three wooden platters. We could all eat more and there would still be enough left for the next day. Laughing Deer insisted that, as the warrior, I should have the best part, the head. Up until that point, we had largely eaten stews to make the paltry amounts of meat we had go further. The fish felt like a substantial meal and that night I felt almost full.

With the cloak and spears making a lean-to and the remains of the fire before us we lay together. I had my back to the fire and then Laughing Deer lay against me and Stands Alone on the other side. There was a difference that night for Laughing Deer faced me and her arms wrapped around me. She kissed me and her tongue tantalised me. I felt myself becoming aroused and forced those thoughts from me.

When she realised that I was not responding Laughing Deer whispered, "Have I offended you?"

"No, but Stands Alone is there and I would not cause the memories which are fading to be resurrected."

She kissed me again, "You are a good man and you are right. Soon we shall be on Bear Island and we can be as one."

The Norns were spinning and when we left the next day the wind became more unpredictable and we were hit by rogue waves which soaked us. I began to fear that we would not reach the island and then, through the murky spray, I saw the island. "Laughing Deer, we must paddle for the boat is struggling." As I dug in with my paddle, I looked for the masts of the two drekar. The fact that I could not see them did not worry me for Fótr and Padraig might have decided to step the masts, especially if there had been a storm. Being so close to the island I forgot my hurts and the aching in my arms and I dug the paddle in to power us through the water. I saw Stands Alone take the third paddle and try to help. That she did not move us much mattered not, she was part of the crew and fighting.

We were just three hundred paces from the entrance to the bay when I saw that the ships were not there. Until then I had deluded myself that they were hidden by the land but as we entered an empty bay without even a single animal clucking, then I knew they had gone. They had returned to the east. We paddled in and Laughing Deer turned and frowned. I could not lie to her. "My clan has gone, and I am abandoned. My life and yours is now bound here in the west.

Just at that moment, a freak wind whistled through the hall Gytha and Snorri had used. The door was open and it sounded like a voice as it wailed. It was a sign. Gytha had tried to warn me in the dream and I had misunderstood. The clan had gone and I would remain. *Wyrd.*

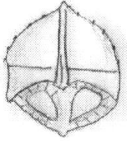

Chapter 2 Fótr

I am Fótr Larsson and I now lead the Clan of the Fox. I did not choose to do so but after the disaster of the roaring water where my two brothers, my nephew and the best warriors in the clan died, then I had no choice. My father had led the clan and he was followed by my brother, Arne Larsson. It was he who had led the clan to the battle we need not have fought but it was my brother, Erik, Erik the Navigator, who had saved the clan. I had mourned my brother Arne's death, but Erik was a harder loss to bear. I had now been given the responsibility of sailing the ship back to the east to seek the Land of the Wolf. Only I had made that voyage and I had been little more than a child when I had done so. Padraig and Aed were the other two who had skills as navigators and they sailed *'Njörðr'* and *'Jötnar'* while I steered *'Gytha'*, the drekar which we had made when we had lived on the island. I was the one with the compass and the hourglass. They had copies of the maps which Erik had so meticulously made. In the middle of the ocean, they would be of little use but we had a long voyage to reach the vast emptiness of the ocean. We would retrace our course, the one we had followed when we had come to this New World. We would sail north and east along the coast until we came to the island where Erik and I had been attacked by fierce Skraeling. Then we would head east by northeast back to our former home. Aed estimated almost a thousand miles before we reached the last spit of land where began the abyss of the ocean. I took out the spell which Ada and the volva of the clan had spun. They had incorporated their hair, my son's and mine. They had woven runes into it and given it to me to keep me safe. I was now the navigator and while I did not feel that I was the one to lead them, the clan did and I would not let them down.

We took animals with us. We could not take all of them for we had too many people. We had two cows and four ewes along with a pig and some hens. Before we left we slaughtered the bulls and rams and salted their meat. It was sad to have to do that but we needed the meat and they would die alone otherwise. This way they served the clan. Aed, on the snekke, had one of the ewes. That way we would all have milk. I knew that, once we left the land, we would have to feed them grain and that would not sustain them. At some point, we might have to slaughter the ones we carried, and I did not relish that prospect. It took days to take all that we could. There were many things we left behind for people were more important than objects. We packed as much as we could below the decks and then tied the barrels of food, ale and water on the top. The animals were at the prow and the barrels spread out to give balance.

As we left Bear Island, I felt great sadness. The dead were buried on our island home and they would be a reminder that the Clan of the Fox had made a mark. The turf and wood buildings would crumble, and the forests would reclaim the fields we had cleared but we had made a mark. I had left my brother's belongings in the home he had shared with Ada. His bear cloak lay on the sleeping platform he and Ada had shared. I am not sure that Ada believed he was dead for she said that she wished to leave behind all that he had used. She had his son and his daughter to remind her of her husband. I had thought to take his spare seaxes, seal skin boots and hide jerkin but something made me leave them there, along with his mail. When I thought about it I knew that I had enough for we might be fighting the sea; we would not have to battle other men. Until we reached land then we could forget other clans and men. When we left Erik's hut intact it was as though it was a memorial to him. I would keep his memory in my head.

That first day we sailed in familiar waters for I had steered **'Njörðr'** when we had hunted the whale. We sailed north and east keeping the land to the west. I led and Aed kept the snekke between Padraig's **'Njörðr'** and me. Although the decks of all three ships were filled there were but twenty-eight warriors who remained and they were spread out. Erik had told me that the winds generally helped when sailing east and I hoped so for, if we had to row, then it would be boys and women who would have to man the oars with the handful of warriors we carried. I had Ebbe with me and the Skraeling who was now a member of the clan. Bear Tooth had been saved by Erik and that, in turn, had saved us. The two of them were with me at the steering board. For Bear Tooth the voyage meant he was leaving the land of his birth to join us but he was happy to do so. He believed in his own version of the Norns. His family was all dead; we had killed his father and his brothers, but he did not hold that against us and was as much a member of the clan as any. As yet he did not look like a Viking, but I knew that, over time, he would.

"What is your plan, Fótr?" The newest member of our clan was more curious about the voyage than afraid. When we had hunted the whale he had been terrified but having faced that ordeal, all else seemed easy.

I laughed, "A plan? That suggests that there is some order in our life and there is none!" I sighed and calmed myself. I was young but I had to behave as though I was older. When Erik had first steered a drekar then he had been younger than I. I was a pale imitation of my brother, but I had to grow! I forced myself to be ordered and logical as I had assumed him to be, "We still have land to the west of us and we can use it to land and to conserve our water. I intend to land before it is dark and camp ashore while we can. My brother's maps show land for at least four, perhaps five days."

Ebbe nodded, "That is what Erik did!" He suddenly looked embarrassed as he realised what he had said, "I am sorry. I meant no disrespect!"

I laughed, "Ebbe, the shadow of my brother is a long one and I fear that I will walk in it my whole life."

He looked relieved that he had not offended me and added, "Do we sail to the land of ice and Fire?"

I shook my head, "I do not see the point. Erik and I discussed this many times. We know that sailing east, we will find land eventually. The danger will be if the winds turn against us or we take too long and run out of food."

Ebbe pointed astern, "We should have lines for fish and rig hides above us to collect water."

I was now the one who felt embarrassed, Erik had told me that was how they had survived on the voyage back to the Land of Ice and Fire."

"Then let us do it. Organize the boys!"

As he hurried off to set the handful of men and the boys to do as I had commanded, I looked at the skies. There was still no sun and so the compass was useless. It was fortunate that we still had the land and Erik's map, allied to Bear Tooth's local knowledge gave us some sense of where we were.

I think Bear Tooth must have sensed my doubt for he came closer to me and said, quietly, "Fótr, the tribes will be heading inland soon, for the winter. We would see the smoke from their fires if they were close. When we hunted the whale, I was always looking to the land for, especially that first voyage, I was fearful. There are many beaches which we can use. The island of which you speak is not known to me and Erik told us that they were attacked there. It may be the tribe which lives on that island is not be the same as mine. Just as the Penobscot are different to us so we may be different from the tribes who live further north."

"I know but that island is the one we must use for it is the last piece of land before we cross the Great Sea." I shrugged, Erik had made this voyage and had not known the end of it. I would do the same although the weight of the clan was on my shoulders. If I failed, then the whole clan would die. Just then some seabirds screamed overhead, and a chilling thought struck me like a dagger. Suppose Erik had not died with his sword in his hand; none had seen him die. If he had fallen without a sword then his spirit would be flying above us! Touching my hammer of Thor, I said, "Brother, if that is you above me, guide us to safety!"

The wind which took us was not a powerful one and that helped for most of the children had not sailed before. They had been born on our island. The women busied themselves keeping the youngest ones occupied. Ada, my brother's widow, had her hands full with Lars and with Ýrr. At least now that Ebbe had set the boys to fishing they would not be racing around the deck like mad things. The women all sat together. Arne's wife had killed herself when Arne had died and his three children were now being cared for by Siggi's wife, Gefn and the other women. Arne, Siggi and Maren were all less than five summers old. The women of the clan had cursed Freja for abandoning her children. The three were now the foster children of the clan. When Gefn took another husband and was married the children would become her husband's foster children. If she did not marry, then the clan would care for them. Vikings did not abandon any child. The Clan of the Fox looked after its own.

The gentle motion of the ship soon had the babies and young children asleep. We had made shelters from old sails and hide. They would help to collect water and also give some shelter. We had many furs for the land we had left had given us much. They had cost us dear, but it meant that the babes and infants were comfortable. Ada left the nest the women had made and came over to me for Bear Tooth had joined the fishermen. She looked astern, beyond the other two ships.

She was silent and I knew her well enough now to know what was going on inside her mind for she had loved my brother, her second husband, "You are thinking of Erik?"

She nodded, "He is in my thoughts always, but I wish we had Gytha with us for she had the power to see into the spirit world. She would have known if he was in Valhalla or wandering the skies. With the volvas on three ships then it is hard to combine our powers." She smiled at me. "Call me foolish for leaving all of his belongings in the hall we shared. His bear cloak, shield and wood axe are there." She laughed in an embarrassed sort of way. "I even left ale and mead for I know that if he did not die and he returns then he will be thirsty."

"You think he will return?"

"As I said, I do not know and we three volvas are still learning how to use our powers. When we are closer to the land of our birth then we will gain in strength. We are not Gytha."

I gestured towards Anya who was playing with Maren. Anya was Helga's younger sister and they were the daughters of Gytha who had been the matriarch of the clan, "Has she shown any signs of inheriting her mother's powers?"

Ada nodded, "And she may have the greatest of all powers for Helga used a sword and that diminishes the power of a volva." She stroked my hand on the steering board, "You are young, but the clan believes in you. Erik would be proud of you. He did all that he could to protect you from Arne."

"My brother Arne was not himself at the end, but he was my brother and I wish that he had not died. When we land might you be able to see into the spirit world?"

"I fear not for it is a ceremony and a ritual which takes time." She waved a hand at the children who, when they woke, would have energy to burn. "When we land, we will be cooking and trying to watch these sprites!" She looked thoughtful, "If we do find the Land of the Wolf then we can seek the help of Ylva for she is the greatest of all witches. She may be able to visit the spirit world. I heard that she and her grandfather met a Norn. She might be able to help us."

I laughed, "Then all I need to do is navigate across this wide ocean and find a tiny dot far to the east! I am humbled by your confidence."

She became serious, "When we lay together, Erik told me of the voyage for he was sad that it had caused the death of my son, Dreng. He went through the voyage in great detail. He told me that he learned to sail by sailing. Each day on the ocean he learned a little more about the sea and his snekke. It is good that this is a benign wind and that we are close to land. I know from Erik's words that when we head east then we will face seas like mountains and bottomless pits of black water. He did and he survived."

"But not your son."

She smiled, "The sea did not kill him; it was the land and something he ate there. Besides, it was *wyrd* and his death, sad though it was, brought me happiness with your brother and Dreng died with a sword in his hand. He is with his father."

Anya shouted, "Ýrr wakes!"

Ada shook her head and patted my hand, "She will want food. You cannot fill her!"

That first day passed but Ada's words had given me comfort. Each mile that we sailed and each landmark which we passed made me more confident. I had now sailed **'Gytha'** further than Erik for she was a new ship and he had barely sailed her for hours. I would learn to sail along with her. Erik had let me sail her for most of her sea trials. I had learned, already, that she was slower than *'Njörðr'* but that she was more stable. There was less movement. She was also brand new so that the mast and the decks were still changing. The drekar would become different as she sailed through the seas. I did not yet know her completely, but she was beginning to speak with me and I felt comfortable.

Ebbe returned to me and I realised that he needed lessons. Once we left the land, we would need another helmsman. Æimundr Loud Voice was one who could sail if he had to for he was a leader. I had Harald of Dyroy, and he had stood a watch once or twice with Erik. I needed to train them while we had the safety of the land. Our hurried departure had meant that we could not prepare as well as Erik and I had planned; the Norns!

"Come, Ebbe, it is time for your lesson. You can take the steering board while I make water." He looked nervous and I smiled, "Speak to her for she is a woman and likes gentle words."

He nodded and said, somewhat self-consciously, "***'Gytha'***, I am young, but I would be honoured if you would allow me to steer you."

As I dropped my breeks and faced away from the wind, the sail seemed to sigh and I said, "That was well spoke and she is happy."

We had ship's boys keeping watch. None had done the job before and once I was happy that Ebbe was steering well I walked down the drekar. I had been a ship's boy for my brother and knew that it was a frightening prospect. Danr, who straddled the cross tree and mast still gripped it with two arms as though he feared to fall. After a few more days he would relax and just use one, "Danr, when you spy a beach which has no smoke near it then hail me. We look for a campsite."

"We are camping soon, Captain?"

It seemed strange to hear me addressed thus for I was not yet twenty, "No, but it will do no harm and it will keep your eyes on the land. Do not worry about the sea. There are no enemies there!" As I headed to the bow, I knew that was not true. We had hunted whales and knew that they could damage us, but this was not whale season. We had been here long enough to know that.

It was Petr who watched at the bow, and he was lying along the sheerstrake with his arms wrapped around *'Gytha's'* prow. She would not mind for Gytha had ever been warm. He grinned as he turned, "Captain, there are fish as big as our snekke and they dance before us as we fly across the waves. How do they do it?"

"I know not but if you see anything bigger then shout it out for I have no wish to be struck by a whale!"

That night we found a sheltered beach. Danr had heeded my words for it was deserted. The Norns must have been in a good mood for the high cliffs around it meant that there was no danger of us being attacked and we lit fires and the women cooked. The ships' boys of our three ships scurried amongst the rocks gathering pails of shellfish. We would save our salted meat for as long as we could. The women also cooked some barley and oat bread. They did not make loaves. They made flatbreads which were cooked on the sides of the precious cauldrons. I sat with Aed, Padraig and Æimundr Loud Voice.

It was Æimundr Loud Voice who spoke first. I know that he felt responsible, in some way, for the deaths of my brothers, cousin and nephew as he had brought back the survivors and left my brothers and cousin, Siggi, to their fate, "Today went well. Erik has trained you well, Fótr."

"Perhaps but we have yet to face the open sea. I had Ebbe take the steering board today. Tomorrow I will see if Harald of Dyroy can handle her."

Padraig nodded, "She is bigger than *'Njörðr'* but I can see that she is slower. We had to reef our sail to avoid running you down."

"I spoke with Bear Tooth today and he said that our last stop, the island my brother first found, might be the most dangerous place for he does not know the tribe there and he lacks knowledge about their ways."

Æimundr Loud Voice asked, "Do we need to stop there?"

"We do and we need to collect water unless it rains twixt here and there. That is something which I remember."

"Aye, when we sailed to the seal islands before we found the Land of Ice and Fire, we discovered that problem." Padraig and

Aed had sailed with my brother, Erik, and they had learned from him.

Aed had the loneliest job for he just had his family on board the snekke. I did not know how he would sail at night. "And how will you get relief, Aed?"

"I will take the night watch and my son Erik Aedsson and my wife, Maren, will follow you."

Æimundr Loud Voice put his hand to his hammer, "A woman steering a ship?"

Aed laughed, "I am Hibernian and not Norse. We have women who can steer, and Maren is Finnsdotter. He knew how to steer."

Æimundr Loud Voice nodded, "Aye you are right. It is strange that all those who could steer have died before now. Apart from you three, we are all warriors."

"Perhaps it is our time."

Padraig said, "We have not spoken of this but what do we do if we are separated? It could happen; there are fogs, storms and other hazards."

I had thought of this and I remembered when the snekke had been thought lost. "We heave to for one day and then continue on the course we have begun. Once we leave the last island, we head due east, across the Great Sea. According to my brother's map that will bring us to the land where the Franks have their great river and were Hrólfr the Horseman rules. It is not where we wish to be, but the alternative is to land in Hibernia."

Padraig said, "That is our land and we know the waters."

I could tell that he wished us to do that but I did not. I nodded, "And I would sail there but it is north of east and that is a harder course to keep if we are separated."

"Then let us sail east until we have travelled for a moon and then change the course to north by east." Padraig was a positive person who always sought the best for us all.

If I had been Arne, I would have argued for that was his way but Erik would have done as I did. I nodded, "That is a good plan for Erik thought that the voyage would take between two and three moons. If we become separated, then we wait for one day and then continue to sail due east." It was a plan and, at the time, it sounded like a good one but the Norns were spinning!

Reginleif, my wife smiled and lifted the blanket for me. Erik lay between us and we spoke in whispers so as not to disturb him. I cuddled with her, feeling guilty that I was having to ignore my pregnant wife and young son.

"I am so proud of you, husband. Today all the women spoke of how happy they are that you lead us."

"But I feel so young and I fear to make a mistake."

"They say that Erik was younger when he sailed away and although we are now leaving this land, they know that it was good that we came."

I nodded and kissed her, "I know that we had to come to this land and I still wonder if we could have stayed."

"There are many who believe that had Erik led the clan then we could have stayed for he was wise beyond his years and could have made peace with the Skraeling. He was the one converted Bear Tooth to our ways. The land was a good one and we could have made it our home."

"But you wished to return east?"

"Aye for I feared that the jarl would lead the clan to destruction. You felt it too."

"You are right, and if we had stayed and Erik had found the maiden of his dreams what then?"

"You are thinking about Ada?" I nodded. "She would have understood, and she would have shared Erik. Do not forget that Ada is wise and had lost a husband and a son already. When she married Erik, it was like being reborn and she knew that their time together was a gift from the gods. She is content."

"And you, are you content for I cannot give you all the time that I should?"

"I am luckier than many for I still have my man and Erik still has a father. When our next child is born there will be others who can help me while you sail the ship."

"Is the baby imminent?"

She shook her head, "No, you goose, for there are three moons, at least, before my time but I know that we may be at sea longer than you said and I must be prepared. Fear not, Ada and Egilleif will be close by for we are family."

I kissed her, closed my eyes and fell asleep. My dreams were troubled for I saw Erik, alone and fighting off the Skraeling.

Unlike Arne I was not a true warrior and I saw little glory in his death.

We left as the sun rose in the east and I took the sun as a good sign. The worst sunrise for us would be a grey and overcast one for that would herald a storm and winds from the east. The few men on each ship had to help the boys to haul on the ropes and the sheets to raise the sail. As yet it was an untidy process but Erik had told me that it took time for boys to learn to handle sails. He, Arne and Siggi had had a cruel and harsh taskmaster on their first voyage who had been uncompromising. Erik had always been patient and I tried to be the same. As yet there was no hurry and it was better to coddle and nurse them while we could pull in each night and rest on the land. Once we were at sea with no comforting land to run to then the adjustment of the sails would become critical and need lightning-fast hands and reactions.

Chapter 3 Fótr

That second day at sea I began to let both Harald and Ebbe take the helm. It was strange teaching a man who was fifteen years older than I was and, at first, I was nervous, but Harald knew his limitations. He was a fine weaponsmith and a fair warrior. He could sail but it had been on the snekke when he had fished with Aed and Padraig. I think teaching Harald of Dyroy gave me confidence because things I told and taught him which seemed simple and second nature to me were revelations to him. Erik had been a better teacher than I had known. Perhaps it was because he had begun work when I was so young. I had sailed with him on the snekke and he had helped me little by little. I was patient with them as I took a sight from the sun which had decided to make an appearance. It meant we had a better idea of our position. I marked the map and then put the compass and map in the chest by the steering board. Both Ebbe and Harald knew to watch the hourglass and to turn it. They would make the mark on the wax tablet we had made. To the others what we did seemed to be unnecessary but Erik had taught me that the marks and scratches we made were vital to the success of the voyage.

Once I was happy with his work, I left Harald with Ebbe by his side and walked the drekar again. I knew that, once we struck land, I would no longer lead the clan and I was happy about that but for now they looked to me for Erik had imparted all that he knew to me. He would have been a better jarl than Arne and I would use what I had learned from Erik allied to the knowledge of the many mistakes which Arne had made. I listened and I watched. Erik had told me how he tried to spot when someone was fearful or nervous for such people make mistakes. We were all, quite literally, in the same boat and the weakness of one could harm the whole. We had widows on board. With so few men it was unlikely that they would find a man until we landed and found others. It was the lonely widows to whom I gave the most attention and spoke kindly to them. I was aware, as I passed them, of Ada, Reginleif and Egilleif watching me, I smiled and Erik who was now dangerously active rushed to grab my leg. My nephew, Lars, grabbed him by the arm, "Come and play with the stones!" Distracted, Erik obeyed.

Petr shouted from the masthead, "Captain, I see smoke over the land!"

"You have good eyes, Petr!"

The fact that we were not going to land for at least twelve hours meant that the sightings were not needed but it kept the lookouts alert. I spoke to the other lookouts and then stood on the gunwale and held on to the forestay; I peered at the land. By my estimation, we had another four or five nights, at least, before we reached the island. If all were as peaceful as the first night then I would make a blót to thank the gods. I had never made one but I knew that one who ignored the gods risked all. Arne had discovered that. I could not remember his making one but my father had.

It was as I came back to the steering board that I saw Bear Tooth speaking and laughing with Anya, my cousin. They looked to be close and I wondered at that. She had chosen to be on my drekar while Tostig, her brother, had asked to sail on *'Njörðr'*. Tostig had been close to Arne and Siggi. Siggi's wife, Gefn, was on the *'Njörðr'* with Helga her sister in law. I now saw why Anya had chosen my drekar. It was strange for Anya was older than Tostig and me. Anya had been close to her mother, Gytha, and had nursed her when she was dying. Perhaps the young Skraeling had been her salvation during that time. Whatever the reason I saw affection between them. It was *wyrd*. I had worried that Bear Tooth would miss my brother but now I saw the threads of the Norns in all of this. Bear Tooth watched over Lars, my nephew and Anya would be his reward. She deserved happiness too.

We had a trouble free first week as we sailed up the coast. The ships' boys grew into their role and the animals became used to walking down the gangplank to graze. We had ships' boys who disposed of the dung. While we sailed up the coast, we deposited it on the land but we would soon have to use the sea. The winds were good ones. They freshened up and we made good speed. I know that the other two drekar could have completed the same journey in a shorter time. My drekar was slower and overloaded.

It was on the fifth day that we left the mainland to head, for the first time, across open water. When we had sailed to this new land we had headed south and west. I had been the one with the wax tablet then and I knew it to be a relatively short voyage but for a few of those who had been babies, this would be the first time they left the sight of land. Danr and Petr had proved to be the best of my lookouts and I had them looking for the dark smudge which was the island.

It was Danr who shouted, "Land, Captain! Due north!"

The sun was in the sky and I knew that he was accurate and had seen land for with the sun there were darker, clearer shadows. "Ebbe, shout to Aed and tell him what we have spied and then take the steering board! I am the only one who has been to this island and I have to remember where we landed."

Once relieved I went to the prow and I lay along the figurehead. It seemed so long since Erik, Dreng, Rek and I had landed on the first land we had seen since leaving the Land of Ice and Fire. It had been where Erik had almost died when he had been knocked out by a deer. How different would the lives of the clan have been had he died? Dreng, Rek and I would be dead and the clan would still be enduring a harsh life in the Land of Ice and Fire. I knew that the tribe who lived on this island were fierce. As we had left the mainland, I had told the men and boys to prepare their bows and their weapons for we might need to fight. I remembered that the natives had not attacked us when we had landed which suggested that they did not live near the coast. That was small comfort.

As the thin grey smudge became more solid and dark, I peered to look for a feature I recognised. The closer the land came the more my spirits fell for I did not recognise anything. I turned and shouted, "Ebbe, steer north by west and reef the sail a little. I want to approach the land slowly." This was necessary but also extremely dangerous for the natives would have more time to reach the water and we could not land if there were natives there. The fact that I saw no smoke did not fill me with confidence. The animals who were tethered at the prow began to make noises as they smelled the land; it was distracting. I spied a waterfall cascading from a cliff. I vaguely remembered it but could not recall if that had been north or south of the place we were attacked. The cliffs meant we could not land and, as the afternoon wore on, I despaired of making landfall and then I saw a headland and birds swooping down to the water. "Ebbe, take us closer to shore but do it gently." I saw that there was a small river which emptied into the sea. The sun was getting low in the sky and we needed to land. I stood and said, "Petr, take over. If you see any rocks or foaming water, then let me know!

"Aye, Captain!"

As I walked down the drekar I saw the expectant faces looking up at me. I smiled back with a reassurance I did not feel. Had we been lulled by a week of easy camps?

We nudged our way into the shore and I saw that the river was little more than a large stream but it would suit our purposes. There were rocks and there was also sand. I waved Aed to use the sand while Padraig and I edged next to what appeared to be a large flat rock. The ship's boys leapt ashore with the ropes which would hold us to the land and Harald of Dyroy joined them. He had his weaponsmith's hammer and two large metal spikes we had brought from Larswick. He hammered them into a crevasse in the rock. They would hold us. The warriors then lowered the gangplank and leapt ashore with bows and spears. We had seen no danger but here there were no cliffs to protect us. There was a path which zigzagged down to the water but that would not slow down Skraeling who were trying to get at us. We would need to look for signs of recent use; we did not know the tribe who lived here and they might not be like the Mi'kmaq.

When Æimundr Loud Voice came back with his helmet in his hand. It was as clear a sign as we could wish for that there was no danger. He stopped in the shallow water and shouted, "We have seen no sign of Skraeling. Bear Tooth and Mikel have headed a little further inland."

I nodded, "Then let us get ashore and feed the animals. This is our last stop before we sail the Great Sea!"

I saw the looks of apprehension on the faces of the women who were closest to me. It was one thing to talk about this leap of faith but quite another to actually embark on the voyage.

Once the animals were ashore then I had the ropes loosened to allow for the tides. I would not risk my drekar on the rocks. I was the last to leave. I placed the compass, map and hourglass in the chest. They lay atop Erik's old mail shirt. He would never need it now and I was loath to put it on until I had to.

"Petr, you stay aboard and shout if you feel there is any threat to the ship no matter how small and inconsequential. I would rather you call me a hundred times than fail to call me once!"

"Aye, Captain!"

As I waded ashore, I saw fires being lit for hot food. I did not wish fires to be lit as it would alert the Skraeling to our presence, but I understood the need. From now on we would be eating cold food; it would be salted or in vinegar, but it would still be cold and the Great Sea could be as icy as winter in Norway, or so I had been told.

Within the ships and the clan, there were smaller groups. The ones like mine were family-related. Others were because the warriors or their wives were friends. Padraig and Aed had their extended family around one fire and I saw that Ada, Helga and Gefn were busy organising our cauldron. Anya and the older girls were busy watching the infants and babes. Ebbe, Tostig along with my young son, Erik were the only males around the fire for the others were collecting shellfish. It was one reason that Helga had travelled on *'Njörðr'*. We wished to have a volva on each ship but now that we were ashore the volvas would stay together. When they had time, they would spin a spell to keep us safe and they would also try to speak with Gytha. Helga was the one who was most upset about the lack of communication with her dead mother. She felt she should be able to and I knew that she was keenly aware that she was not as powerful as her mother had been. That was the conversation I overheard as I approached.

"I curse the times I practised with the sword, Ada, for it weakened my power. If I had not done so then my mother would be able to give us her guidance."

"That is not the reason, Helga, for Gytha said, many times, that she felt closer to Erik than to her own children. It was *wyrd*."

"But if Erik is dead then why can she not communicate with us?"

We all remained silent for Helga's words suggested the unthinkable, that we had abandoned Erik in the savage wilderness. He might be alive and that was a quagmire we would all avoid. My wife, Reginleif, carried over some slices of salted meat to add to the shellfish which Danr and the other boys were collecting. She put her hand to her back and Ada said, "You should sit. You have a child within you."

"I have sat enough on the drekar and I need to walk." She looked at me, "When we are on the Great Sea will we be able to walk along the deck?"

I shook my head, "It will be hard for the animals take up almost a third of the ship and the children…"

She nodded, "Then I shall make the most of this last time ashore."

"Is Erik behaving himself?"

"He is. Each day he seems so much older. He is no longer a baby and I miss that."

Ada laughed, "And soon you will have another and this one will be a girl."

I looked at them, "How do you know?"

Ada beamed, "We are volvas and we know such things!"

Helga shook her head, "Stop teasing, Fótr, for he has much on his mind has he not?" She looked at me, "We listen to the baby within Reginleif and we can hear the heartbeat. The heartbeat is that of a girl. Does that disappoint you?"

I shook my head, "So long as she has the required fingers, toes and the like I care not!"

I looked up as Anya shouted, "It is Bear Tooth, he returns!"

Gefn laughed, "And, of course, she was not watching for him was she?"

They all laughed and it confirmed what I had thought. Bear Tooth and Anya were a couple Technically Tostig was the head of their family but he had seemed distracted of late. I said to him, "If Bear Tooth and your sister, Anya, choose to be together then you would have to give your permission."

Tostig was of an age with me but he always seemed younger. He shook his head, "It is nothing."

Something in his voice made me ask, "But if they do wish this then what would you say?"

"I would say no, Fótr, for it was the Skraeling killed my brother and the Jarl. I cannot forgive those people."

"But Bear Tooth is of our clan. He fought the Penobscot with us!"

"It matters not and that is all I have to say."

Now I understood why no approach had been made. Anya was a sensitive woman and she would know the answer she would get. So long as they did not broach the question then the liaison could be ignored.

The men all gathered as Bear Tooth and Mikel Finnbjǫrnsson returned from their scouting expedition. Mikel was the husband of Ada's daughter Egilleif and was one of the best trackers we had. He and Bear Tooth made a good team.

"Well?"

Bear Tooth was the better tracker and he shook his head, "We saw no enemies and the signs they had made were more than a month old but…"

"But?"

"But that does not mean they will not return for some tribes like to wander month by month. They pick the berries and harvest the sea and land before moving on."

I heeded the warning in his voice, "Then we should keep a watch this night?" He nodded.

Harald of Dyroy said, "Let us do as we did on Bear Island. Let us set traps and have men on guard. There are twenty-four of us. Eight men will watch at a time."

I knew exactly how many men we had, "There are twenty-eight warriors, Harald."

He shook his head, "The captains do not watch and Ǫlmóðr Ragnarsson has still not fully recovered from his wound."

It made sense but I would sleep with one eye open. Harald organised the watches and, after we had eaten, I curled up with Erik and Reginleif and slept. It was Erik, my son, who alerted us. He cried and woke me. I asked him later when we were at sea what woke him, and he said it was an old woman with white hair and he was scared. In my heart, I believe that was Gytha.

As I was awake, I went to make water and, knowing that I would not be able to sleep again once woken, I strapped on my sword. I could hear the noises from the animals who had been penned by a wall of shields and brushwood. They must have been making the noises all night, but we were used to that and it had not disturbed our slumber. I headed away from the camp for all were sleeping and I stood close to Bear Tooth. After I had made water, I went over to him. "Quiet?"

He whispered, "Aye, but as you came across here, I turned my head to see who it was and when I looked back, I saw a movement."

"Where?" He nodded to some scrubby fruit bushes and straggly trees whose shadows lay just two hundred or so paces from us. There was no breeze and any movement either had to be an animal or a man. I was suspicious. "Alert the other guards and I will wake the men. This may be a tribe who do attack at night!"

I headed for Harald of Dyroy and shook him awake. His eyes opened and I hissed, "There may be trouble!"

He said nothing but rose and the two of us went to wake the other men one by one. Inevitably some of the women, thankfully the older ones, were also disturbed and I said, "Remain quiet but be ready to move!"

I felt painfully naked as I headed back to the line of warriors for I wore neither mail nor helmet. Both were still on the drekar with Petr. Some warriors took the time to don mail and so I was not the last to reach the line. I stood next to Bear Tooth who said, quietly, "I was right; there are enemies out there and I can smell them."

Harald joined me and I said, "Bear Tooth has confirmed there are Skraeling out there."

Ebbe must have heard the noise and he ghosted next to me, "Should I get the ships' boys to get their weapons, Fótr?"

"No, Ebbe, have them prepare the ships for sea. Try to get some of the smaller animals aboard but do it quietly and if we are attacked then get your mother to organize the women. If we must leave, then it will have to be done quickly."

He hurried off and I stared into the dark. We now had all our warriors around the camp and that meant the women and children would be protected but for how long? We stood for a long time and I was aware of the noises of animals behind me. Ebbe and the boys were moving the hens, sheep and goats onto the drekar. Perhaps the Skraeling whom Ebbe had smelled was just a scout and he was watching us.

Æimundr Loud Voice appeared at my side and his mouth was close to my ear as he spoke, "Bear Tooth is right I have smelled them too and seen movement. I think they wait for dawn so that the beach will be lit by the sun and they will attack from the dark. We should begin to load the ships."

I chewed my lip, "But will that not alert them?"

"It might but then they will have lost their advantage of attacking into the light. We cannot risk the women, Fótr Larsson."

I nodded and turned where I saw Danr close by and I waved him over, "Find Ada and ask her to begin to board the women and the children on to the drekar. When that is done load the cows."

"What of you and the men, Captain?"

"We will load but we need the three ships ready to leave." He nodded and disappeared. I wondered if the tide would be right and I cursed myself for not returning to the drekar and checking the ropes which tied us to the land. Would we be able to remove the spikes which held us to the land, or would we have to sever ropes and abandon the precious metal? Inevitably, there was more noise when the children began to move. They were excited or irritated or just children and were not silent.

The Skraeling were not Vikings. If they had been then they would have begun their attack silently and sent their arrows into the dark to catch us unawares. The Skraeling began their attack by screaming loudly and running at us. Only Bear Tooth and I did not have shields. We both wore hide vests and it was that and the fact that the arrows which came from the dark were both ill

The Bear and the Wolf

aimed and stone or bone tipped which prevented hurts. A Viking attack would have yielded casualties but neither Bear Tooth nor I were hurt. I felt two arrows hit my chest. I would be bruised but that would be all. As well as my sword I also had my seax and I had fought before. Like Erik, I was not the warrior Arne had been, but I had fought Skraeling and knew their weaknesses; they had poor weapons and no armour.

I heard cries and screams from my right as the first of the wild warriors were slain by true Viking warriors. To my left was Danr Gandálfrson and he had a shield and a metal-studded byrnie not to mention a helmet. He was little older than me, but he had survived the disaster of the falls and fought in the battle of Horse Deer Island. It gave me comfort. His father, Gandálfr, one of the oldest of our warriors, held the right end of our thin line.

And then I had no time to think for warriors raced at the three of us. They would outnumber us, and I saw that they held bone tipped spears. If they struck flesh, then they could do terrible harm to us. I swung my sword in a long sweep. The sharp edge hacked through the wood of two spears rendering them ineffective and then I slashed with the seax across their naked middles. It tore through the stomach of one and ripped into the side of the second. I brought my sword down to smash into his skull as he tumbled. Bear Tooth had a short sword and a small hatchet. He had an advantage over me for he had often fought other Skraeling and knew what they would do. Danr Gandálfrson was also doing well for his shield blocked every attempt to spear him and his helmet afforded him protection too.

A tall Skraeling with a shaven head and painted face ran at me with a bone knife and stone club. I guessed he saw me as the weakest of the three and was attempting to break our wall for already there was a line of bodies before us. I had been told that when my brothers and Siggi had fallen some of the Skraeling had been like berserkers and fought as though they cared not if they lived or died. I faced such a warrior who screamed as he hurled his huge body at me. I slashed across his middle with my sword and saw the red line widen as my blade bit home, but it did not halt him. He brought his stone club down at me and I barely fended it off with my seax. He had a free strike with his bone knife which was sharp, and it ripped a long line up my right forearm. Its tip stuck in my hide vest and his weight knocked me to the ground. The Norns were spinning for, as I tried to use my left arm to slow my fall my seax tore up under the warrior's chin. I hit the ground hard and the breath was knocked from me but the seax had killed him. Forcing his body from me I rose.

At that moment I heard the horn sound from my drekar. It signalled a retreat. Æimundr Loud Voice was the most experienced warrior and he shouted, "Clan of the Fox, fall back! Sword foot. Shield foot. Sword foot. Shield foot."

I was aware of blood dripping down my right arm, but I ignored it as I did as I was ordered. We all moved as one and we were all in step for our circle of warriors would begin to shrink and if we were not in step, we might trip over each other.

To help us Æimundr Loud Voice began a chant and we all joined in.

> *"Clan of the Fox*
> *March to war*
> *Clan of the Fox*
> *Hear us roar*
> *Clan of the Fox*
> *We fight this day*
> *Clan of the Fox*
> *The Viking way!"*

It worked and, as we walked backwards, the Skraeling who had to negotiate their own dead and wounded were forced to attack us as individuals and our superior weapons and protection meant that we won. I noticed that there was more light in the sky to the east and that meant the sun was rising. Ebbe must have organised the ships' boys for arrows began to drop amongst the Skraeling. We, too, were now using bone and stone arrowheads but the Skraeling wore no mail and each arrow which struck found flesh.

Æimundr Loud Voice shouted, "Fótr, Aed, Padraig, get aboard your ships and we will hold them!" As we obeyed, I heard our men cursing and swearing at the Skraeling; this was a battle for vengeance and to atone for the deaths at the falls. As I ran up the gangplank, sheathing my sword, I saw the sword of

Æimundr Loud Voice take the head of a Skraeling. They were brave warriors but the sight of the head flying through the air shocked them. I saw Harald of Dyroy use his hammer to knock the metal spikes holding us to the rocks. He and Gandálfr picked them up and our men began to run up the gangplanks. *'Jötnar'* had already pulled away for there were just Aed, his wife and his sons on board. I saw men with wounds clambering aboard, but I ignored them and my bleeding arm as I ran to the steering board, "Let loose the sail! Haul in the ropes!" I saw that Æimundr Loud Voice was the last man aboard.

The ship's boys dropped their bows and ran to obey me. I heard Ada shout, "Women, pull on the ropes!" We were one clan and our clan fought together!

Arrows fell on the deck as we began to edge slowly away from the shore but mercifully none found either the women or the children. Skraeling tried to climb up the side of the drekar but hands and arms were severed by our warriors who had just returned to the ship. I saw that *'Njörðr'* had also pulled away. We were safe from the land and, as I turned us into the sun, I knew we faced another enemy, the Great Sea!

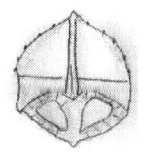

Chapter 4 Fótr

It was Reginleif who spied my wound and she shouted to Ada. When she came and saw the wound Ada shouted, "Ebbe, take the steering board!"

"I am fine!"

"Your arm is cut almost to the bone! Even I can see the bright sun and that is the east! My son can sail!"

In our clan, the women had great power and I allowed Ebbe to steer. I sat on the deck and allowed my wife and Ada to tend to me. In truth, I felt a little dizzy and I knew not why. I saw Bear Tooth approach and his hide vest was bloody, "Are you wounded?"

He shook his head, "The Penobscot warriors are fiercer."

"Are any others hurt?"

"Yours is the worse wound, Fótr, you should not have risked yourself, for now you are the navigator!"

"No Bear Tooth, I am not. We needed Erik for this and, as I look ahead into the vastness of the east, I fear I will not be up to the task."

Reginleif held my left hand in her two and she watched the volva heal me. Ada had washed the blood from my arm and now had a piece of cloth held tightly to it to staunch the bleeding as she said, "Listen, brother, Erik believed in you. He is no longer here but he told me that he was happy for you to sail back to the Land of the Wolf. In the long nights of winter, as we lay together, he spoke of his voyages. He said that you were the one who could do as he had done for you had sailed with him and he trusted you. Gytha believed in you too and while we may not be

The Bear and the Wolf

able to speak with her, here, in my heart and in my head, I know that she is with the clan for Gytha was the heart of the clan and her death has not diminished that." She looked up, "Bear Tooth, hold this cloth tightly while I fetch the honey and the vinegar." As he did so she added, "I will have to sew the arm, Fótr, and we do not have enough ale to make you drowsy. You will have to endure much pain."

I forced a smile as Reginleif squeezed my hand, "I am a Viking and I will bear it like a man."

Ada snorted, "Then thank the Allfather that you are not a woman for then you would have to suffer the pain of childbirth!"

She was right. I looked up at the sail which was full and billowing. The stays and sheets were taut and Ebbe was going a good job. I looked up at him, "You are doing well, Ebbe."

He shook his head, "I should have fought with the other warriors for I am a man. I might have stopped you being injured."

Laughing I said, "No, for this was just the Norns. I will be stiff and suffer a sling for a while but the Allfather watched over us for we emerged from the battle with fewer hurts than we might have expected."

We had been lucky and had lost neither men nor animals and the attack had made us leave earlier than we might have done. The wind was from the south-west and *'Gytha'* was flying. What could have been a disastrous end to our time in the west was a hopeful start. The other wounded warriors were being healed and women were distributing food. I prayed that all would be well, but I knew that I would have preferred to speak to Aed and Padraig before we had left just to ensure that we all knew the plan. We had been over it enough times, but the sudden departure was unexpected, and I hoped it would not jeopardise our journey.

The first test came towards dusk when I ordered the sail reefed to slow us down and to allow the other two vessels to close to us. They came to within two lengths of us. For the snekke, this would be a risky time as the two drekar were much bigger than the snekke and any collision would be fatal for Aed and his family. As darkness fell, I saw that it was Aed at the steering board. We rigged the pot we had made from river clay;

The Bear and the Wolf

it had a hole in the back so that the burning seal oil could be seen by the other ships. I was not certain how effective it would be or how long the oil would burn but it was worth trying. I had rested during the day and despite their protestations, I insisted upon taking the watch during the hours of darkness. It was a clear night and there were stars to help me steer. Reginleif brought young Erik to speak to me before she put him to bed. I saw the concern in her eyes. As much as she wished to return east, she now understood the decision we had taken was momentous. Already the seas were growing, and this was calm weather. When we had a storm, it would be far worse.

After I had said goodnight to Erik, she kissed me and said, "Take care, Fótr, for as much as you are the hope of the clan you are our life and we would not lose you."

I smiled, "And you will not for I am going nowhere. When you wake, look to the steering board and you will see me here."

I had two lookouts on my watch, Petr Haraldsson and Leif Mikelson. Leif was at the prow and Petr stood by me. If I needed to make water, then he would hold the steering board. At first, the drekar was noisy as for the first time people prepared to sleep abord the drekar. The children were excited, and the animals showed signs of distress. They had expected to be taken off and grazed. I knew that before the end of the voyage we would have to slaughter some of them. I hoped that we could keep the cows alive until we reached land but that was hope more than an expectation. I sent Petr around the ship each time I turned the hourglass. From now on we would keep a record of the hours and they would be marked on the wax tablet I used. So long as there were stars then we could use the compass. This would be a test for Petr. Thanks to my wound I could not hold the compass, but it would be good training for him. I had done the same for Erik. As well as watching our course I studied the sail and the sea, and I felt the ship beneath my boots and my hand. She was speaking with me and all was well.

Petr brought me the horn of ale in the middle of the night. I had told him when to do so for I knew I would only have one horn of the precious nectar during each watch. When the ale ran out, we would be reduced to drinking the water in the barrels and then rainwater. When we had landed on the island, we had filled the barrels with fresh water from the stream. We could do no more.

"What will it be like in the Land of the Wolf, Captain?" He had been little more than a baby when we had left Larswick.

I shrugged, "I have only seen it from the sea, and I know not. Sámr Ship Killer and Ylva the witch rule the land of Dragonheart and keep it safe from the clutches of kings and warlords. That is why we seek it. From what I have heard it has many mountains, but the rivers and waters teem with fish. We had a land which had nothing, that was the land of Ice and Fire and we have had Bear Island which was full of natural riches. The Land of the Wolf is a haven and whatever life is like there it should be safer than Bear Island."

He lowered his voice, "Some of those on board think that we are cursed and that without Erik the Navigator we are all doomed."

Petr was young and I was not insulted by his words, "And you, what do you think?"

"I never sailed with your brother save on the voyage from the Land of Ice and Fire. Then I was but a child and it was all an adventure. I did not think it was real. It felt like a game." I nodded. Petr was on the cusp of manhood. "I trust you, Captain, and I believe we will see land again but when I was on watch at the prow and saw the vastness of the dark ocean, I felt fear."

"We all feel that way. Let us trust to the drekar and the Allfather and pray that the Norns are in good humour!"

For the next three days, all went well: the wind continued to aid us, the seas did not swamp us, we kept formation and the sun shone so that we could keep a record of our position. I slept during the day, or rather, I did as Erik had done and I snatched sleep in short spells. That was not merely concern about our progress but, as my arm ceased to ache and started to heal so it itched and a lengthy sleep was impossible. Ada, who inspected it each day told me it was a good thing but as I was not allowed to scratch it then I disagreed.

On the fourth day, my itching arm woke me and Ebbe sent Danr to Reginleif for my water and food. I always took my single horn of ale while I watched. We had now established the ritual. Ebbe pointed behind us, "Fótr, the black clouds have been gathering over the land we have left. Is the Allfather angry?"

"He may well be but those are, unless I am mistaken, storm clouds." Danr handed me the horn of water and I drank half and then began to chew on the raw fish which had been caught while I had slept. "If we were alone, as we were when we came west, then I would keep the sail full and make all speed to race before the storm, but we must travel with the other two and we are slow. Before you rest, Ebbe, have everything tied down and secured. Assign two boys to sleep close to each of the animals." He nodded. "Danr, I will need Petr as well as Leif for this night's watch."

"Aye, Captain."

I finished the water and hung the horn around my neck. I took the clay pot and, using my flint, lit the seal oil which had been refilled during the day. I saw Aed begin to close and I signalled to him to alert him to the clouds. He nodded and I watched him repeat the signal to the boys on *'Njörðr'*. Both Aed and Padraig knew the sea, but it had not cost me to warn them of the storm. Taking over the steering board as Ebbe hurried to do what I had asked him I looked afresh at the seas. The troughs were just a little deeper than when I had fallen asleep and the crests were white flecked, higher and definitely more threatening. The storm was coming and the question in my head was how big would it be? For the first time since we had begun the voyage, I was grateful that Erik had made the drekar so wide. Up until now, we had been the slow one but in a wild storm, we would be the stable one.

When Reginleif brought Erik to me to say goodnight I told her to tie herself to the mastfish and to secure Erik to her. She gave me a surprised look, "A storm is coming, and it may be a hard one. We put the women and children around the mast and mastfish for a reason; it is the centre of the ship and the most stable. I helped to build the drekar and know that it is the strongest part. If the storm comes then the men will be busy saving the ship. Do as I ask and then I shall not worry about you."

"And what of you, my husband? Who will watch over you?"

The Bear and the Wolf

I pointed above me, "The Allfather and the spirits of those who have gone before." When they had gone, I took out the woven spell and kissed it before tucking it back inside my tunic. Taking out my seal skin cape and laying it beneath me I sat on my chest which was secured by thick ropes to the solid bolts on the stern of the drekar. I was ready.

Erik had told me, often, that a drekar was a living beast which could talk to its master, its captain and **'Gytha'** did not disappoint. Even before the winds began to grow and the rains started to pelt us from the west, she had warned me of the storm. It came as a voice inside my head and as I heard the reefed sail flapping, I knew that the storm would go from windy to wild in a heartbeat. The hourglass told me that Ebbe and the other men had only had three hours of sleep but that would have to be enough.

"Danr, have the men woken and then reef the sail. The storm will be upon us soon."

He looked fearful for he could see that the seas were much higher, and our motion was becoming exaggerated. As he left, I stood and placed the hourglass in the chest. I donned and tied my sealskin cape although even that would not help me if the seas began to crash over our stern. Looking behind I saw that **'Jötnar'** could no longer be seen. I hoped that they could still see my light for I would be able to do nothing if she rammed me. We would be damaged, but she would be destroyed.

I was pleased when I saw that Ebbe, Bear Tooth and some of the other younger warriors helped my boys to completely reef the sail. I believe that is what saved us. The men began to help the women who had a safe little nest around the mastfish. Capes and old sails were fixed and fastened to the barrels which held our water and our food. Even as I was congratulating myself on our actions the storm struck us. Waves crashed and cascaded down onto the deck. I was in danger of losing control of the steering board, "Ebbe!"

Ebbe and Bear Tooth slipped and slid along the already slick deck to come to the steering board. They both joined me and, with one on either side of me we held on to the steering board to keep us with the wind directly behind. We needed no sails and the slow and stately **'Gytha'** became a wild colt racing and skipping from crest to crest, plummeting into bottomless troughs to, unbelievably, rise to the top of the next one.

Bear Tooth screamed above the roaring wind and the thundering rain, "We are all doomed! I will die here in the deep ocean!"

Ebbe shouted, "No, you will not for we have Fótr and the spirit of Erik the Navigator will watch over us."

In my head, I prayed that was true, but I had not felt Erik's spirit since the battle of the falls. I had spoken to screaming gulls in the hope that one of them was he, but I did not know. I heard some of the younger women and children crying as we descended into a seemingly bottomless trough. My stomach felt as though it hung in the air above me and then, almost as quickly, we soared up the side of a cliff of water. And the dark night just went on and on. Had there not been three of us clinging to the wood of the steering board then I am certain that we would have perished for if we had gone beam on to a wave we would have been swamped. I remembered now the meticulous care Erik had taken with the construction of the drekar and the love with which Snorri had carved the figurehead. I was grateful in that storm for the efforts of both of them. I began to fear for the other drekar and the snekke. They had been built by our father, Erik and Arne but Snorri had not carved their prows. Would that make a difference? When dawn finally came it brought no relief except that the storm and the seas looked even more terrifying in what passed for daylight. The darkness had hidden the scale of the storm. Now we could see the swells and the crests; we could anticipate the falls and rises. However the fact that I could see more of the terror seemed to make it easier, but we were all more fearful because of the emptiness of the ocean. *'Jötnar'* and *'Njörðr'* were no longer to be seen and our clan was no longer whole.

By the next night, we were all exhausted. Harald of Dyroy took the place of Ebbe so that he could get some sleep. We were all salt rimed and soaked. The seal-skin capes just protected our clothes and shielded us from the wind. They could no longer keep out the rain which poured down our necks. Harald tried to cheer me up as he joined me, "At least we will have plenty of water to drink!"

I had to laugh, "Aye, Harald, if there was any way to collect it."

He nodded towards the women and children who were gathered around the mast and the mast fish. Ada had them directing the water from the sails and the capes into the cauldrons. "See how the women of the clan help us? It is a good sign."

I nodded. The collected water would be slightly salty because of the seawater but it would occupy the children and could be used for washing and to give to the animals. We had lost one sheep which had escaped the clutches of Arne Haraldsson; it had leapt to its death when the storm was unleashed. If we lost just one, then I would be thankful. Even as it had leapt overboard, I wondered if the gods would consider that a blót. When we could I would make one in any case. It could not hurt.

At dawn of the next day, the storm appeared to be marginally easing although that was hard to judge. Æimundr Loud Voice relieved Bear Tooth and I and Ebbe took over the steering. "Fótr, you and Bear Tooth have not slept since before the storm began. Even Erik needed some sleep. I promise to wake you if the storm worsens!"

Reluctantly I obeyed but while Bear Tooth went to lie close to the women, I curled up in my fur next to my chest. I drank some water but did not bother with food. I slept but my sleep was haunted by dreams. It was not one continuous dream it was flashes of images and people. I saw Erik's face and the Skraeling who had laid open my arm. I saw my father and I saw Gytha. A silent Arne screamed at me and I saw the body of his wife being washed away by the sea. When I awoke, despite the cold and the rain, I was sweating. I looked at the sky and saw that it was still light, "How long have I slept?"

Æimundr Loud Voice shook his head, "I am not sure, but I know not how you managed to hold on to this steering board for so long. I am exhausted already!"

I smiled, "I will make water and then relieve Harald. Ebbe, how is the storm?"

"It appears to be easing."

The Bear and the Wolf

"Then, Æimundr Loud Voice, when I have made water Ebbe can relieve you and you can go around the drekar to give comfort and to see how **'Gytha'** fares."

He nodded, "You are the only one who could have done this, Fótr. Erik chose his successor well."

As I made water, I reflected that none of us had spoken of Erik's present circumstances. The volvas had not sensed his spirit and that made us believe that he was not in Valhalla and was a lost spirit. Yet, even as I pulled up my sodden breeks, I wondered at that. Erik, if he was lost, would have tried to follow us and yet none of the birds, which we had long ago lost, had spoken to me. As a rogue wave hit our steerboard side making everyone lurch and the women and children scream, I put those useless thoughts of my brother from my head. I had to save what was left of the clan!

It took another day and a half for the storm to abate sufficiently that I did not need to have two of us on the steering board and, when the next day came it was as though the storm had never been. There were blue skies with a few scudding clouds and the waves were barely halfway up the drekar. I was able to send Danr to the masthead and we used a reefed sail to keep the way on her.

I patted the gunwale and murmured, "Thank you **'Gytha'** for you have saved us."

I waved Ebbe to the steering board and, after taking out the hourglass, compass, wax tablet and map, walked down the drekar. We had lost barrels, but they were mainly the smaller ones. I would have to find out what exactly had gone. We had, miraculously, lost not a single member of the clan. The one sheep had been our only casualty. Reginleif and Ada rose to greet me. My wife kissed me first, "Thank you, husband."

Ada smiled and hugged me, "I told you that you could do this. Erik's trust was not misplaced."

I nodded, "Let me know what was lost and what this will mean. I hope to have a better idea of our position by the morrow."

She looked around, "And where are the other ships, the drekar and the snekke?"

"It was a wild storm and they could be anywhere. Let us just put *'Gytha'* in order and then I can work out what we need to do next. When you have time, I would have the volvas of the clan weave." Even as I walked to Æimundr Loud Voice and Harald of Dyroy, both curled up asleep, at the prow I saw that we had lost ropes. They were a precious commodity. The damaged ones would have to be saved for they could be re-used but we would need to put our few replacements in their place. The mast and crosstree looked sound, but I would need to scale the mast to see for myself. Thanks to my command to reef the sail early we had no damage to the sail.

Æimundr Loud Voice's son shook him awake as I neared him. He looked up at the sky and, clutching his hammer of Thor, kissed it, "Thank you Allfather for giving Fótr the skills of his brother." I smiled. He looked around as Harald rose to his feet, too. The area around the animals stank although the seawater had removed much of their dung and piss. Æimundr said, "The others?"

I shook my head, "Danr has not spied them yet but we knew this might happen. The circumstances are more dramatic than we might have expected but we will do what I said we would do. We will sail in a long circle this day and at dawn I will continue east."

Harald shook his head, *'Njörðr'* might have survived but the snekke? I fear Aed and his family will be dead."

"We know not, Harald of Dyroy. Keep those thoughts to yourself. Until we have evidence then they are alive. Smile for the women and children look to us."

I returned to the steering board and I spoke to as many of the clan as I could. I remembered Erik doing this when we had sailed from the Land of Ice and Fire; I was young but now I was the navigator. Reginleif and Erik awaited me at the steering board with a horn of ale and some salted meat and cheese. "Eat and drink for you have deserved it."

I smiled, "Ebbe, take a sight on the sun and I shall steer. Mark our course for I intend to sail in circles until the middle of the afternoon. I can eat and drink while I do so."

I saw that Ebbe was delighted with the responsibility and the fact that I trusted him. In truth, he had done well. Bear Tooth had merely followed Ebbe but then Bear Tooth was a warrior, as he had shown when we had been attacked. Reginleif and Erik stayed with me as I ate but soon my son became bored.

"I shall have to go, husband, but know that my thoughts are always with you."

I nodded, "And the baby was not hurt by the storm?"

"A Viking baby is born with a heart which is ready to fight for life. All is well."

As we began our turn I shouted, "Do you see anything, Danr?"

"The empty sea, Captain."

"Watch for wreckage!"

I saw some of those who had relatives on *'Njörðr'* turn at my words and I cursed myself. I should have sent Petr up to pass the message on.

"Aye, Captain."

We sailed two wide circles; the clan saw what I was doing, and the sides were lined with them as they sought our consorts. Ebbe said, quietly, "Fótr, we have reached the point where we began our search."

I had seen him making the marks on the tablet and already knew. I nodded, "Then we head east. We will keep the half-reefed sail. The wind is not strong, and they may be ahead of us."

As soon as the clan realised that we would be heading east then some of them turned to look at me for they knew what a momentous decision it was. I was abandoning the other two vessels. This was the real responsibility of leading the clan and, as soon as we reached land then I would relinquish the role. I should have known that the Norns were spinning as their threads still held us together and that meant they had not finished with us.

I managed to get a couple of hours of sleep before darkness once more overtook us and then, under reefed sails, I sailed east. The boys who had begun the voyage as novices had been tempered by the storm and now knew their business. They scrambled up the mast, sheets and stays as though born to it. They no longer had a nervous air and were even able to joke and banter with each other. They knew my routine and, with the hourglass once more in use, they knew when to bring my ale and my food. I allowed Ebbe a little longer asleep and waited until full dawn before I roused him. It was good that I did for Leif shouted, from the mainmast, "Captain! Wreckage ahead to steerboard!"

"Loose the sail!"

My shout woke the warriors and even before the ship's boys had scrambled up the mast to obey my orders the sides were lined with the warriors seeking a sign of *'Njörðr'*. I could see nothing but that was because of the watchers lining the side. I would just steer the ship.

"It is a sail and it looks like *'Njörðr's'*. That was an easy conclusion for the drekar had a much bigger sail.

"Reef the sail and try to gaff it!"

"Aye, Captain. A little more to steerboard!" I nudged over the steering board as Danr leaned out with the hooked gaff we used. "I have it!"

As the soaked sail was hauled on board, I resumed our eastward course. "Ebbe, go and check the sail to see where lies the damage." If the sail was whole, then it did not bode well for the drekar. I hoped it would be torn for that would just be storm damage. A whole sail would suggest that the ship had gone down!

Although it was my turn to sleep, I would not do so until I was certain that there was no more wreckage. Ebbe came back to me, "The sail has been torn. It is now too small for us to use."

I nodded and felt relief as it meant that there was a chance that the drekar was still afloat. The whole of the clan aboard my drekar now watched for we were seeking a large object, a drekar. When Petr shouted, "Wreckage ahead!" I expected it to be followed by shouts telling me that it was the drekar. The words, when they came, were shouted by Petr, "It is *'Jötnar'* and she has been dismasted.

Chapter 5 Fótr

Once again, I would have to shout words which I knew the women would not wish to hear but I had no choice, "Are any aboard?"

"Aye, Captain, I see movement but there is no sheep!"

I shouted, "Lower the sail and be ready to board the snekke!"

We sailed quickly even though the wind was little more than a breeze, but it still seemed an age until Ebbe shouted, "We are almost there, Captain!" I saw the half-submerged snekke.

Rather than raising the sail to stop us, I put the steering board hard over to almost put us into the wind and then reversed my action. The result was that all of the way went from us and we edged east on the gentle breeze. I saw Ebbe nod and smile. He was becoming a sailor and appreciated the skill. This time Harald and some of the other men were clinging to the outside of the drekar with their feet on the strakes. When I saw their heads disappear and the damaged ropes we had salvaged hurled, I knew that they were securing the drekar. When Aed's three children were rescued, followed by his wife, Maren Finnsdotter I spied hope for the first time since we had awoken to an empty sea. Aed was the last to be hauled aboard.

"What do we do with the snekke, Fótr? It is waterlogged!"

"Is it holed?"

There was silence and then Harald's voice came to us, "No, Fótr."

"Then Leif and Petr, go aboard and tie her to the stern. Bail her out. We may need her yet!"

I knew not why I kept the snekke, but I did. I suppose she had been made by my brothers and my father and that was the reason, but I genuinely thought that we might have a use for her. The Norns were spinning.

Once the boat was secured and bailed, I had the sail lowered so that we could go at full speed. We would lose some speed due to the tow but that mattered not. I handed the steering board to Ebbe so that, before I took some much-needed rest, I could speak with Aed.

He looked up at me as I approached, "Where is Padraig and *'Njörðr'*, Fótr?"

I shook my head, "We thought you both lost until we found you. What happened?" I needed to know to discover what we had done that they had not.

He shook his head, "You are younger than we, Fótr, but Erik trained you well. You are a better sailor. We saw you reef your sail and I was slow to react. My brother was slower. In the dark, we were travelling so fast that I had to put the steering board over to avoid your stern. We overtook you and you knew not for we were both too busy trying to reef our sails and the night was as black as the Morrigan's heart! Once we had passed your drekar we briefly saw my brother, but the wind was blowing so hard that it was like trying to ride an untamed stallion! We lost the sheep that first night and the hens followed soon after. It was all that Maren could do to keep the children inside the snekke and I had to fight it all the way. The sail and the mast lasted but a day and a night and then the winds sheared them. We would have been dragged to our deaths had Maren not used my sword to hack through the rope. Our food, water and ale were swept away. Until yesterday I had not slept, and I clung on to the steering board as though it was life itself. When the storm blew out, I could not help myself, I just fell asleep. We were so exhausted that had you not seen us we would have perished upon the seas. We owe you our lives, Fótr, for you did that which you promised."

I nodded, "I am just sorry that your family had to suffer so."

It was as though he suddenly realised that he had another family, "And Padraig? Where is he?"

"We have not seen them, but we found part of their sail. They may have suffered as much as you did, perhaps more." His face fell, "We will continue to search but, for now, we will reef our sails and I will get some rest for I must steer this night. From what you say, Padraig will be ahead of us for we deliberately sailed in a circle to seek you. If he did as you then he will be to the east of us."

I confess that exhausted though I was I found it hard to sleep for, as well as my itching arm, I wondered if I could have done anything differently. Had I not sailed in the circle then I would have found Aed sooner. Suppose I was too late to find Padraig and his drekar was already swamped and sinking? When we made landfall then I would relinquish the clan for I was not meant to lead, and I just wanted to be a husband and a father. Arne had been the leader and he was gone. I was not woken during the night but, despite my exhaustion, I woke naturally while the sun was still high in the sky.

I saw that it was Aed at the steering board and he shook his head, "I see that you, too, are troubled and cannot sleep." He peered ahead, "I fear for my brother, yet I think that he is still alive." Aed and his brother were Hibernians and that meant that their religion was different from ours. I knew that Morrigan he had spoken of was their god of war. He and his brother had a connection like that of Erik and Gytha.

I stood and made water over the stern. I looked at the waves and saw that the swells were getting larger. The skies did not look stormy, but the seas were growing and the snekke was bobbing up and down. That gave me hope for the snekke was smaller than *'Njörðr'* and yet she was still sound. "You think he is ahead of us?"

He nodded and, as I pulled up my breeks and turned, he said, "I do not think that he is dead, and I do not sense him to the west. I think his size would have carried his ship further ahead of us. What I cannot understand is how this drekar avoided damage."

I shrugged as Aed's son, Erik, brought me a horn of water, "Perhaps it was the Norns although I had not realised the difference a few moments could make when reefing the sails. We

The Bear and the Wolf

had already tied down all that could be tied, and I had boys watching the animals."

"My brother and I sailed with Erik but did not learn as much as you. We were and are fishermen. This deep-water sailing fills us with fear and dread." He shook his head, "I confess that despite the riches of the land we have just left I shall be glad to get back to waters I know. This vast ocean is not meant to be sailed."

As I walked the drekar I thought about his words and realised that he might be right. We had fled a king whom we had thought to be a tyrant and yet the freedom we had found in the New World had been soured by our own tyrant, my brother Arne. If we had stayed there, then he would have sought more power and more conflict. Arne had been different to my father and to Erik. I saw then that Siggi would have been a better jarl. As I nodded and smiled to the women and children I thought back to Erik's tales of when the three of them had first sailed and all became clear; if Siggi had been the leader we might have managed to make a home in the west.

Galmr Galmrsson was at the prow, "Have you seen anything?"

"There were small pieces of wreckage, Captain, but nothing that suggested a drekar was close by."

Just then I heard from the masthead, "Wreckage to larboard. It is ahead of us!"

I looked up at the mast and saw that Sven Folkmansson was pointing just off our bow. I shaded my hands from the sun and peered ahead. After a few moments, the speed of the drekar took us closer and I saw that it was a barrel. I shouted, "Aed, take us to larboard. Reef the sails. Galmr, take the gaff and see if you can snag it."

The barrel would be proof that *'Njörðr'* was ahead of us for we were in the middle of the ocean and I doubted that any other ship had sailed this far west. As Galmr leaned out I grabbed his leather belt in my hand. I heard the barrel bump alongside us and then Galmr pulled. Harald of Dyroy leaned over and his mighty arms helped Galmr haul the small barrel aboard.

"Full sail!" It was as the sail billowed that I felt the strength of the sea. The ocean was gaining in strength. It might not be a cataclysmic storm, but we were in for some rough seas!

Mikel examined the barrel, "I recognise it as one of ours. See, here, there is a rune and it tells me that Faramir made this."

Harald lifted it up, "It is still filled and that means it was not abandoned." None of us thought for one moment that our drekar would waste even an empty barrel but Harald's words told us that the barrel had been lost accidentally.

"We keep a good watch! *'Njörðr'* is out there!"

Having found Aed and the barrel we all had reason to be vigilant. When we landed, we would need all the men that we could muster and we had, thanks to Arne, precious few left. The ship's boys had shown me that we had the raw materials to make warriors but, as I knew, it took time. As I walked back down the drekar I saw that Anya and Bear Tooth were together and were watching to steerboard. They were close and I saw that their fingers touched. Tostig and his sister, Helga, were on the other drekar. Bear Tooth would have to speak with them if he wished to join with Anya. Despite my responsibilities, I would need to speak with him for he did not know our ways. I doubted that Helga would object but Tostig was a different matter. He had been wounded by the Skraeling and, like Arne, had had a poor opinion of Bear Tooth.

I ate and spoke with my family and Ada. It was not sleep but I felt more rested than might have been expected. In my mind, I heard voices crying for me to come to them. I did not recognise them, but they spoke Norse and they were my people. Somewhere, in the vastness of the ocean, the rest of the clan was still alive! As darkness fell, I relieved Aed who went to the prow to sleep with his own family. He hoped that his dreams would take him closer to his brother.

Although the seas had grown in strength there had been enough sun for us to take regular sightings and I had a reasonable idea of our position. If we had been alone and not seeking Padraig, then I would have changed course to the northeast for the winds would have sent us to the Land of the Wolf more quickly. As it was, we were heading for the land of Hrólfr the Horseman. The movement of our drekar became more exaggerated. We were sailing with the barest of sail. We sank into troughs and climbed up salty cliffs. There was no rain, but the wind was stronger than at any time since the storm. We had learned the lesson of the storm and everything was tied down. The damaged rope had all been used and we had even used some of *'Jötnar's'* rigging to secure all that could be secured. Our women and children had built nests and mothers had tied themselves to the mastfish and mast with their children in their arms.

When dawn finally came it was not with the promise of a fine day. The clear skies had become cloudy and although there was a hint of red in the east it was not the sign of a good sunrise for, as the old sailors said, *'Red sky in the morning, sailor's warning.'* I glanced behind and saw clouds gathering. We were in for another storm and I prayed to the Allfather that it would not be as devastating as the first. Our rolling motion, even though we had built a drekar which was as stable as possible, made movement on the deck for most, impossible. Danr was at the masthead and I knew that less than a month ago he would have struggled to hold on, but he now did so with ease and it was his sharp eyes which spotted *'Njörðr'*. He was so excited that he forgot to give me its position!

"I see *'Njörðr'*! She is dismasted and almost beneath the waves, but I see people on her!"

"Let fly the sail! Where away?"

I looked and saw him pointing to the northeast, "To the larboard, Captain!"

"Warriors to the larboard side and all others to the steerboard! If she is sinking, then we must save as many as we can as quickly as we can."

As we sliced through the waves, rising and falling in the troughs and crests which were increasing in size, I saw the debris from the ship. I saw bodies! They were face down and not moving. I had delayed too long. My long circles seeking them had doomed many of our clan! I could now see, each time we climbed a crest, the doomed drekar. I did not see many people and I saw no animals. The ship had had almost half of the clan aboard her and I could see nowhere near that number. Aed was at the prow peering ahead as he precariously perched on the figurehead of Gytha. I watched him tie a rope to the figurehead and knew what he intended. Harald and my other warriors were also tying ropes to the stanchions and thwarts on the larboard side. When we reached the drekar then we would have to act swiftly. As we knew from Aed's rescue those who had been shipwrecked would be exhausted and unable to help themselves. We had all slept, eaten and had drunk water and ale.

Even as we neared the sinking ship, I saw Erin, Padraig's youngest, slip from her mother's arms and fall into the water. We were so close and yet one had died. Suddenly I saw a blur as a naked Bear Tooth dived into the seas and begin to swim towards the child. We were so close and yet two more of the clan would die. I held my course and shouted, "Take in a reef! Prepare to bring them aboard and quickly!" I could see that the whole of *'Njörðr's'* deck was below the water. She was sinking!

As we bumped into her, harder than I intended, I hoped and prayed that we had not sprung a strake. I could do nothing to help my men except to hold us as close as I could to the drekar. I used the wind and the steering board to do so and I found myself fighting both as we rose and fell with the sea. I heard shouts and calls, but I dared not divert my eyes from the masthead and prow as I tried to keep both on a straight line. In a perfect world, there would have been hands to help me but everyone was trying to save the survivors. Each time we grated against the hull of the doomed ship I winced for I knew not what damage had been done to the drekar I commanded. Waves now cascaded over us as we no longer rode the crests. I saw some survivors being carried across the deck, but I had to watch for the slightest deviation from a straight line. I also wondered what had made Bear Tooth take such suicidal action. Few men would dive into a calm sea unless life depended upon it and to enter such turbulent troughs was foolishness of the highest order.

I heard a cry, "She has gone!"

It was followed by Ebbe, who ran across the deck toward me, "We have all the survivors, Fótr! We can sail again!"

Even then I was reluctant to give the order to use the full sail, "But Bear Tooth!"

Ebbe grinned, "That madman and Erin are aboard! He used *'Njörðr'* to his advantage. He swam to her and we hauled him aboard. The drekar clung on to life until he and the child had boarded her and then climbed to safety!"

Even as I shouted, "Unreef the sail!" I said a silent prayer of thanks to the old drekar who had finally given her life for the clan.

The seas continued to punish us and prevented me from being able to discover who had survived and whom we had lost. It was night before the rough seas calmed and the women and children were able to untie themselves. Ebbe and Harald of Dyroy came down the deck to speak with me. Ebbe's face was not the delighted one with which he had greeted me when he had told me of Bear Tooth's survival. "Fótr, you need rest. I know it is night, but Harald will help me to steer and besides, Helga wishes to speak with you."

"She lives?"

"Aye, she lives."

Helga had helped my mother care for me as a child and, in the same way that Erik had felt a close bond with Gytha, so I had with Helga. I nodded, "The stars will soon appear. Keep us as close to north and east as you can. Those seas may have taken us from our course."

I saw now that we had too many people on board. I was grateful that so many had survived but I had to pick my way between the sleeping bodies on the deck. We might have to slaughter the animals to make room. I was now thinking like a captain and I ran through every solution even as I spoke to the women and children and sought Reginleif and Erik. I saw Ada kneeling over my wife, and I dropped to one knee, "Is she…"

Reginleif smiled up at me, "The baby in my womb does not like rough seas. She kicked more than usual."

Ada also smiled, "The babe lives and with rest, your wife shall be well." She looked around, "I fear that rest will be hard to come by."

I kissed my wife on the forehead and then rose, "I will see what I can do." As I headed toward the huddle of warriors close to the prow and the animals I wondered if we could have salvaged enough of *'Njörðr'* to make a raft. Then it came to me, we could use *'Jötnar'* as a sleeping snekke. With no barrels and chests then she could accommodate eight warriors. They would be able to descend if we hauled it close enough to *'Gytha'*. During the day or when we needed them as crew, then they could return. It would not be easy, but we were Vikings!

I saw that many of those rescued were covered with cloaks, capes and blankets. They were asleep. Helga and Padraig were there with their children around them and Aed and his wife were close by. All of Helga's family had survived. Helga took my hand and kissed it, "You found us, Fótr. In the middle of the ocean and you found us. I prayed that you would come."

I nodded, "I heard voices in my head, but I am sorry I did not come sooner! I sailed for a day in a circle trying to find you."

Padraig shook his head, "That was our plan before we sailed and it was right. My brother and I are not the sailor that you are, Erik! Your skill has saved the clan."

Helga squeezed my hands, "It was the Norns. They spun and they plotted. Had Ada, Gefn and I been together then we might have…" she shook her head, "This is *wyrd* and was meant to be. You cannot bemoan what is out of your control." She nodded her head to where Bear Tooth and Anya lay asleep together, covered by a fur. "When your brother saved Bear Tooth, we did not know the strength of the thread. Had he not then Erin might have died, and my sister might never have found happiness."

"You approve?"

She laughed, "Of course!"

"And Tostig?"

Her face became serious, "He died. He was swept over the side along with many others in the clan. They were the ones who did not heed my husband's advice. They were the ones who did not trust in me. My brother was weak. I think my mother knew that. He lost faith in you and others believed him. Arne's children all died too. Tostig had them with him when the wave took him. Lars Eriksson and your son, Erik Fótrsson, are the last of the blood of Jarl Lars."

I looked at Padraig, "What happened to you?"

"The same as Aed except that we were even slower to lower the sail. As we headed into the blackness of that storm which was sent to kill us our sail began to tear, and it was torn away before it could be reefed. *'Njörðr'* was a well-made drekar and fought the storm but the mast was ripped from us and the

The Bear and the Wolf

animals swept overboard. We tried to use the oars to keep us straight and that was when Tostig lost his mind. I believe had we been able to use every man on the oars then you might have found us, but he ranted and raved and argued. He said we were cursed. Men and their families were swept overboard. When the storm abated then I would have sailed in a circle too, but the steering board withy was severed, and we did not have enough men left to use the oars. That was Tostig. I am sorry for he is dead but he had weaknesses in him and they cost him his life. We drifted while I repaired the withy."

Helga smiled at Padraig. "My husband is a hero for he slept but an hour during that whole time and without him, we would have died."

"I had just finished the repair when the seas became rougher. That was when we lost Tostig and the others who died. They panicked and were swept overboard. I was at the steering board and I could do nothing."

I stood, "And now you should rest."

I turned to Æimundr Loud Voice, "We have too many on the deck. Have eight of the crew of *'Gytha'* sleep aboard *'Jötnar'*. We can use a double rope to secure it."

He beamed, "You are a navigator! That is a good idea. I will arrange it and you need to sleep. We now have Aed and Padraig who can sail with you. The other warriors and I have felt useless for much has been laid upon your shoulders. There is now help." He nodded down to Bear Tooth and Anya, "You and your brother Erik have been proved right. We needed Bear Tooth to come into the clan." He clutched his hammer of Thor, "The Sisters weave and they spin; who would have thought our threads and that of a Skraeling would have bound the clan together?"

I spoke to all the survivors who were awake and then made my way back to the steering board. There we had a little more space than in the rest of the drekar. I nodded to Ebbe and Harald and curling up in my cape fell asleep. My sleep was fitful and shallow; it was not filled with dreams but pictures and thoughts. We did not have enough food and water to last. I had a picture of the map come into my mind. By my reckoning, we were halfway across the ocean. We had had two encounters with the sea,

The Bear and the Wolf

and they had almost destroyed the snekke and they had sunk a drekar. Would a third kill us?

When I awoke, it was the next day and I did not feel refreshed. As I stood and made water, I saw that Æimundr Loud Voice and seven warriors lay beneath capes in the snekke. I had been obeyed and that still amazed me for I was one of the younger warriors. It was not Ebbe and Harald at the steering board but Aed.

"Well Aed, I am guessing that while I slept you were assessing our problem?"

He smiled, "You have a wise old head on those young shoulders, Fótr. Aye, I have." He pointed to the east, "I saw seabirds this morning."

My heart leapt, "Seabirds?" He nodded. "Then the land is somewhere over there!" I looked at the sky which was still cloudy. "We need the sun so that I can work out where we are. We will keep on this course. Do we have enough food?"

"Maren and Gefn say that there is enough salted meat and now that the storm has gone, we can fish." He nodded to the boys who trailed lines astern of us. We have finished the ale, but the storm gave us water. It is the animals who are in danger. They are almost out of grain. We cannot feed them all. Some must be sacrificed. Helga suggested that we keep the cow for the milk and slaughter the sheep. The sea will help us preserve them but even if their meat cannot be eaten, we will have more space and the cow might live."

I nodded.

Aed said, "Helga said we should kill them one by one here at the stern to avoid upsetting them."

I knew then what I had to do, "I will kill them and the first shall be a blót. I will thank Njörðr for saving us."

"That is good, and you are wise. You will make a good jarl."

"No, Aed, I am the captain and command at sea, but I do not want this weight upon my shoulders. When we land, if we land, then I will ask for a Thing to choose a jarl. I am not a warrior and do not have the wisdom to lead."

The winds were still, generally, from the west and we made good time. We were helped by the fact that we now had three experienced navigators. Although Ebbe had learned much he was still not as skilled as the three of us. The blót was made and the wind strengthened enough to show that the god had listened. That first evening, as the boys cleared the last of the animal waste over the side and then used the guts and offal for bait, I sat with Bear Tooth and spoke of his rescue.

"Why did you risk your life, Bear Tooth? It was brave but the clan needs you."

He smiled and Anya squeezed his arm, "And Erin, the clan does not need her? I am not of your people, so it matters not if I die. Besides she was a child and I could not let the gods of the seas take her without a fight."

I shook my head, "Anya, have you asked Helga about your marriage?"

She smiled, "Last night, we told Helga and she approved. Last night we lay together. We are now one!"

I clapped Bear Tooth on the back, "This is good, and Erik will be watching from the spirit world. He too will be happy!"

For some reason, that news brightened my spirits and I found myself grinning. Had Arne been the Jarl of the clan then he would have disapproved and stopped the marriage. It would have caused dissension amongst the clan and might even have destroyed it. Even though we were fewer in numbers the clan had never had a better spirit and purpose. Our adversities and even our losses appeared to have made us stronger. We had hope.

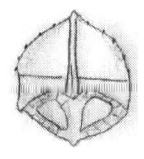

Chapter 6 Fótr

It was four days later, not long after noon, that Danr shouted down with the welcome news that our journey was almost over, "Land to the north!"

It was not a real surprise for we had been followed, for the last days, by seabirds. We still had animal waste and our fishing had yielded larger fish. The bones and guts we would have used in a stew were discarded for we ate our fish raw. Aed, Ebbe and Padraig joined me. Aed had been asleep for he had recently been on watch.

Padraig said, "It is to the north and not the east?"

I nodded, "It could be the south coast of Hibernia or Mercia. It might even be Hrólfr's land, but I doubt it." The hourglass was useful, but it was the sun which marked our position more accurately. Looking at the map Erik had made I saw that the land of Hibernia and Om Walum lay just a day or two apart. "We turn north and land on a beach at night. We have come a long way and the last thing we need is to fall foul of Mercians or Hibernians. We have less than twenty who can fight, and the voyage will have taken the energy from our legs. Until we reach the Land of the Wolf, we shall be cautious." We had lost warriors in the storm and the ships' boys would now need to become warriors.

As soon as we turned north there was a buzz of excitement throughout the drekar. Land could not come too soon for our cow. She had suffered badly, and I feared that we might have to slaughter her as soon as we landed. We reefed the sail so that we closed with the coast towards sunset. Danr had proved to have

The Bear and the Wolf

really good eyes and he had spied a beach with grass close by. I turned the drekar so that we approached it from the east. We did not have as good a wind, but we no longer needed speed.

Æimundr Loud Voice was the senior warrior and he organised the warriors he would take ashore. He did not choose me. I shook my head when he told me, "Æimundr Loud Voice, until we have a new home then I still lead the clan and as much as I would like to rid myself of the weight I bear, my father and brothers would not rest easy knowing I had not done my duty. I will come for I need to see that which you see. My eyes are those of a sailor and may see that which you do not. I will just be one of the warriors you take."

He smiled, "You have grown immeasurably, Fótr Land Finder. I believe that Arne held you back and that is sad for there was no greater warrior in the clan than Arne but being a great warrior does not always make a man a good leader."

We both clutched at our hammers for it did not do to speak ill of the dead.

I had the sail reefed and we used oars to edge into the bay. Petr was at the prow and he used a piece of rope with metal attached to test the bottom. We did not wish to rip out our hull on rocks! It was sandy and, therefore, safe. There were just five of us who went ashore: Æimundr Loud Voice, Bear Tooth, Eidel Eidelsson, Danr Gandálfrson and me. I took my helmet, shield and sword. I did not bother with mail. Once we had jumped into the waist-deep water, Padraig had the drekar rowed off the beach. They would wait for our return.

As I had expected none of us were able to walk steadily at first and if we had been attacked then we would not have been able to defend ourselves. The Allfather watched over us and we made the grass without being attacked. Bear Tooth was not from this side of the ocean, but he had shown that he had greater tracking skills than we did and Æimundr Loud Voice allowed him to lead. The Mi'kmaq was impressively silent while we seemed to make noise just walking. We travelled at least a mile and a half, following a path which had been made by man. We all knew that it would lead to houses or a farm and when we neared it, even I could smell the woodsmoke. It meant there was a settlement close by. We wished to be invisible. Animals could be heard in the fields and that meant the people would have men watching them. There were too many enemies to leave a field unguarded and so Æimundr Loud Voice restrained Bear Tooth and he waved us all to the ground. We crawled on all fours until I heard voices. If we could make out their words, then we could return to the ship. Annoyingly, when we stopped so did the voices. We had to be patient. Finally, we were rewarded. I did not understand the words, but they were clearly Saxon. The two shepherds were young boys and we would learn nothing from them. We headed back to the drekar.

When we saw the water and could risk speaking Æimundr Loud Voice asked, "Shall we land?"

This was the main reason I had come as I did not wish a second-hand report. We had not seen the settlement but the woodsmoke had not been so powerful that it suggested a major town. I guessed it was a farm or village, but this decision would be mine. "Aye, for we need it. Bring all ashore, including the cow and we will risk a fire and hot food. If you have men here, they can give good warning." I smiled and my teeth shone in the dark, "It will give me a chance to clear the stink from the decks." He nodded his understanding. It had not been just the animals who had fouled themselves on the deck, some women had been fearful of hanging over the gunwale and did not relish using the clay pots.

I signalled Padraig and he brought the ship in. We did not hammer in the metal spikes for that noise would carry to the farm. The wind would not take our smoke in that direction as it was coming from the south and west. As people stepped down the gangplank, I commanded them to be quiet and to speak in whispers. I could do nothing about the grateful lows of the cow as it ate grass for the first time since the island so many days and nights ago but I hoped the noise of a cow would not be unusual in Mercia. I stopped the boys from going ashore, "We clean the ship. I want the barrels and chests organising and the deck swilled with seawater. When that is done, we can go ashore but we go in shifts. I want at least three of us aboard all night in case we need to make a sudden departure."

Once the ship was organised, I headed ashore. I would eat first and return to the ship. Reginleif and Erik had kept a space

The Bear and the Wolf

for me close by Ada. She handed me my bowl of stew and Ada leaned in, "Had you not demanded silence then the whole clan would have cheered you for you have done that which you promised and that is good in a leader."

I shook my head as I ate the first hot food in a long time, "I am not the leader; I navigate and when we reach the Land of the Wolf then I will become a father and husband once more."

She nodded and ate her own stew. There were pieces of brined mutton and some shellfish. It made for an interesting taste. "And when you relinquish the life of a leader will you be as Aed and Padraig? Will you become a fisherman?"

I confess that I had not thought that far ahead. My aim had been to reach the east and I had done that. "I do not think I would like to spend a long time away from my family. I believe I would be a farmer."

She beamed, "And that is what Erik would have done had he found the maiden."

"He did find the maiden."

"But he died. You are both alike and yet the two of you have much in common with Arne. He was the eldest and therefore became jarl but the two of you have better qualities." She shrugged, "I am just a woman. What do I know? Yet the Norns spin and they have saved both you and the clan. Think on that."

She had given me much to think about, but I still had many days of sailing left ahead of me. Once I had eaten, I returned to the drekar with Leif and I went around checking the ropes, sheets and stays by touch. The other boys returned when they had eaten. The tide was coming back in and so I sent a message to Æimundr Loud Voice to begin loading the drekar. I did not want to be stuck on the beach at low tide and I knew that it would take time to load the drekar. Despite the allure of solid ground and a fire, the clan obeyed so that, as the tide began to go out and the sun rose in the east, we were ready to leave. It proved to be not a moment too soon for Saxon warriors, Mercians by their garb, appeared in the distance. We had not made too much noise, but the smell of our fires must have alerted someone. It was an important lesson. We headed west, along the coast.

We had managed to miss Syllingar and the treacherous line of rocks when we had made landfall, but we would have to negotiate them now. Ebbe and Padraig stood by me with the hourglass, compass, tablet and chart. We sailed as close to the coast of Om Walum as we could as Padraig thought that there was a passage we could use close by the last tip of Mercia and Om Walum. It was a risk, but we had all heard the stories of the witch of Syllingar and none of us wished to risk her wrath. Had Gytha still been alive then it might have been a possibility. We were helped by the fact that we could not travel quickly for the wind was from the south and west; we had to tack. I had made the decision not to make another landfall before the land of the Walhaz! Mercia had too many burghs and they also kept a watch for Vikings. Even though we had no shields along our gunwale they would still view us as a threat. We hove to at night for I saw the maelstrom of wild water which marked the passage. If we were going to risk it then I wanted high tide and daylight. We waited and I slept.

We now had experienced watchkeepers and I slept better than when we had sailed the Great Sea. The next morning, I had every boy watching the water and the warriors manned the oars. The women and children were crowded around the prow and the mainmast. Ebbe stood on the gunwale and clung to the forestay. His left arm would guide me. It would be like when we had hunted the whale. The waters became more turbulent as we neared the rocks and I hoped that Ebbe was confident enough to make the correct call. He had sailed the drekar enough to know its limitations. The sail was half-reefed and if we had to reverse our course, we could do it quite easily, I hoped.

The first signal was to sail to steerboard and the coast, but I trusted Ebbe. Almost immediately he made me straighten up and the drekar lurched alarmingly as a wave which had struck a rock bounced back at us. We were buffeted from both sides by waves. From what Padraig had told me the passage was less than a mile long, but he had never sailed it. His knowledge was based upon what someone had told him. The next signal took me to larboard, and we travelled further before Ebbe corrected the course. This time the buffeting was not quite as bad, and we kept on the same course for at least two hundred paces. Our oarsmen were stroking easily for there was no need for power and then Ebbe signalled a turn to steerboard. When he kept signalling, I needed one-half of the oarsmen to back water and we seemed to head towards a rapidly approaching cliff. This was a true test of the confidence Ebbe and I had in each other. The women began to scream as the cliff approached and then when the cliff was less than one hundred paces from us, he signalled a sharp turn to larboard. This time I anticipated the need to use the oars and ordered the opposite action. And then we were through. The water still bubbled but Ebbe's hands in the air told me that there was no longer dangerous water ahead.

I grinned and felt like a ship's boy again as I shouted, "Full sail! In oars!"

Ebbe came back to me and grasped my left arm, "Thank you for trusting me!"

"And thank you for believing I could pull off those manoeuvres."

Padraig appeared and said, somewhat shamefacedly, "Had I known how hard it was then I would not have suggested that course. That was fine seamanship from the two of you!"

"It was *wyrd*, Padraig, and you have saved many miles. Now you can steer for a while, I feel the need to sit and recover my strength. My legs and arms feel like those of a freshly foaled colt."

It was getting on to dark when we saw the coast appear ahead. We were in the estuary of the Sabrina, that mighty river which can crush a drekar as though it is nothing. Once again, we headed for land and this time we landed before dark so that we could see the bay. It was surrounded by high cliffs and reminded me of the place we had used on the island in the west. Men were sent ashore and determined that it was safe. The cow, which had benefitted from one night ashore, was then let off the ship first. Her milk had ceased some days ago and we wanted her grass-fed. With warriors watching the women and children left the drekar with their cauldrons. We had had to use one of the sheep which we had preserved as bait for fishing as it had gone rotten. The result was that we had caught a large shark and we would enjoy a fine feast. I sat on the drekar with Æimundr Loud Voice, Aed, Padraig and Ebbe. I had considered asking Helga to join us for we were now within a few days of the Land of the Wolf. I would wait until I had spoken with the men first.

The Bear and the Wolf

"The map shows that we have the island they call Ynys Môn and then Man before we reach the Land of the Wolf."

Aed shook his head, "Avoid them, Fótr, for we were nearly undone when we left Larswick."

I nodded, "Then we have to sail between Hibernia and Ynys Môn. Can we do that in one day?"

Padraig licked and then lifted his finger, "The wind favours us and *'Gytha'* seems to be faster than when we left Bear Island."

I nodded, "Then, Æimundr Loud Voice, we have the men mailed and weapons to hand. We use the barrels and chests to line the sides and afford protection for the women and children. Aed is right and this is the lair of pirates. I would hate to fall so close to the end of our voyage."

"That is wise, and we will make it a fortress once we have eaten."

We had seen the last of the big seas and the barrels and chests would be protection for the women and children. When we left, the next day, we had to row for a while as we had a headland to negotiate and then the wind was from our larboard quarter. The warriors were happy to row for the voyage had meant they had not had to use their arms as much and all of the clan knew that if we were not welcomed in the Land of the Wolf then we would have to fight for a home once more.

We did not sail close to the coast as we were heading for the channel between the island of Ynys Môn and Hibernia. I saw a delegation of women approaching. It was Helga, Ada and Gefn who were the three most powerful volvas on the drekar. I had seen them spinning each day since we had sighted land and I had thought nothing of it. Now, as they approached then I knew there had been a purpose to their spells. Ebbe was standing close by and when Helga said, "We would speak with the leader of this clan, Fótr Land Finder."

It was the second time I had been called that and I wondered if the clan was about to rename me. I nodded and said, "Ebbe, take the steering board. I will watch the sails." Ebbe was not quite as obsessed with the sails and the ship as I was. I constantly looked and listened for the snap of the sail which told me it needed adjustment. Ebbe would not worry about such a sign. We went to the larboard side of the stern where they gathered close to me so that we could confer without being overheard.

"You have done well, Fótr; better, in fact, than any could have expected but the Norns have spun. We were sent here quickly for we were summoned." Confusion must have shown on my face for I truly did not understand how we could have been summoned. We had been on the far side of the world. Helga smiled, "My mother was powerful. She may have been one of the three most powerful witches in our world. When she passed over to the spirit world, she could speak with those in our old world. The three of us had flashes of her while we endured the storms and the seas. Since we have neared the land, we heard her voice." She shook her head, "No, that is not quite true. We thought it her voice, but it was another. It was Ylva the granddaughter of the Dragonheart. That is not surprising for we all know that she was once taken by the witch of Syllingar and imprisoned beneath the seas."

Now I was really confused, "Ylva? The one we seek?"

Helga nodded, "Aye, but the Land of the Wolf is in turmoil. We know not why but know that the Norns have spun, Fótr, and your work is not finished. It is you who will have to make the correct decisions and make them quickly. Your brother Erik was lucky, he had my mother to help him. You, I am sorry to say, just have us and even together we are not my mother." She handed me a piece of material. "We have spun. The old spell was used up when you rescued me and my family. This new one will help you and you should know that if there is trouble then the three of us will do all that we can to help you."

They went back to the mainmast and I was left with a maelstrom of a mind! Ebbe asked, "What was that about?"

"Trouble and I will heed it. Sail a little longer while I don my mail."

"That kind of trouble. I shall get your brother's sword when you are ready."

It did not take long for word to spread. The warriors had worn their mail since we had first sighted Mercia but now the younger men, the ones who were yet to be blooded as warriors, now sought their weapons. Bear Tooth joined me and asked what was amiss. I told him.

"Then I shall prepare my weapons too." He tapped my mail, "I am not sure I could ever fight in mail like this."

"You have the hide vest with the metal and that will suffice but if you are to fight in this new land then you will need a helmet."

He looked fearful, "This metal you have is like magic, Fótr. It is unnatural."

I nodded, "True, but unlike your people, we change the world in which we live. You will see buildings made of stone for, like the bjorr, we alter our world to make it serve us." He went to gather his weapons and, as we approached the channel, every man, youth and boy was armed and ready.

It was late afternoon when we spied the trouble. We had passed the island and Man was some way to the northeast of us when we saw a knarr. Petr shouted down from the masthead that the Norse knarr was being attacked by two Hibernian pirate ships. I confess that had Helga and the volvas not spoken to me then I would have avoided them and not risked the women, but I did not hesitate.

"Women and children behind the barrels. Warriors, we go to the aid of the knarr. They are of our people and the pirates are not!" I donned my helmet. The sail needed no adjustment as it was taut and taking us to them quickly. If nothing else the crew of the knarr would spy hope.

Ebbe joined me, "You have a plan?"

"Lay us alongside one of the pirates and kill as many as we can."

He laughed, "I can see that you are no warrior!"

"No, I am a sailor, but it is all that I can think of."

Bear Tooth, Aed and Padraig joined me at the steering board while the rest of the men gathered at the prow. The boys and the youths had slings and bows. They would line the larboard side and protect the women. Our approach meant that I was able to ascertain the enemy numbers. The low Hibernian ships were not ocean-going vessels. They were the type which raced out from an estuary to catch an unwary, lumbering merchant ship. The size of the ships had so far saved the knarr which had higher gunwales and the Hibernians had not managed to board her yet. I could see that would soon end as one of the knarr's crew fell backwards.

The wind had helped us considerably and we were rapidly gaining on the nearest Hibernian. "Reef the sails! Use the oars as fenders!" We could afford broken oars but not sprung strakes!

As we neared the battle, I saw Hibernians turn to look at us. The ship on the far side was in no danger but the captain of the one closest to us saw his dilemma. I heard a shout and the ropes tying the pirate to the knarr were severed but they were facing the wrong way and could not use their sail. Even as we approached the ship, they ran out their oars and attempted to flee. We did not need our own oars to protect us as we struck the oars on the Hibernian pirate. As they shattered and splintered, pirates were speared and spiked by shards of wood.

Æimundr Loud Voice did not hesitate; as the pirate ground against our side, he shouted, "Clan of the Fox!" and he and a dozen of our warriors leapt aboard the pirate. The men who followed him each had a shield and mail. The pirates did not. It was a short and bloody battle but there could be only one result. However, despite the brief nature of the fight, I was almost hit. One Hibernian, realising that I steered the drekar, loosed an arrow at me. It struck me in the chest, but I wore good mail and the hunting arrow merely stuck there. Had I not chosen to wear the mail then I might have been hurt.

I shouted, "Aed, go aboard the pirate! We can use that vessel!"

On the other side of the knarr, the other Hibernian cut his own ropes and they began to row west. The women and children all began to cheer. The last time the clan had fought had been a disaster and many men had died. We had fought our first battle since then and we had routed our enemy and taken a ship. Aed steered the ship so that it came to our steerboard side. It meant we could use the sail and lighten the load on **'*Gytha*'**.

The knarr nudged closer to us and the captain, bloodied and wounded, raised his arm, "We owe you our lives! Had you not come then we would have perished. I am Snorri of Beinn na bhFadhla."

"And we are the Clan of the Fox. We have volvas onboard, do your men need healing?"

He shook his head, "Lars is beyond help and we can tend to our own. Where are you headed for? I have not heard of the Clan of the Fox."

"We have sailed from across the far side of the Great Sea!"

The crew all forgot their hurts and clutched their hammers, "Truly?"

"I speak the truth."

"Then you did not fall off the edge of the world." He shook his head in wonder. "I would love to speak with you. Where are you bound, for when I return from Lundenwic I would hear the tale and pay for it with Frankish wine?"

"We are heading for the Land of the Wolf."

The crew all looked at each other and the Captain said, "Have you not heard?" I did not state the obvious, that we had been on the far side of the world and I merely shook my head. "The King of Norway has taken the land of the Wolf. Sámr Ship Killer and Ylva, great-grandson and granddaughter of Dragonheart have disappeared. The Dragonheart's son, Gruffyd and grandson, Ragnar were both given the blood eagle and their home, Whale Island, is no longer an open port. Only those who bend the knee to Harald Fairhair are allowed to trade."

My spirits sank to their lowest point since I had heard that my brothers were dead. Then the thought came to me that the volvas had heard Ylva's voice. She might be alive. "Where did Ylva live?"

"It is said that she lived in Myrddyn's cave which lay to the west of the Rye Dale, but none has seen her for this last year. The Land of the Wolf wears the yoke of Norway." He looked at the sky, "The weather changes and we have tarried long enough. May the Allfather be with you!"

"And with you!"

As they sailed south and east all eyes were on me. Aed brought the pirate around to our steerboard quarter and Æimundr Loud Voice said, "Do we head north, then, to Orkneyjar?"

I saw the three volvas looking at me and my hand went unconsciously to their spell, "No for that is Norwegian too. We came to find Ylva and Sámr. I believe that the witch is alive, and I would seek her." I turned to Padraig, "Is there not a small beach on the west coast of the land of the Wolf which we could use?"

He grinned, "Aye, Fótr! There is, I believe, an old Roman Road which heads east."

"Then, while I still lead the clan, we will seek the witch!"

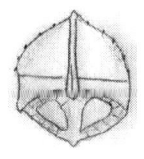

Chapter 7 Fótr

We reached the mountainous west coast of the Land of the Wolf a day later. The Hibernian ship was not as well made as *'Gytha'* and we made slower progress than I would have liked. After looking at inhospitable rock-lined bays we found a suitable beach and the deserted huts showed us that once there had been fishermen for they had a wooden quay. We tied up and, after Æimundr Loud Voice, Bear Tooth and our men had explored the land around and found it deserted, we landed. I took the momentous decision to unload the drekar. I knew that it was dangerous, but I needed to examine the hull for damage. We had shelter for the women and children and when we discovered no signs of people, I gathered the men around me.

"You have trusted me thus far and I would ask for you to continue to do so." Helga, Ada and Gefn flanked me and it felt as though I was wearing the strongest of mail. "Our volvas have spoken with Ylva and she lives. I think that, as she has spoken with us, then we should try to make contact with her."

Eidel Eidelsson had been the most outspoken of the advocates to return to the east and he spoke first, "If the King of Norway rules this land should we not bend the knee? We all agreed that a new land was preferable but look at the cost. We lost men at the battle of Larswick and then the Land of Ice and Fire. The battle at the falls was the Allfather's way of telling us to endure a king."

Æimundr Loud Voice shook his head and, as he did so I saw the three volvas smile, "To do so, Eidel Eidelsson, would be to laugh at those who died, Lars, Snorri, Butar Beer Belly, Arne,

Siggi and Erik. We owe it to them. And what of the Dragonheart? I never met him, but he made the Land of the Wolf a haven for fair-minded warriors who wished to live without a lord commanding them. His heirs are Sámr and Ylva and we would honour the Dragonheart if we tried to restore his land."

I sensed that the clan was divided. I could see it on their faces and so I spoke. It seemed to me that the words did not come from me but from somewhere inside my head, "Let us ask Helga and the volvas what they think we should do."

Helga smiled and put her hand on mine, "You are a good leader, Fótr Land Finder, and it is true that while this land presents dangers and threats, we are the Clan of the Fox. The wolf and the fox are brothers. If that was all then I would say let us sail away and find the land of Hrólfr the Horseman but Fótr is correct. Ylva is alive. Each night since we have been within sight of land the three of us have spun. We have taken potions to dream and each night Ylva has come to us. It is she who has led us here and she is alive! We spoke with Fótr about this and we believe that he is the one to find her." She looked at me, "You say that you wish our advice? Then here it is, you, Bear Tooth and Ebbe should travel to the cave of Myrddyn and speak with Ylva. While you are gone, we will make this our home and we will prepare **'Gytha'** for sea for it is a wise clan which prepares for the worst but hopes for the best."

"But I am no warrior!"

Ada smiled, "Nor was Erik but, like Erik, you have been chosen. My son was chosen by Erik as was Bear Tooth. The three of you are the hope of the clan." She cast a disparaging look at Eidel. Ada was afraid of no man.

Æimundr Loud Voice nodded, "This is *wyrd* and I trust Fótr. He says that he is the leader for the sea and not the land, but this will be a test. If he succeeds," he smiled, "when he succeeds, then that will be the proof that he is jarl."

I had no choice although I saw the fearful look on Reginleif's face, "For myself, I accept the labour you give me, but I would have Ebbe and Bear Tooth answer for themselves."

Ebbe nodded, "I am honoured to be chosen."

Bear Tooth put his arm around Anya, "I know not what you wish us to do for I am not of your people, but I am of your clan. I owe you all and I believe that my seed is now in Anya and that I am a branch of the tree that is this clan. I will follow the brother of the warrior who gave me life."

And as easily as that it was decided. We had weapons we had taken from the Hibernians and so Bear Tooth was given his first sword and his own helmet. He also saw a seax which he liked. To a warrior who had only used bone or stone weapons, his new weapons were truly magical. Ebbe was given a short byrnie and his father's shield. I still had my own shield. Ebbe had his sling and Bear Tooth his bow. We had taken some ale skins from the Hibernians and so we each had one. We were given the last of the good meat and the clan would hunt and fish while we were away. I had no idea how long it would take us to reach the cave. Its exact position was unknown to us. All that Padraig knew was that it was one or two days march east from the coast and lay near two bodies of water. That was not much help.

Ada provided us with the most sensible advice. "The folk who live in the Rye Dale will be Dragonheart's people. Unless Harald Finehair has slaughtered all Dragonheart's clan then the ones you find, the ones who are not warriors will be people to whom you can talk. Ylva is the most powerful witch in the Norse world. Those who live close to her will be her supporters. You will just need to convince them that you mean her no harm. We will spend as much time as we can in the dreamworld and will warn her of your arrival. You head for the Rye Dale and hope that Ylva can find a way to guide you thence."

Ebbe said, "If she is the most powerful witch then surely, she will know that we come!"

Ada's face showed shock and terror in equal measure, "My son, do not harbour those thoughts! Have you not heard my words? She does have great power, but we can aid both you and her! Take care."

I kissed my wife and son and then leaned down to speak to our unborn child. The volvas were convinced it was a girl, "My daughter, I pray that you wait for my return before you enter this world but if you are in a hurry to see the Land of the Wolf then know that I will return and then we shall all be together."

Even as we left, I knew that the Norns were spinning and would make a mockery of my words.

The Bear and the Wolf

It was dawn when we headed east. All that I had was a few vague places we might pass. The most crucial appeared to be a Roman Road and a long deserted Roman fort. We headed east along man-made trails knowing that if we met anyone then I would have to talk my way out of trouble as just three of us could not risk a fight. I was fighting for the life of the clan and there was no more important task. We saw signs that, like the deserted village the clan had occupied, there had been many people living here. We found deserted homes as we followed the man-made road. We found one clutch of homes with the skeletons of four warriors; identifiable by their hammers of Thor. One had a broken spearhead lodged in his ribs and another had a split skull. Tendrils of hair and flesh remained on some. It explained much. We crossed a shallow river but, as the road continued east, we followed it. After we had walked six or seven miles we were rewarded by a bigger river. There were huge stones in the river, and we used them to cross for we saw the road continuing east on the far side. Once on the other side we drank some of the water and nibbled some of the salted meat.

Bear Tooth said, "This looks nothing like my land. Where are the biting insects? Why are there no trees which rise so high into the sky that a man cannot climb them?"

I shrugged, "I confess that I know not. On Orkneyjar there were few trees and at Larswick there were just small woods and a mighty river. This land is a special one, Bear Tooth." As we continued up the road which ran along the river, I told him all that I knew of Dragonheart. All of it was in the form of sagas and songs. We all knew the songs. They were not ours and so we never sang them while we rowed but in the Land of Ice and Fire the warriors like Butar Beer Belly had sung them and they had heartened us in the depths of that icy land. Ebbe had been too young to hear them and so I sang the only one I could remember; I had liked the story. It was the song of Ylva's rescue by her grandfather.

The Dragonheart sailed with warriors brave
To find the child he was meant to save
With Haaken and Ragnar's Spirit
They dared to delve with true warrior's grit
With Aðils Shape Shifter with scout skills honed

They found the island close by the rocky stones
The Jarl and Haaken will bravely roar
The Jarl and Haaken and the Ulfheonar
Beneath the earth the two they went
With the sword by Odin sent
In the dark the witch grew strong
Even though her deeds were wrong
A dragon's form she took to kill
Dragonheart faced her still
He drew the sword touched by the god
Made by Odin and staunched in blood
The Jarl and Haaken will bravely roar
The Jarl and Haaken and the Ulfheonar
With a mighty blow, he struck the beast
On Dragonheart's flesh he would not feast
The blade struck true and the witch she fled
Ylva lay as though she were dead
The witch's power could not match the blade
The Ulfheonar are not afraid
The Jarl and Haaken will bravely roar
The Jarl and Haaken and the Ulfheonar
And now the sword will strike once more
Using all the Allfather's power
Fear the wrath you Danish lost
You fight the wolf and pay the cost
The Jarl and Haaken will bravely roar
The Jarl and Haaken and the Ulfheonar

They were both silent when I finished and then Bear Tooth asked, "What is a dragon?"

I let Ebbe tell him the answer for I had spied, ahead, a road which looked Roman. "Come, let us move for I see the road and perhaps the fort. If we find them then we know that we are on the right path."

Ebbe and Bear Tooth were like chattering magpies as we headed up the side of the river. I saw the steppingstones and we crossed the river beneath the place that the path twisted and turned before reaching the Roman Road. For Bear Tooth it was as magical as anything. He had never seen such precisely cut stones laid out to form a surface upon which he could walk. He was so fearful that both Ebbe and I had to step upon them first before he would risk it. The magpie was silenced. The going was much easier now that we were walking on a straight and hard road and when we found the half-ruined fort I almost shouted with joy. Once again it was Bear Tooth who became so fearful that he could barely move. Both Ebbe and I had seen stone buildings before but the Skraeling had not. Rather than try to explain its function I hurried him on. Soon the road descended, and I saw the Land of the Wolf laid out before us. I spied, to the northeast of us, a mighty mountain with a sheer, craggy face. This was as spectacular as anything I had seen in the land of the Skraeling. As the road descended, I spied a tendril of smoke rising from a hut in the distance.

We stopped and I took off my helmet and my shield. I handed them to Ebbe and Bear Tooth. "Keep these for me. I hope that I may speak to these people. If I am harmed, then you must continue east without me."

"Let us all go and that will guarantee your safety."

"No, Ebbe, this needs words and not violence."

Bear Tooth nocked an arrow, "We will follow."

"Do not begin a fight unless I tell you to."

I kept my sword sheathed as I walked from the road down the path to the small hut which lay by the stream. I deliberately kicked stones as I walked for I did not wish to surprise whoever lived in this remote valley. The door of the hut was open and a dog, which lay across the entrance, growled. I reached into my leather pouch for some dried meat, "Peace, for I am a friend."

The voice which came from inside the hut was old, but it was a friendly one, "And until I give him the command then no amount of food will let you pass." The man who stepped out of the door was white-haired. He had a scar on his face, and he was stooped, "Who are you and what is it that you want? If you are from Finehair then my answer is still the same as it was before, I will not bend the knee!" I stood in silence and he laughed, "You have too honest a face to be one of Finehair's killers. Speak."

"I am Fótr of the Clan of the Fox and ..."

He rubbed his chin, "The Clan of the Fox? Did I not hear that they were driven from their land by Harald Finehair?"

The Bear and the Wolf

I nodded, "I will tell our tale but before I do can my two companions come for one has an arrow aimed at your chest and I would not, for all the world, have his hand slip."

He laughed, "And that confirms that you are not from Finehair, fetch them and I will bring ale. I will not ask you to come inside for my home is mean and rude." He turned to his dog, "Friend. Now you may feed him."

The dog stood, wagged his tail and came to me. I gave him the meat and then shouted over my shoulder, "It is safe. The man means us no harm."

Ebbe and Bear Tooth ran and the dog growled. I said, "Walk and put up your weapons."

The old man came out, "Well, Fótr of the Clan of the Fox, I am Egge of Skelwith. This is Skelwith and once it had six families living close by." He handed us horns of ale, "Let us toast this meeting for you are the first friendly faces I have seen in this last year."

We toasted him and he pointed to a log, "I have no seats but the Allfather felled that one in a storm. Tell me your tale for the dog's stories are all the same; feed me, play with me, stroke me!" He shook his head, "And although he cocks his head to the side when I speak I fear he does not know my words."

I looked back the way we had come, and the sun was setting. We would go no further that day. I began at Larswick and told him the tale. When I came to the part about Bear Tooth, I stopped for the old man was curious. Bear Tooth allowed himself to be examined and then Egge said, "So there are men in this world we have not seen. I can now die a happy man for I wondered about that. Continue."

When I had finished, he stood and turned to make water, "I pray you to excuse me for I have an old man's bladder. It is too late for you to go further this night. I have a stew I have been feeding for a week or so. We will finish it and you can cut some wood for me as payment. While you do, I will tell you my tale."

He fetched an axe and Bear Tooth claimed it. He actually enjoyed cutting the wood for Egge and it allowed Ebbe and I to listen to him. "I was one of Dragonheart's warriors. These scars were honestly earned. I retired here to raise a family and we had many sheep on the fells. When Sámr inherited the land my three sons followed his banner. All went well until the day that King Harald Finehair decided he wanted the sword which was touched by the gods. Sámr and the Dragonheart's son and grandson fought them all off until they were lured away from the protection of Ylva. It was said a witch was used and the three of them were taken. Sámr was captured and Ragnar and Gruffyd tortured and killed."

"Why did they not kill Sámr Ship Killer?" Ebbe knew the stories of the Dragonheart's family as well as anyone.

"Finehair hired Danish witches and they used their magic to contain Ylva. She defeated and killed all but one. There were still many men who opposed Finehair and so he threatened Ylva. He had his own witch lay a curse upon Sámr. If any of the Clan of the Wolf tried to rescue him or fight Finehair then Sámr would be killed." He turned to me, "Pass me the salt, it is in that bowl." As he seasoned the stew he said, "Sámr is the last of the Dragonheart's blood for his son and grandson were taken with him. We know not what happened to his family. They may have escaped for the three would have sacrificed themselves to help their families live but the rumour persists that they were also killed."

I nodded as Bear Tooth brought in the wood he had chopped, "And what happened to your sons and the people who lived here?"

"Harald Finehair is a man without honour. Even when none tried to oppose him after he had Sámr in his power he sent a warband to execute warriors. We thought that we were safe and then they came. I was not here. I was in the hills watching the sheep. My sons and my wife were killed. Their wives and children were made thralls. That was a year since." He suddenly looked at me, "Why are you here?"

I sighed, "We have three volvas but the most powerful witch in our clan died in the land to the west. Ylva wishes us to speak with her."

His eyes widened and I saw hope in his eyes, "You are the one Ylva said would come! You are the hero who will save the Land of the Wolf! When Sámr was taken the rumour was spread that there was a warrior would come and Finehair would die. It was said the hero would come in the form of a wolf."

I laughed, "Egge, you have lived alone for too long! I am a navigator and I am not a warrior! My clan is that of the Fox! Do I look like a wolf or a warrior?"

He would not be cast down, "The Dragonheart had humble beginnings! He was a slave and look what he achieved!"

"He was a warrior!"

"He learned to be a warrior!" Come, sit, eat and have more ale. This night you have brought hope to me for while you cannot bring back my family you can wreak revenge upon their murderers!"

Despite my protestations, he refused to become depressed again.

"Ylva lives and even Finehair knows where. It is why he slew all those who lived in the Rye Dale. The men of Windar's Mere live still for they have good walls, but Hawk's Roost is where they keep Sámr and, some believe, his sons. The rumour is that they are chained and guarded by Danes whom Finehair had hired. They are Skull Takers and they have a blood feud with the family of Dragonheart."

I had finished the stew and I used the bread which Egge had provided to mop up the juices. It might have been an old stew, but it was delicious. The ale too was the first since one of the watches in the Great Sea. "And do you know where Ylva can be found although I confess that I am fearful of bearding a witch in her lair?"

"You will be safe for she sent for you, but I know what you mean. I would not enter the cave either, but you are chosen." He smiled, "It is less than two miles from here. I will take you tomorrow, but I will go no further than the path which leads to its gaping maw. I will show you the cave and then return here."

I had not known that we were so close. We drank more ale and Ebbe and I questioned Egge about Finehair and his men. We discovered that Cyninges-tūn was also occupied by Danes but the Clan of the Wolf still harboured thoughts of throwing off Finehair's shackles. It gave me hope but I still could not believe that I had been chosen. Perhaps I was to be the messenger and I was to sail somewhere, I knew not where, to fetch help.

We slept beneath the stars and my dreams were haunted by haggard-looking women who screeched and screamed. I was assaulted and assailed by skull bearing Danes and when Ebbe and Bear Tooth shook me awake I knew that I had been shouting in my sleep. It was not good preparation to meet a witch.

For an old man, Egge was remarkably spritely. I suppose watching over his flocks with his old dog for company would make any man healthy. We tramped across his land and he took us down trails and paths we would not have found ourselves. We crossed another river and then climbed up through trees. I saw Loughrigg Fell, for the old man named it, rising above us and, when we reached an open piece of wood, I saw the crag called Nab Scar across the Water of Rye Dale. We were growing nearer and all of us felt a weight upon our shoulders. It was as though we could not breathe.

Seeing our discomfort he said, "What you feel is the power of Ylva." Egge stopped and shook his head, "I can go no further for my legs will not go closer." He pointed, "The path rises and then twists around a shelf of rock. Before the cave it is flat and there is a pool of water. Do not touch the water for it is enchanted." He looked at Ebbe and Bear Tooth, "I am not certain if you should venture inside with Fótr as it seems to me that he is the chosen one, but each man chooses his own path. May the Allfather be with you and if you survive and return to your people then call in to speak with me. If you have not returned in a month, I will take word to your clan for they deserve to know your fate." With those cheery words he left us, and I led the other two, with leaden feet, up the twisting path.

Once we left the forest into the open we were almost blinded by the light and I saw, above us, the rocks which hung over the entrance to the cave. My shield was on my back and it felt as though it was dragging me down. When we reached the flat rock before the cave I stopped and said, "I will enter the cave with just my sword. Help me take off the mail."

It was a relief to remove the mail, shield and helmet. I took a deep breath and stared at the black pool of enchanted water. The cave looked as frightening a place as I had ever seen. I turned and looked at Bear Tooth and Ebbe. Bear Tooth was clutching the bear's teeth necklace which Erik had given to him and Ebbe gripped his Hammer of Thor as though his life depended upon it.

The Bear and the Wolf

I smiled, "You need not come with me. This task is appointed to me and I am content."

Ebbe said, "But I should come with you!" He did not sound enthusiastic.

Shaking my head, I said, "I think that if you take fear into the cave then that will consume you. Stay here and light a fire for I do not know how long I will be within." I saw the doubt on their faces. "What can you two do against a witch? If I am to die on this quest, then you two can return to Helga and tell her that I tried."

I saw relief tinged with guilt on their faces as they nodded and then I turned to approach the cave. I kept to the rocks at the side for the pool was larger than I had assumed. The cave was filled with darkness and I wondered if I should use my flint to make light. I was glad I had taken off my mail and my helmet for if I slipped and overbalanced then I might touch the enchanted pool. I edged into the darkness. The cave appeared to be empty and I stopped to allow my eyes to become accustomed to the darkness. Thankfully I saw the water and was able to avoid it.

"Hello?" My words echoed around the walls and danced across the water. They came back to almost mock me. There was no-one there and Egge had been wrong. Sámr Ship Killer and the Clan of the Wolf were doomed. I was about to leave and then thought better of it. If there was no witch, then the cave was safe, and I moved deeper within it. I suddenly stopped for I could smell animal and not just any animal but a wolf. I remembered a story my father had told me of Dragonheart's son who had come to this cave to kill a wolf. Had the wolves returned?

Unconsciously my hand went to my sword and then I heard a voice in my head, "You are safe, Fótr, son of Lars. Take your hand from your sword."

I could see nothing save the pool and darkness.

"I have come as I was asked but I am no warrior. I cannot help the Clan of the Wolf!"

I heard echoing laughter and suddenly the cave was bathed in a soft blue light. I saw the figure of a thin but tall woman at the far end, and she was seated on a high-backed chair. A skeletal finger beckoned me, "Come Fótr, and let me see you a little more closely."

I saw that there was water between us; was this a trick to trap me? "But there is water and it is enchanted!"

She laughed again but it was not a frightening laugh for it sounded like music and lifted my spirits, "This whole chamber is enchanted but it will not harm you, come and meet Ylva the Terrible. Ylva who Finehair so fears that he slaughters all who may help me. Are you afraid to help me; you who have braved the most terrifying of seas?"

I forced my legs to walk, "That was on a ship and there I knew what I was doing."

"And yet you and your brother are the only two men to have navigated those seas. You are both remarkable men."

I shook my head, "My brother is dead!"

"There you are wrong for he lives and will soon be a father again!"

If I had been struck in the face, I could not have been more shocked. We had abandoned Erik. He lived!

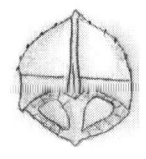

Chapter 8 Fótr

Before I could even think of a reply she had stepped down from her chair and approached me. I was terrified for she appeared to be almost translucent and I was not even certain if she was alive or a spirit. That she was beautiful was beyond question, but she was also the most terrifying figure I had ever seen, and I found myself quaking before her. She was the creature who had visited my dreams! She stepped close to me and took my hand.

"This is hard for you, Fótr, but you have been chosen. My cousin is held by the evil King of Norway and his Danish mercenaries. I have great powers, but I am powerless against the threat to Sámr Ship Killer for there is a witch who has placed a spell on him. She and her sisters were powerful and it took all of my power to destroy the others. The one who remains is almost my equal. When Gytha died I spoke with her and we sent for you and the clan. I know it meant abandoning your brother, but he was willing to make that sacrifice. Gytha, who loved Erik as much if not more than his own mother knew that the sacrifice was worthwhile and your brother lives. He lives so that you and your clan can save the Clan of the Wolf."

I was so confused that I knew not what to think. "I am not a warrior!"

Smiling she said, "You know not what you are. Erik did not know he was a navigator until he took that first step to the Land of Ice and Fire. You must trust me."

What I said next was either very courageous or very foolish, "But I do not know you! You might be a wight or an evil spirit come to trap me!"

She laughed and the laugh was so terrible that it chilled my very blood and filled me with even more terror, "You are brave, Fótr, and I can see how you fought the seas but know that I have such power in my hands and my mind that if I so chose I could destroy you where you stand." Her face became softer. "I was there when my grandfather faced down a Norn so I know what you are feeling, but I swear I will not harm you and that your family will be safe." She put her arm in mine and led me to a dark recess in the corner. "I will show you something that only Sámr has seen."

I know not how she did it but as we went into the dark corners light emanated from her body and we could see the interior of the cave in a soft blue light. There was a stone slab and upon it was a body covered by a wolf cloak. She pulled it back and I saw the body of a Viking warrior with a sword held in his hands. His features were still discernible; he looked old for he had grey hair and his scarred face was wrinkled but he had a smile upon his face. Even I recognised a mighty warrior, "That was a great warrior."

"He was the greatest for this is Dragonheart, my grandfather."

I gasped, "But he looks as though he died just yesterday and yet he died long before I was born."

"This cave is magical and was magical in the time of that greatest of wizards, Myrddyn. Do not question his state but gaze upon him and the sword. It is the sword which Harald Finehair seeks. This is the sword which was touched by the gods and if he had it then all of this land, Englaland would fall to him. We cannot allow that."

I nodded, "I accept that, but I am Fótr who is, at best, Land Finder; you need Fótr the King Killer and I am not that warrior."

She looked to the roof of the cave and nodded, "You were right, Gytha, Erik and Fótr are made of the stuff of Dragonheart." She looked at me, "Will you trust me?"

I smiled and shrugged, "I have little choice for I would die for my clan and you hold their lives in your hands. If I am right, then if I can rescue Sámr my clan will have a home in the Land of the

Wolf?" She nodded. "Whatever you wish of me I will do but I would do it alone. I would not risk the lives of any of my clan for we are now few in number."

She shook her head, "This is the time of the Clan of the Fox. Hitherto you have been defeated. You have won minor clashes but you have run away each time you lost."

Her words were true but they cut me to the quick, "That is unfair!"

"You are clever, Fótr, think about it. Orkneyjar? Larswick? The Land of Ice and Fire? Bear Island? You lost and you ran. If your clan wishes to live, then men must die, and you must fight for a land. My grandfather and Prince Butar did that."

She was right and I wanted the best for our clan. I would do as she asked, "I am yours to command, Ylva!"

"Then let us begin for time is precious and we must not waste it." She led me to the body of her grandfather. "This cloak is as famous as the sword and the Danes who guard Sámr fear it." She whipped it from the body and placed it around my shoulders. "When you rescue Sámr you will wear this with the head on your helmet."

"But I am not Ulfheonar!"

"They will see what they expect to see. If you bear yourself like my grandfather and appear with the bear cloak, then they will think that you are Dragonheart come back from the dead to rescue his great-grandson." I was dubious about that, but I nodded. "However, what will convince them is if you wield the sword that was touched by the gods."

I shook my head, "You cannot risk that for I can use a sword, but I am no warrior."

"The sword you see is not the real one for that lies at the bottom of the Water and will remain there until the end of time. It will remain where the Dragonheart ordered it but you will wield this." She picked up the sword from his body and handed it to me. "It is not the real one, but my grandfather had it made by the weaponsmith who made the real one. Bagsecg Bagsecgson was an artist and this was the last weapon he made before he died. The scabbard is the same, it is a great sword but not the one the King and the Danes want."

I touched the sword and I felt the power. "But…"

The Bear and the Wolf

"You are not a warrior, yet, but you will practise here while Bear Tooth and Ebbe return for the warriors from your clan." She waved her hand around the chamber, "Here the spirit of the Dragonheart will make you into a warrior."

I nodded, dumbly, for I was in her power and I knew it. How could I refuse to obey such a powerful witch who was inside my head? Yet I knew that I would fail her and many of the clan would die but what could I do?

Her voice when she spoke made me jump, "It is those doubts which will ensure that you succeed. A confident warrior might fail but your caution and your fears will get the deed done. Now the night is almost done. You must go and tell Bear Tooth and Ebbe to return to your clan and fetch ten warriors. They will meet you at the bridge of Skelwith where Egge lives. By the time they return then you will be ready."

I nodded and headed out of the cave. I saw that the entrance was lighter and that showed that dawn was approaching. The light of their fire illuminated the two cloak-covered bodies. I found myself moving silently over the rocks at the entrance to the cave. Had I been bewitched already? Bear Tooth stirred as I approached but I had to shake Ebbe awake.

"You live!"

I nodded, "And I have seen the witch, Ylva. You two must return to the clan for she has a quest for our men." I told them the details of their task, but I did not tell them of the sword, the cloak nor of my training.

"We are to leave you here?"

"Fear not, Ebbe, I will be safe and you two just need to bring the warriors to Egge's hut. You need not put yourselves in danger."

Ebbe shook his head, "Even I can see that our threads are bound, Fótr. You cannot cut them."

Bear Tooth nodded, "And what kind of warrior would I be if I let my two friends face death alone. Bear Tooth will come for he has now planted his seed. Perhaps that was why I was sent to this land. There will be a child who is of my tribe and yours." He smiled, "What is the word you use, *wyrd*?"

I laughed and put my arm around his shoulder, "Aye, Bear Tooth; this is meant to be, and it is *wyrd*."

They left as the sun rose over Nab Scar and I returned to the cave. I had thought to run but knew that was useless. Ebbe was right and this had been determined by the Norns and by the witch. I was merely a man and I could not fight such forces. Ylva was waiting for me and she had laid the wolf cloak on the floor next to the tomb. She had, in her hand, a drinking horn. "Drink this; it is a potion and will prepare you for your meeting with the spirit of my grandfather." She saw my fearful look. "I have told you, Fótr, that you are safe and it is in my interests to keep you so. Drink it and you will dream." As she handed me the horn she said, quietly, "You will see your brother, Erik."

That convinced me and I drank it. There was a sweet taste to it. She had mixed the potion with mead. It had been some time since I had drunk the nectar of the gods and I enjoyed it. I lay down on the wolf cloak which I had expected to smell but it did not. Within a few moments of closing my eyes, I was asleep, and I began to tumble into a deep cave; before I reached the bottom I was in the forests of the land close by Bear Island.

I saw a white-tailed deer and suddenly an arrow flew and struck the doe which galloped a few paces and then crumpled in a heap. It was then I saw Erik. His hair was longer, and it was tied behind his head. His arms, neck and face were burned brown by the sun, but I knew him. Then a Skraeling maiden and a child appeared, and they began to gut and skin the deer. I tried to speak but no words came, and I could not hear Erik's words as he laughed and spoke to the maiden and the girl. It was a bright day but a fog began to rise from the ground and enveloped them and the forest. I tried to clear it with my hands then, as though by magic, the mist evaporated, and I saw the forest, but it was not the New World for there was a large water and the trees were not the same. I saw Danes and knew them by the skulls that adorned their totem, they were Skull Takers. They walked the palisade of a stronghold which rose from the water and was surrounded by trees. I could hear no words but saw that they were vigilant as they walked the fighting platform. To my amazement, I saw the old man whose cloak I slept upon. He seemed to walk amongst them, but they did not see him. When he passed through two of them, I knew it was his spirit I saw. But they saw me and they loosed arrows and hurled spears at me. I seemed to bear a charmed life and they all missed me but then they leapt from the palisade and ran at me, I found that I had two swords, one in each hand and I fought them. No matter how many I slew there were always more of them and their blades, axes and spears hacked and chopped at my body, but I did not die. Then I saw a witch, it was not Ylva and she was chanting and weaving; I could no longer move my arms and I knew that I would die. Suddenly an arrow grew from her forehead and she fell. As she did, I tumbled to the ground and darkness swept over me.

When I woke, I spied the fire in the cave and saw Ylva stirring a pot. She was watching me. "You dreamed." It was not a question and I nodded. "The dream world is one which can sometimes fool us for the spirits do not always show us what will happen. There is some truth in all that you saw. Your brother is alive and with the maiden and her sister. You will never see him again. The spirits allowed that one glimpse for my sake," she smiled, "and, I think because Gytha wished it too. Now we begin the work to make you a warrior. We have less than three days and this will be hard. I have made a stew. All the food which I used was chosen for a purpose and will make you both stronger and more skilled. Now eat."

As I ate, I plucked up the courage to speak to her, "Are you alive or are you a spirit?"

She laughed, "The sleep and the dream have made you bold. The truth is, Fótr, that I live in both worlds and soon I shall leave this one entirely. When you have brought Sámr back here I will speak with him and then no other human will ever see me in this world. I will be here, in Myrddyn's cave but none will see my body. You and Sámr are the last two who will ever see me alive."

"And will I live?"

"You are alive now and, I hope, you will still be alive when you rescue Sámr, but I do not know for the Norns spin. I have not dreamed your death, but you go to fight against a witch and her spell. There have been warriors who have killed witches and they have been cursed. That is why you must take Bear Tooth with you."

The Bear and the Wolf

I shook my head, "His wife is to have a child and I cannot put his life in danger."

"He is witch's bane for he is not of our people and the witch's spells and curses cannot harm him. Why do you think your brother spared him? Why did he not return to his own people? The Norns spin, Fótr, and their threads can stretch across oceans. Bear Tooth must take his bow and an arrow which I will dip in a potion. He will kill the witch and the spell which binds Sámr will be broken."

"How do I get into the stronghold? I am guessing the Danes in my dream showed me where Sámr is held?"

She poured some stew into a wooden bowl and said, "We will leave that for now. You need to focus your mind on the task at hand; learning to wield the sword. Eat while I prepare to enter the spirit world and to summon the Dragonheart. When you have eaten then take the copy of the sword that was touched by the gods and begin to familiarise yourself with the weight and the feel. When next you see me, I will no longer be Ylva, daughter of Aiden and Kara, I will be the spirit of the Dragonheart."

She turned and left leaving me fearful and apprehensive. I knew how to use a sword and I had killed our enemies, but I had never fought a mighty warrior and I knew that the men who guarded Sámr Ship Killer would be great warriors indeed. I ate the stew which was delicious despite the unusual taste. I then stood and took the sword from its scabbard. I had never seen the real sword and had nothing with which to compare it, but the scabbard and the blade were as different from my sword as my sword from a seax. As soon as I picked it up, I could feel the perfect balance. When I tried a sweep, it felt as easy as waving my arm. I took some practise swings as I had seen warriors do before a battle and it felt so easy that at first, I did not notice that Ylva had reappeared but when I saw her she looked different from when I had seen her in the cave. It was as though I could see the wall behind her and when she spoke it was not her voice but that of a warrior. It was a kindly voice and reminded me of Snorri Long Fingers, for it was gentle and reassuring.

"Thank you, Fótr. They call you Land Finder but when you have saved my land they will call you Fótr the Wolf." I found it hard to breathe for the mouth and the face belonged to Ylva, but

The Bear and the Wolf

the voice was Dragonheart. I knew that even though he had been dead before I had been born. "The sword you hold is identical to the one which men feared while I was alive. It was powerful before Thor sent his lightning bolt to make it invincible. Swing so that I may watch you."

I did as he commanded.

"I can see that you are not yet a warrior, but you have natural skills. Imagine that you are on your drekar and in the Great Sea. Use your legs to keep your balance and then sway. I have no sword, but I will use my arms as though they are weapons. Do not move your feet but block my arm with your sword and sway."

"But I do not want to hurt Ylva!"

"And you will not for we are now in the spirit world and have neither form nor substance. What you see is Ylva's spell."

I did as I was commanded and, at first, it was hard not to step back but I managed to hold my ground and found that my leg muscles, which had stood me in such good stead during the storm, were stronger and I was able to sway away from the blows of the spirit arm.

"Good. Now you will not be using a shield. Take your own sword and use it as a shield. Holding the steering board of your drekar has made both your arms as strong as each other. You just need to use both weapons as one. Do the same as you did before."

This time the spirit of Dragonheart used both arms and, at first, my left hand was slower than my right, but I persevered and eventually I managed to forget I had two swords and I blocked all the blows. I was tiring and the Dragonheart's spirit must have sensed it for he said, "Now rest and while you do make yourself two scabbards to wear across your back." There was a smile and it touched me, "I cannot thank you enough for what you are about to do. I know what it is to be alone and fighting for another. When I was young, in Norway, I fought and defended Old Ragnar and then the clan. It made me the legend I became. This will make you something greater than either your brother, Erik or your father Lars."

Before I could say anything, the spirit had disappeared. I saw that there was leather, a bodkin and thin leather thongs by the fire and so I sat and worked on a double scabbard. By the time I had finished Ylva had reappeared. She looked tired but she beamed, "My grandfather is well pleased. Now sleep for we have another night to complete your training."

This time, when I slept, I did not dream, and it was only later I realised that she had not given me the potion. When I woke, I asked her about that. She ladled stew into my wooden bowl and said, "The Spirit World can be dangerous, and the potion can change you. We need you to be alert. If you wish to dream one more time, then we will do that when you return. For now, let us concentrate on making you a wolf warrior whom men fear." She took a helmet from behind her. "This is the helmet of the Dragonheart. It will convince the Danes, along with the cloak and the sword that you are the spirit of the Dragonheart. It will put fear into their hearts and slow their reactions. The witch will see through it but that is why you will have Bear Tooth. Now don the helmet for you will need to become accustomed to it. Then practise!"

The helmet did restrict my vision a little, but I liked the protection it afforded. I went into the routine I had developed the night before. When I had stopped my muscles had ached and now, as I began, they complained. I knew the experience for sailing a drekar across the ocean meant that I often had to work long beyond the pain barrier.

"The helmet will seem a distraction at first, but it is necessary. The Danes must believe that you are my spirit." The voice was that of the Dragonheart!

Once again, I jumped, and I knew that I would have to rid myself of such emotions if I was to succeed. I still did not believe that I would but Ylva did as did the spirit of her grandfather.

"This night I will teach you to use moves to go with the swaying motion you have mastered. When I fought, I tried to be unpredictable. If you use the swaying motion too often, they will anticipate it. I am teaching you to fight as I did and that will keep you alive long enough for your friend to slay the witch. Once she is dead then Sámr can be freed. Let us get into the rhythm of the combat. I will try to strike you and you must keep your feet planted on the ground." This time, despite the weight and distraction of the helmet, I found it easier and my guide stopped it. "Now, instead of swaying, when I strike, I want you to step forward on your right foot, pivot and bring a sword around to my back. It matters not which sword you use."

Of course, when I swung, I did no harm to the spirit and we spent, I know not how long using right leg then left leg, right arm then left, left arm then right, until my muscles burned. It was then he showed me how to strike below the shield of a foe into the legs which were not protected by mail or to stab at a foot. The moves we practised did not tire my body but they made my mind ache as I tried to take in the experience of a lifetime.

"That is enough. You could not stand in a shield wall and fight but, as Ylva will tell you, you do not need to do that on this quest. Once you are inside Hawk's Roost then you must move as quickly as a striking serpent. Your aim is to get to Sámr and the witch before they know you are there. The few moves I have taught you, the helmet, sword and wolf skin are the tricks which will give you an advantage over the Danes. They have guarded Sámr for more than is good for warriors who must fight constantly to keep them sharp. These Danes will be dull!"

I took off the helmet and, at that moment, Ylva seemed to disappear. I replaced the swords in their scabbards and placed the helmet close by. Ylva reappeared. "It is daylight now. You will not sleep until night time. I have food to prepare. Go outside and climb Nab Scar. I am comfortable here, but you need the Allfather's sun on your skin and to feel the land. From the top, you can see Windar's Mere as well as Rye Dale Water and parts of the Grassy Mere. The water is your friend. You will not need to sail to Hawk's Roost, but the Water beneath Olaf's craggy gaze will help you." With those enigmatic words, I turned to leave. Her voice was commanding, "Take the swords and wear the mail for you are now the warrior and not the sailor."

Climbing the crag was not as easy as it had looked. Whilst it was not very high the path was steep with many twists and turns. Ylva was right. Each turn gave a different perspective and view. It helped me to think about people. I had hated Arne but that was because of my position; I was below him and he treated me badly. Erik was more of an equal and did not hate him as much. Gytha was his superior and she was able to dismiss his faults and appreciate his skills. I would need to use my judgement if I was to complete this quest and then lead my people. The last thought struck me when I reached the top and, turning, spied the three bodies of water. It was as I sat down that I realised I had thought of leading my people. I had said when we had sailed east, that I would relinquish the clan but now I saw that I could be the leader. *Wyrd*!

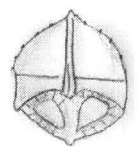

Chapter 9 Fótr

When I returned there was an enticing smell from within; all the food I had eaten had been delicious. Ylva was smiling and looked pleased. For some reason that made me feel pleased too. She smiled, "You found the climb harder than you expected?"

I nodded, "My legs need more work. I think I sat at the steering board for two days continuously. My arms burned but my legs had little to do."

She ladled food into my bowl and then, as I was eating, she began to interrogate me, "This Bear Tooth, what is it you called him?"

"A Skraeling. They are like us and have tribes and clans. He is now of the Clan of the Fox."

"Do they all look the same?"

"There are similarities between clans, but the tribes look different from each other. The Penobscot shave their heads at the side and the top sticks up like a cockerel's comb. They each paint their face differently. Why do you ask?"

"Bear Tooth now looks like a Viking, does he not?"

"He does. He has his hair in pigtails, and he wears breeks as we do. He wears seal skin boots instead of the mockasin."

"Then when you meet him, he must revert to the way he dressed when he lived in the west. Have him shave his head at the side and paint his face as the fierce tribes do. I want the witch to be terrified. You say he wears bear's teeth around his neck?"

"He does, Erik gave them to him."

"Then he should wear them too. And you, Fótr, will need to wear red cochineal on your face for that was how the

Dragonheart was seen. When the fire is out we will cover your mail in the soot for the Dragonheart, when he could, fought in black mail."

I had finished the stew and, putting the bowl down, I nodded, "And now, Ylva, how do we get into the stronghold for in my dream it looked to be an impossible task."

She smiled, "Already you are more confident, Fótr, and you seek ways to succeed for when first you came you did not. You are right it is an almost impossible task. Sámr and his oathsworn, Baldr, laboured hard to make it difficult for an enemy to attack but they also made it easy for a friend to enter." She went to the pool and took out some rocks which she placed along the edge. "You will know north from south?"

"I am a sailor."

She smiled, "Good, then at the northern end of the Water there is the stronghold. The rocks represent the wall. At the point where the wall is closest to the Water, here," she pointed, "if you wade in the water to your waist you will find a rock which was placed there by Sámr. Three men can move it and then slip inside under the wooden palisade. Two of your men must enter there, using the water for cover, while the rest wait by the main gate. The main gate will be guarded but at night time there will be just two Danes. You will need to stand in the trees which lie just forty paces from the gate. How you judge the time is up to you, but your men must be in a position to slit the throats of the two Danes when you use a light to illuminate yourself. You will say, through the helmet, *'I am Dragonheart, come from the dead to seek my blood!'*"

"But I do not sound like Dragonheart!"

"They have never heard his voice. The tales and the sagas describe him but not his voice. You must trust me that appearing like a wraith from the dark, appearing like the Dragonheart, will fix them and their gaze. Your men can kill them and let you in."

"I will send in four men and that guarantees success."

"See, Fótr, already you become the leader and you will become Fótr the Wolf."

"Where will I find Sámr?"

Her face hardened, "They keep him in a cage which is exposed to the elements. It is between the main hall and the warrior hall. They have built a shelter for the witch who watches him at all times. They need no guards on him for he is bewitched."

I nodded, "And Bear Tooth must kill her." When I had first come, I had been sceptical but now I saw the threads of the Norns. It was clear to me that the Clan of the Fox, despite our lack of experience, were the only hope for Sámr Ship Killer. Even if we did not seek a land, we still owed Sámr for he had saved us when we had left Larswick. We might die in the attempt but if we succeeded then we had done something noble and worthwhile. I was committed. "When we rescue, Sámr," I had to believe that we could do the impossible, "what then? We will be few in number."

"There are men in Cyninges-tūn who can fight. When the disaster happened, I took the shape of a wolf and warned as many as I could to feign obedience to Finehair."

"And that is why I wear the wolf cloak for I am to be the symbol of the clan."

Ylva laughed, "You do remind me of Sámr when he was young. I read your thoughts and see how you have changed since first you came. Others misjudged Sámr because of his youth and I think they do that with you. Your father sired two great Vikings."

"Arne was not all bad!" I said, defensively.

She nodded, "And you have only come to that conclusion since you stepped into this cave. On the road here you still harboured harsh thoughts of him."

I looked up guiltily. She was right.

"Now let us blacken your mail. There is an old fire over there. Roll the mail in it and then put the byrnie in the fire which we used to cook the food. We will bake on the soot."

"Will it harm the mail?"

"Quite the opposite, it makes it stronger. Just as the lightning strike made my grandfather's sword more powerful so the fire and the soot will not only add to the illusion that you are the ghost of Dragonheart, it will also make the links harder to break." When that was done, she waved me to the wolf fur, "Now sleep so that I may enter the spirit world and see where your warriors are. You will not dream, at least not one of my

The Bear and the Wolf

dreams but all dreams are sent to give us a glimpse of the past or the present. If you are lucky then you may see the future."

And I did dream but it was nothing to do with war or fighting nor was it of Erik. It was of my wife and son and I saw a blond-haired bairn. I had a daughter. I saw myself tending my fields overlooking the sea as the sun set over it. When I awoke, I wished that I was back asleep for the dream had been the most restful I had had for some time. Did the dream mean I would live once the quest was over? I dared not ask Ylva in case she had dreamed my death. It would be better if I just tried to do what I had been asked and hope that I survived.

There was food waiting and Ylva looked almost fondly at me. As I sat eating my food she stroked my hair, "Mine is a lonely life, Fótr, and your arrival has been a most welcome one for it has allowed me into your world and I envy you the simplicity of your life. Sámr and I have borne the weight of the clan since my grandfather died. When you have brought Sámr back here then I will leave this world. I am not sure that we shall meet again. This is for your daughter when she is born." She took, from around her neck, a necklace and from it hung the most well-made golden wolf I had ever seen. "I was named for the wolf and this was given to me when I was but a babe by the Dragonheart. I no longer need its protection, but your daughter might."

When she handed it to me, I said, "But this is gold! It is too rich a gift!"

"Fótr, you offer me all in doing this quest and you risk your life and that of your clan. This is a beautiful piece of work, but it does not measure up to what you are about to do for us." She smiled, "And I am being selfish for I shall see the world through your daughter's eyes and be part of your world. I will have a taste of a life which my power denied me."

I nodded and fastened it around my neck.

She then handed me two pieces of woven material. "This is for you and for Bear Tooth. The witch will have no power over Bear Tooth but if he wears this in his hair then the witch will know I have woven a spell for him and will guarantee that she is defeated. You know the plan and that you must attack at night. Once you rescue Sámr and free him from the curse then he will give commands. We have a land to recover." She then picked up a red fletched arrow and I saw that the arrowhead was covered in hessian. "This is the arrow which Bear Tooth will use. Keep the head covered until he is about to use it for the potion is powerful. Now let us prepare you for war." I stood. She placed a padded byrnie over my tunic and then helped to put on the mail. She handed me the cochineal with instructions to don it just before we attacked. She placed a head protector on my head and then the helmet. Finally, after she fastened the swords across my back, she fitted the wolf cloak over my helmet and fastened the wolf clasps. She stepped back and shook her head, "Even I am taken in. You are the Dragonheart! May the Allfather watch over you. Until the witch is dead, I cannot help you but when she dies listen for my voice in your head for the potion I put in your food each day has tied you to me, for a while, at least. Now go, your men await you at Egge's farm. Tell Egge I said that he should guide you to the Water at Cyninges-tūn."

She kissed me and I turned to leave the cave. I had entered fearfully not expecting to leave alive and now I felt sad for it had felt like home. Now I had to live up to the expectations of the most powerful witch and the spirit of the greatest of all Viking heroes. I dared not turn for I knew I would try to return. I had a quest and I would fulfil it not only for my clan but the greatest of clans, the Clan of the Wolf.

I had only travelled the path once, but my footsteps never deviated from it; it was as though I had walked it my whole life and when I saw the smoke rising from Egge's cottage I was but half an hour from the cave. I could not resist testing my new powers and I did not approach from the road. Instead, I headed up to the small wood to descend from behind the hut. I heard and recognised the voices: Ebbe, Bear Tooth, Egge, Æimundr Loud Voice, Eidel Eidelsson, Sven Eidelsson, Danr Gandalfrson, Gandálfr, Galmr, Mikel Finnbjǫrnsson, Folkman and Qlmóðr Ragnarsson. I stopped and listened; they were debating how long they should wait and Qlmóðr Ragnarsson was all for going to the cave. Egge began to speak of the terrible power of the witch. I walked slowly from behind the hut. The dog barked and alerted them but when Egge saw me he dropped to his knees, "It is the Dragonheart! His spirit walks this land."

The Bear and the Wolf

The others all drew their weapons. I took off my helmet, "Fear not, Egge of Skelwith, it is just I, Fótr! Well met!"

It was fortunate that I was wearing mail and a padded byrnie for they crowded around to hug me as though I had come back from the dead. When Æimundr Loud Voice finally prevailed on them to let me breathe Ebbe said, "You look different Fótr; what happened?"

I shook my head, "I cannot tell you except to say that I went into the spirit world and met with Dragonheart."

They all clutched their hammers and Egge beamed, "This is the best news I have heard since... ever!"

"We have much to do. Ylva has set us a task and I have to say that not all of us may return for we go up against the Skull Takers. We will be fighting Danish mercenaries. The prize will be a home in the Land of the Wolf but if you do not wish to come then speak now!"

They looked at each other and then Eidel said, "Tell us what we must do. We owe you that for you brought us home and I do not believe any other could have done so."

I nodded and explained our task. I did not try to make it sound easy and I stressed my role in all of this. I handed the red fletched arrow to Bear Tooth. While the others had been amazed at my tale he seemed to know it already. When I had finished, they looked at each other and Æimundr Loud Voice said, "I know not about the others but this seems to me something that we can do. I do not mind dying but I would like to do so for something which is worthwhile. To save Dragonheart's heir is the right thing to do!"

They all cheered, and I said, "Egge, you will need to lead us there!"

He laughed, "I will fetch my sword and join you for if I am to die then what better cause."

I shook my head, "I would rather you lived. Bear Tooth, can you shave your head and look like a Penobscot?"

"Aye, but is it true that the witch cannot harm me?"

"That is what Ylva said but do not fret for the witch will be too busy trying to kill me. You must use your arrow to strike true and forget that she is a woman!"

The Bear and the Wolf

"That I can do for it is for the clan, my wife and my unborn child!"

Egge told us that it would take less than half a day to reach Cyninges-tūn and as we had to prepare Bear Tooth we worked quickly. While Egge and the others gathered what we would need, Ebbe and I helped to shave the sides of Bear Tooth's head and to turn him into a Penobscot warrior. Although we did not manage to shave him as well as we might have, the cuts we inflicted added to the fierceness of Bear Tooth. We fastened the spell in his tufted hair and Bear Tooth added some feathers from the fowl Egge kept. He told us that the warriors who had killed others did this. "Long Sight was our best warrior and I will look like him!" The effect was astounding, and he looked as different from a Viking as it was possible. Galmr, Mikel Finnbjǫrnsson, Folkman and Ǫlmóðr Ragnarsson were the smallest of the warriors as well as being the ones who had fought and killed before and they would be the ones to gain entry into the stronghold. We would need the others to help me to grab the attention of the Danes and then effect an entry. We had a fire in a clay pot with a lid which would burn slowly. When we reached the stronghold, we could fan the flames and use it to light my head and face.

With my helmet in my hand, I followed Egge and his dog as we headed south along the ancient road to the heart of the land of the Wolf. We kept Bear Tooth at the back along with Æimundr Loud Voice to disguise him for as long as possible. Æimundr Loud Voice was the real warrior amongst us and despite what had happened in the cave he was still the real leader. The path we followed was no more than a hunter's trail. Egge told us that before the King of Norway had taken the land from the clan it had many travellers who marched upon it but since the culling of the clan, it was becoming overgrown. The road led us up into the hills above Egge's valley. We climbed and found ourselves in a watery dell surrounded by humps and bumps and we rested for it was not far from the Water we sought.

Egge shook his head as we drank from our ale skins, "This was the land farmed by Ragnar Bjornson and his sons. He was one of the warriors who fought alongside the Dragonheart. He fought hard against the men Finehair sent but it was in vain and he and his sons were killed, their women and children made into thralls and every stick and timber burned so that there is no trace left of them." He shook his head, "We have just two miles to go and it would be better to approach after dark. We can rest here."

As we ate the food we had brought Æimundr Loud Voice asked, "The Clan of the Wolf was a powerful clan. I know that Finehair has many warriors, but the clan had defeated the Danes many times; what happened?"

Egge shook his head, "Aye, you are right but they took the head of the clan first. When they captured the Dragonheart's family the rest of us all tried to fight but we did so in small groups. Ketil's family, in the north, held out the longest for they had the best stronghold, but they fell too."

I nodded, "It would have been better to feign acceptance and then strike at a chosen moment."

They all looked at me and Æimundr Loud Voice said, "Where did you learn such wisdom? We knew you could sail but the strategy of war?"

I smiled, "Let us say that when I was in the cave of Myrddyn with Ylva the witch and the spirit of the Dragonheart I was changed. If Harald of Dyroy was here, he would understand. I was tempered in that cave and the man who walked out was not the same who went in." I watched realisation sink in. "Let us go through this plan one more time for once we are close to the Water then we cannot speak. Egge, you and your dog must return to safety once you have shown us the stronghold."

"I can fight!"

Shaking my head, I said, "We do not need you to fight; we need you as a witness if it goes wrong and to take word to our families. We need not numbers and Ylva's plan relies on surprise and trickery. The fox is a clever animal, but it is not the largest in the forest. It survives through cunning." I saw him nod his acceptance. I had not insulted him by calling him old and that had made it easier to swallow my words. "Galmr, Mikel Finnbjǫrnsson, Folkman and Ǫlmóðr Ragnarsson, yours is the most crucial part of the quest. If you cannot eliminate the sentries, then we will have to battle our way in, and we will fail."

Mikel nodded, "But how will we let you know that we are in? We need a signal."

Galmr said, "If we make a noise then the Danes will hear."

Egge beamed, "Ducks!" My warriors looked at him as though he was mad, but I listened. He said, "There are ducks who live on the eastern side of the Water for there are reeds there and it safer for them. Even though it is night time this is the time of year when they are raising young. They quack. When you are inside then one of you quacks. Make it three times and then Fótr here will know that it is not a real duck."

I liked the simplicity of the idea. "That will work and then I will open the pot forty counts after I hear the duck. Egge, is it far from the walls to the gate?"

He rubbed his grizzled beard, "It is a long time since I was there but if you were swift then you could reach it in fifty steps."

I decided that we needed a little more time and so I said, "Then I will count to sixty and gain their attention by stepping out in the bear cloak. You must open the gate for us but avoid the witch." That, to my mind, was the main weakness of the plan. I knew, from my time with Ylva, the power of a witch. Gytha and Erik had had a bond which kept them close even though they were many miles apart. If the witch sensed us, then all our preparations might be ruined. I touched the spell Ylva had given to me. I prayed that it would work.

We left the tarn and headed towards the Water. We reached it before the sun had set and were rewarded by the sight of Old Olaf watching over the Water. Egge had told us the legend of Olaf and the sun setting behind him appeared to give the craggy mountain a crown. It also shone on the stronghold which Egge pointed to as we sheltered in the trees at the northern end of the Water. I could see that they had used the water and the rocks there as natural defence although there were hewn rocks which I could see. They were unnatural and explained how we might gain entry. There had been growth around the rocks, and I hoped that Ylva's recollection was accurate. I tapped Mikel on the shoulder and pointed to the rocks. He nodded, clasped my arm and then signalled for the others to follow him. They would skirt the water, as the sun set and make their way to the hidden entrance.

I turned and clasped Egge's arm. To my surprise, he hugged me. We left and I saw Egge and his dog hunker down to await our return. He had his sword across his knees. I knew that if we failed then Danes would die as would Egge and his dog. He would disobey me and our families would be forced to wait until all hope of our return had faded.

    Egge had told me of the road which ran around the northern edge of the Water and then climbed above Hawk's Roost. I halted just below the first bend and applied the cochineal to my face. I donned my helmet and the others recoiled as the fading light of the sun illuminated it. I could not see my own face, but they were clearly terrified by my appearance. I hoped that the Danes would be too. We climbed up as darkness fell. We passed the shadows of two deserted huts and they were testament to the ruthless nature of the Norwegian King. Egge had told us that the road led directly to the stronghold and so when we could smell the wood smoke and hear the noises from within the palisade then we knew we were close, and we left the road to enter the wood. I knew from Ylva that Sámr and Baldr had cut back the forest to enable them to see their enemies. We gathered dead wood as we passed through the wood and then stopped at the closest point to the stronghold knowing that we could not be seen. We, however, could see the sentries on the gate and we waited for the Danes to retire. We watched the number of sentries decrease as it became later until there were just the three night guards. I saw that the walls were not high, perhaps they were the same height as two men, but the fighting platform afforded them a good view of the road which lay to our right. I saw that there were three Danes on the gatehouse. That was more than Ylva had expected and I began to fear that the Danish witch had sensed us, and security was tighter than we had anticipated. We had made our plans and if I changed them then men would die. I had to trust that Mikel and the others were inside. Using our bodies to shield us from the walls we added dried material and made the fire in the clay pot brighter. I replaced the lid and then stood between two trees. Ebbe put the wolf's head over my helmet, and while he fastened it around my neck, I drew the copy of Dragonheart's sword and, with the others hidden, we waited.

    The duck call, when it came, seemed inordinately loud and I feared the Danes would be suspicious. I did not hear their words, but one said something and the other two laughed. All was well and I began to count in my head. Mikel and the others would be stealthily approaching the ladder leading to the fighting platform and they would wait until they heard my words before they struck. I had seen the wisdom of Ylva's plan for the Danes kept glancing back into the heart of the stronghold. When I reached sixty, I raised my sword as Ebbe took the lid from the pot and I shouted, "I am Dragonheart, come from the dead to seek my blood!" The face mask on the helmet seemed to change my voice.

The effect was dramatic. The three Danes were dumbstruck, and their hands went, not to their swords, but to their hammers hanging from their necks. I saw four shadows appear behind the Danes and heard the death rattle of the sentries as they had their throats cut. We raced for the gate and as we neared it, Galmr opened it. I took out my second sword and nodded to Bear Tooth who nocked the red fletched arrow. Ebbe took the hessian from the arrowhead. Speed was of the essence and we ran towards the warrior hall. There was no guard and Ebbe carried the clay pot with the fire. Folkman carried the dead wood we had collected when passing through the trees. They would set a fire outside the door of the warrior hall. Æimundr Loud Voice led half of the others towards the lord's hall while I led Mikel, Galmr, Bear Tooth and Qlmóðr Ragnarsson towards the shadow that was the cage of Sámr Ship Killer. There was a burning brand outside of the witch's hut but I could not see the witch. Bear Tooth and I were to the fore for we had to attract the witch's attention and fix her gaze on us. Bear Tooth was a good archer and had become even better since we had given him one of our bows. The arrow he drew had the potion which Ylva has assured me would help to eliminate the witch. I prayed that it would. I had great respect for witches.

I saw the skeleton that was Sámr Ship Killer in the wooden cage and my heart fell for it seemed we were too late. It was then that the witch gave a shout and stepped out. She saw Bear Tooth and her hand went to her spell bag. The Skraeling did not hesitate and the arrow struck her with such force that she was thrown back into the hut. Galmr and Mikel ran to the rope which held the cage and began to lower it. Ebbe had managed to start the fire and the dried wood of the door to the warrior hall was already afire. Viking halls had just one door. The only way out for the warriors was though a fiery doorway. Æimundr Loud Voice and his men were already inside the hall and I could hear the clash of metal on metal. Qlmóðr Ragnarsson opened the cage and, to my amazement, Sámr grinned and spoke, "I know not who you are, but I am grateful. You are the image of my great grandfather and yet I know he is dead! Have you a weapon for me for I will not suffer capture again?"

I reversed the copy of his great grandfather's sword and said, "Will this do?"

He nodded and took it, "Already I feel my strength returning. There is magic in this blade! If we are to escape then all in here must die! How many men have you brought?"

"Not enough but let us die hard, eh?"

Just then a handful of Danes used their axes to break a hole in the wall of the warrior hall and they ran, wearing just their kyrtles, at us. I had my old sword, but I drew my seax in lieu of a shield. Just then Bear Tooth gave a Skraeling scream. It had chilled our blood on Bear Island, and it had the same effect here. The light from the burning hall made him look like a terrible and fierce supernatural spectre. That allied to my appearance, with Dragonheart's helmet, wolf cloak and blackened mail made the Danes pause. It was long enough for Bear Tooth to send an arrow into the head of one and, a heartbeat late, a second into another. We ran at the rest and each faced a warrior. I remembered my lessons and while swaying away from the strike, I blocked the blow from the Danish axe with own weapon as I rammed my seax up through the Dane's ribs. I twisted as I pulled it out and was rewarded with the man's intestines tumbling after. He fell at my feet. Sámr Ship Killer had looked to be dead when I had first seen him but now, I saw that despite his condition he was very much alive, and he brought his sword to hack into the neck of a Dane. Bear Tooth had dropped his bow and was using a hatchet and seax to fight like a berserker. The warrior hall was now fully ablaze and Mikel and Ebbe joined us.

I pointed to the main hall, "Go and help Æimundr Loud Voice and the others!"

The Bear and the Wolf

Just then I heard a voice in my head, *'Fótr, you have done well but you have alerted the Norse in Cyninges-tūn. Bar the gates and trust in me!'*

I caught the eye of Sámr Ship Killer and he smiled, "I see Ylva can speak with you too. She is right. We must make this a fortress. Have your wild man bar the gates."

I shouted, "Bear Tooth, bar the gates."

I then followed Sámr as we ran through the stronghold slaying any that we found. There were not many for the warrior hall inferno had incinerated most of the Danes. We then went to the hall and, when we entered, I saw that we had lost warriors. Eidel Eidelsson and his son Sven lay dead, but they and the others had slain the leader of the Skull Takers and his oathsworn. The Clan of the Fox had been redeemed and the two had died well. The rest of my men were finishing off the wounded.

There was no time to mourn for dawn would soon be upon us and I knew, from speaking with Egge, that Cyninges-tūn was close enough for the Norse there to reach us in a couple of hours and these would be armed and mailed. They would be intent upon revenge!

Sámr took charge for this was his land and his stronghold. "I know not who you are, but I owe you all. For the moment we must defend the walls. There are few of us, but the walls are well made."

I nodded and took off my helmet. Holding out my arm I clasped Sámr's. "I am Fótr of the Clan of the Fox and Ylva and the spirit of your great grandfather sent me. Her words in my head suggest that she has a plan to save us, but you need to eat, Sámr Ship Killer, for you look weak. We will watch the walls while you eat and enjoy some ale."

He nodded, "Aye, Fótr the Wolf, I will but I beg you have the witch's body thrown into the fire for who knows what power remains in her even though she is dead."

Bear Tooth nodded, "I will do so for I have the spell and she cannot harm me."

As he left Sámr shook his head in wonder and said, "I can see that there is a tale here worth the hearing. I hope that I will be able to hear it at my leisure."

"Aye, as do I."

I ran to the fighting platform. Æimundr Loud Voice had spread the men out along the wall and I joined him above the gate. "Your brother Arne would be amazed at the change in you, Fótr. You fought that Dane as though you were one of Arne's hearth weru. You learned that in the cave?" I nodded. Like Sámr Ship Killer I must hear this tale. It makes our voyage east seem like nothing!"

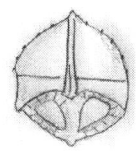

Chapter 10 Fótr

The smell of the burning flesh in the warrior hall filled the air and although it made me nauseous, I also knew that it had saved us for the Danes in the lord's hall had fought hard and killed two of our men. There were many more who had died in the inferno of the warrior hall. Æimundr Loud Voice had sent Ebbe and Bear Tooth to find some bows and arrows. They were now distributed along the palisade. Sámr came up to join us. He had donned some mail and managed to obtain a helmet. I took off the two scabbards from my back and handed one to Sámr. "The scabbard goes with the blade."

"Ylva gave it to you, did she not?" I nodded, "Then it is yours."

"No Sámr, it was given to me to create an illusion and it worked. I am no warrior, and this is yours by right."

"Fótr, I saw you despatch two Skull Takers as though they were novices. You are a warrior, but I shall keep the sword."

Just then Galmr, who was watching the head of the Water, shouted, "I see warriors approaching. They are on the road at the northern end of the Water."

Both Æimundr Loud Voice and I looked at Sámr. This was his stronghold and his land. He would command us. He rubbed his beard, "I have been a prisoner so long that I do not know how Clan of the Wolf fare."

I pointed north, "In the woods is Egge of Skelwith and if he is typical of the clan then there is fight in them. Ylva said that while the Danish witch lived and held you as prisoner then she could do nothing. I believe that she will be taking action, but I know not what."

"I do, she will rouse the volvas of the clan and they will tell their husbands and sons that now is the time to rise."

"Ylva said that many of the clan died. The last warriors to hold out were Ketil's sons."

"We have been hurt, of that I am in no doubt, but we are a resilient clan."

Now that day had dawned, and the smoke had drifted away we could see the interior of the stronghold. Sámr pointed to two piles of bones which had been close to the cage. I had missed them in the dark. "Those are the bones of my father Ragnar, and my uncle, Gruffyd. I have had to watch the flesh being devoured by carrion each day and that seemed to me to be what was happening to our land but Ylva's voice has spoken to me. There is flesh yet on the Clan of the Wolf and your wearing the wolf cloak, Fótr the Wolf, is a symbol of our people. Have your men come to this wall. When we built this, we made the gateway the only place that men could attack in numbers. I should have dug a ditch and had a bridge made but we all have perfect vision when we look back."

Æimundr Loud Voice cupped his hands and shouted, "Clan of the Fox! To this wall!"

We were a handful of men and I did not think we would survive. All that I could foresee was a glorious death, but our hopes would be ended. Just then Ylva's voice came into my head, *'Be strong and have faith! I will not abandon my heroes!'*

I drew my sword as the last of our men arrived. As I had expected, Ebbe and Bear Tooth stood next to me. Sámr looked at Bear Tooth and asked, "And where is he from? Miklagård?"

I shook my head, "He is from the lands beyond the Great Sea, he is from the west."

"You have crossed the Great Sea?" The great Sámr Ship Killer was amazed.

"Our whole clan did and my brother lives there yet."

Ebbe said, "What?" It was the turn of Ebbe to be amazed. I realised I had not told him about my dream.

"It is true, Ebbe, and I have not had time to tell you. He is not dead, and he lives there with his maiden and her sister. I saw him hunting. Ylva showed me."

"My mother always said he lived. I am glad."

Sámr laughed and said, "This gets better and better although before we can enjoy these strange tales, we have much bloody work to do. We will have to defeat these Norse for I am desperate to sit in my great grandfather's hall and hear the tale!"

Æimundr Loud Voice growled, "Aye, Lord Sámr, let us beat them first, eh, and then we can sit and drink mead and tell tales?"

Sámr nodded, "My great grandfather had a warrior like you. Olaf Leather Neck also understood the need to fight first and talk later." He raised his voice, "Unless they have ladders, they will have to use shields to lift their warriors to reach us. Keep them from the walls and use the piles of stones you see around the fighting platform!"

I had not noticed them before but Sámr and his people must have been prepared for a siege. The Danes had obligingly left them there.

Æimundr Loud Voice asked, "Do we know who will lead these warriors?"

"When I was in my cage, they took great delight in mocking and humiliating me. They dared not harm me for fear that I might die and then the clan would rise. The warrior who rules across the Water is Jarl Harald Haraldsson. He is Norse and was one of Finehair's hearth weru. From what the Danes said to each other he is not as good as he thinks he is and since he has been here in my land, he has done nothing."

"Ylva said the same. She thought that the Danes we fought were not battle-ready. Perhaps that was why I was able to win."

"No, Fótr the Wolf, you won because you were better than they were." Just then we heard the sound of men approaching down the road. "They come! Fight hard!"

Æimundr Loud Voice began banging his shield and he started to chant.

Clan of the Fox
March to war
Clan of the Fox
Hear us roar

Clan of the Fox
We fight this day
Clan of the Fox
The Viking way!

We had few voices, but we sang vigorously and, I think, we confused them for they had not heard of our clan. Even Sámr joined in. The column of men halted a hundred paces from us and formed a shield wall.

I shouted, "Bear Tooth do you think you can hit a face for me?"

"Aye! Which one?"

I laughed, "Any!"

Bear Tooth's tribe had learned the art of nocking, drawing and releasing in one motion. He had been able to do it with his own Skraeling bow and the one we had given him was much better for it was longer and made of yew. The arrow flew true and the distracted warrior was too busy locking his shield to notice the missile which smacked into his head and knocked him to the ground. The front rank was disrupted, and the effect was exacerbated by Bear Tooth's maniacal scream. His scream did not stop him from sending a second arrow into the shoulder of a second warrior. Their leader ordered them to fall back and they ran back down the road out of Bear Tooth's range. We jeered as they ran.

"Are you women or warriors?"

"You will never get to Valhalla!"

"We are the Clan of the Fox!"

"Have you filled your breeks?"

We laughed and Sámr turned to me, "You are a brave clan, what could we not achieve with all of your warriors."

I shook my head, sadly, "There is just a handful left with our women! The Skraeling and seas took a heavy toll. We are the last of the foxes!"

"Then when this is over, and we have won back our land, you shall choose your own part of the Land of the Wolf. The Norns spin long threads."

"They come!"

The warriors had rearranged themselves and they had formed a block six men by eight. We had killed two, but we would each

The Bear and the Wolf

have to slay five if we were to win. Sámr shouted, "You have seen what the wild warrior from the west can do let us show him what Vikings can do as well."

Bear Tooth loved a challenge, "Aye, let us see who can claim the most victories."

Although the warriors were protected by shields and they were more than one hundred and fifty paces from us Bear Tooth sent an arrow towards them. They raised their shields, but he had cleverly aimed it below the shields, and it slammed into the knee of the warrior on the extreme left of the column. He did not fall out of formation, but he would be of little use in a fight. I could use a bow and I thought I could use it well, but I was not as good as Bear Tooth. I nocked an arrow as the rest of the men sent arrows at the wood and metal protected column. Bear Tooth had shown me their weakness, and I recalled the advice of the Dragonheart. The Norns' threads were long indeed. Bear Tooth's arrow had made them nervous. Few had facemasks and so when I saw a warrior drop his shield to stop Bear Tooth's next arrow hitting his leg, I sent an arrow into his cheek. He screamed like a castrated pig. We were not killing them, but we were hurting them. One of Galmr's arrows hit a helmet so hard that it was knocked from the warrior's head. He was forced to duck behind his shield, and I knew that when they were closer his head would be vulnerable to stones. The closer they came then the more chance we had of hitting them for we were above them. Added to the fact that their wounds made keeping in step harder meant that they were disorganised before they reached us.

It was then that Ylva's voice came to me, *'Shout to them and say you are the spirit of the Dragonheart!'*

I was not sure that it would work in daylight but Ylva was my mistress and I would obey her. "I am the spirit of the Dragonheart! Flee now while you can!" The effect was extraordinary. Faces looked up and saw the blackened mail, the helmet with the facemask covered by the wolf skin and the red eyes peering from behind. They recoiled and their distraction allowed four arrows to find flesh and hurt warriors.

A warrior with a dragon crest on his helmet and a serpent on his shield shouted, "Dragonheart is dead and Sámr Ship Killer is a shadow of his former self. Let us break down the walls and slay them!"

The words were intended to make the men advance and the enemy obeyed but as they broke formation and ran towards the walls the rest of my men on the fighting platform hurled rocks at them and Bear Tooth loosed his arrows. Some of the enemy fell. Spears were flung at us as well as throwing axes. A spear hit my helmet. If this had been my helmet, then I would have been knocked out or even killed but the Dragonheart had a good helmet and the spear spun off into the stronghold. I shouted, "Is that the best that you can do?"

Before I had been to the cave with Ylva I would never have dreamed of uttering such a challenge but I now felt like I was a warrior. I heard axes striking the wood of the gate and wondered how long it would last. I picked up a stone and threw it down. The warrior who had lost his helmet was trying to use his shield for protection, but I threw it from the side. His head cracked and crunched like an egg and he fell to the floor. I am not certain if they might have broken the gates for we were not hurting them enough but, suddenly there was a cheer and angry warriors fell upon the rear of the column.

Sámr cheered and shouted, "It is the men of Cyninges-tūn! The tide it turns!"

Æimundr Loud Voice shouted, "My blade demands blood! Let us get amongst them!"

Our blood was up, and we descended the ladder, opened the gates and threw ourselves at the Norse warriors who were suddenly assailed on all sides. Æimundr Loud Voice showed me that day why he had such a good reputation in the Clan of the Fox, and he fought Harald Haraldsson one to one. I only saw it briefly for I had my own battle. I still had no shield, but I remembered the lessons from the Dragonheart. As the warrior I fought brought his sword over, I swayed to the side and ripped my seax across his face and, as he reeled, I lunged with my sword and tore it up through his skull. A second warrior who had the same design on his shield as the first screamed and raced at me. Swaying was of little use and so I spun so that he passed me, and I brought my sword around in a sweep. He had mail but my blade broke the links and then cracked into his spine. He seemed to shiver before he fell. And then it was over. There was no quarter given. These were invaders who had made thralls of the women of the Clan of the Wolf and they were not only slaughtered, they were beheaded and emasculated.

As we were walking amongst the bodies, I heard a dog bark and I saw Egge with a bloody sword take the manhood of a young Dane. He looked up as I approached and grinned, "You did not obey us then?"

He laughed, "When I saw the fire, I ran to the farms close by and roused the warriors. I knew you had succeeded. Riders are already racing to fetch men to fight alongside Sámr, our jarl. We were tricked and beaten once but we have learned that lesson! The Clan of the Wolf is roused!"

The warriors of the Clan of the Wolf just wanted to speak to Sámr and that was understandable. We were forgotten but there was mail and there were weapons. We had young men who would need to become warriors. Danr, Petr, Leif and the others would reap the reward of the deaths of Eidel and Sven. We were not greedy, but we did take the better mail, weapons and helmets. None of us wanted the dragon-topped helmet. Firstly, because it would attract attention in battle and secondly because it was easier to knock from a warrior's head. We collected what we needed and Æimundr Loud Voice sent Galmr to find a cart or a wagon. We had just loaded it when Sámr strode up.

"You are the heroes and you are being ignored. I apologise for my warriors. They did not mean to be ungrateful, but they now have hope and have risen up."

I shook my head, "Do not worry, Sámr Ship Killer. We were glad to help. We came to this land for we wanted a home and we owed you for the time you saved us." I looked around at the burned-out stronghold. "Will you stay here this night?"

He shook his head, "We will return to Cyninges-tūn. The women will prepare food." He glanced at the cart and laughed, "I can see that you are wise warriors. Come, by the time we walk around the Water, it will be dark. You can tell me your tale as we walk!"

My warriors took it in turns to pull the cart and Sámr's warriors surrounded us to protect the leader they had thought lost. The tale was a long time in the telling and darkness was about to fall when we stepped through the mighty gates of Cyninges-tūn. He waved an apologetic arm around the interior, "I know that it has been fouled by Finehair's men, but I would ask you to stay with me in my great grandfather's hall this night."

"We would be honoured, Sámr Ship Killer."

Bjorn Asbjornson was the leader of the warriors. He had many battle bracelets and he said, "The women began to cleanse it, lord, when the Norse left. We slew those that they left behind."

Sámr nodded, "And then tomorrow I will go to pray for my dead wife and children at my great grandmother's grave."

"But they are not dead! Finehair took them back to Norway with your mother and many of the other women. Did you not know?"

Sámr looked angry for the first time since I had met him. "How would I know that, Bjorn Asbjornson, I have been in a cage since I was taken."

Bjorn recoiled in the face of Sámr's words, "I am sorry, lord."

"Then when we have driven the last of Finehair's men and mercenaries hence we will gather ships and bring back the family I have lost!"

"But Whale Island is filled with the best of the Norwegian King's warriors!"

Sámr's eyes narrowed and he pointed at me, "This tiny clan sailed across the Great Sea, they returned here, and it was they rescued me! If they can do that what cannot the mighty Clan of the Wolf do?"

As we sat around the table Sámr shook his head, "I know not why I was angry with Bjorn Asbjornson. I had thought my family lost and he brought me news of them."

I smiled. I was half Sámr's age and yet I felt both older and wiser, "Sámr, I left my brother in the land of the Skraeling. There is little point in becoming angry at such things for it is the Norns. We are their playthings and all a man can do is the best that he can and hope that the Allfather approves. You know where your family lies, and you can fetch them back, but you are right; we have a battle here if we are to have a home. We are a small clan and cannot sway the scales, but we will fight alongside you."

He nodded. "Since my rescue, Ylva's voice has grown stronger and she speaks to me. Warriors are heading here in their hundreds. All was lost but your clan has brought hope. The King of Norway had three strongholds. This one was easily taken but the other two, Whale Island and Olaf's Stad on the Eden are stronger. When my men are here, we will try to take Whale Island. There are drekar there and we can use those to take Olaf's Stad. You and your band have done enough. You need not come with us. I know, from your words, that you all have families. Believe me, I understand that better than any."

I nodded, "When we set sail from Bear Island, we had a goal. We wished a home in the Land of the Wolf. That dream is still to be fulfilled. We will fight alongside you, but we are being selfish for it is for the clan that we do so!"

That night as we went to sleep, I reflected that I had become the leader of the clan without wishing to do so. I knew I could not relinquish the power, but I would learn the lessons of Arne. I would listen for I knew that Erik would have listened. That he would have made a better Jarl than either Arne or I was now clear to me but the Norns had spun. Erik was lost to me and I would not sail west to find him. Others might make that journey but not I.

Warriors began to arrive the next day. Not all wore mail but they each had a determined expression upon their faces. When they arrived, they were greeted by Sámr. They wanted to know that he was alive. I could see that Sámr needed to rest and recover his strength for he had been mistreated badly in the cage and deprived of sustenance, yet he clasped the arm of every warrior who came to swear to drive the Norse from the land. We kept apart from them not because we were excluded but because we knew the importance of the bond that was being reformed. We, too, had been a fractured clan; ours was the fault of Arne but we had had to speak with each other to heal the hurts. I thought it ironical that the one who had wished to return to the east the most, Eidel, had died along with his son and he had been the one willing to bow the knee. *Wyrd*. The rest, myself apart, had mixed views on the return. I had had time to think of my motives and I now saw that the need to return had been planted in my head. The Norns had spun and Ylva had summoned me. Once Gytha had died then we had been pushed into the race to come home by events beyond our control. In many ways that gave me peace for since I had seen Erik alive, I had felt guilt at abandoning my brother. I now saw that it was *wyrd*.

Although we kept to ourselves, practising and, in Bear Tooth's case, learning how to fight with a sword and a shield, we were not isolated as the tale of our journey was spread. Added to that was the fact that Bear Tooth was a cause of great curiosity. He took the stares in good part. Now that he wore a kyrtle again and wearing a helmet he looked a little less like a Skraeling when we practised. It was when we sat by the Water taking in the majesty and beauty of the land that he was seen as different and the folk of Cyninges-tūn would wander to the shingle beach to see us. The men asked us about the voyage while the women appeared fascinated by Bear Tooth. The maidens, in particular, seemed quite taken by him.

All of us wore mail and had a helmet and shield. I still wore Dragonheart's helmet, but I knew that I would return it to the cave once the quest was completed. The lessons from the spirit of Dragonheart had been the start but now I knew I needed to work harder to become a warrior. I had never fought in a battle and Sámr told me that we would have to fight shield wall to shield wall if we were to drive the Norse from the Land of the Wolf. Æimundr Loud Voice was still the leader of the warriors and he began to tutor us so that we could fight in a shield wall. We had taken the ash spears from the dead Norse and we now trained to use them. If I thought it would be easy, then I was wrong. There was a point of balance which had to be found. The shields had to be locked and, hardest of all, we had to march in rhythm. Ebbe, Bear Tooth and I had never fought like this and some of the others had not fought in the front rank. When we met the Norse the Clan of the Fox would fight together and so Æimundr Loud Voice had us march back and forth on the shingle covered beach of the Water. The slippery stones trapped the unwary and we learned after a few falls to be careful. We used chants to help us and we became familiar with those next to us. I was between Ebbe and Bear Tooth and we were on the extreme left of the line. I knew that was the safest place and Mikel had the most dangerous position, on the right.

"Hold your spear so that its shaft rests upon your shield. When we strike it must be as one and remember, the Norse will be doing the same to you. It will take skill and courage to strike Norse flesh while avoiding being skewered. I doubt not your courage but your skill?"

Æimundr Loud Voice was right; we had tricked the Danes and used magic to defeat them. Bear Tooth's skill with a bow had also aided us. The battle we would fight against the Danes would find our weaknesses. I found myself holding the two spells, the one from Ylva and the one from our volvas, in my left hand as we fought. I would need all the help I could get.

After three days Sámr came to speak to us, "Tomorrow we march to Whale Island. I have enough men now and we need to strike before Finehair brings more of his men from the islands. I come here to say, once again, that you have done enough now and need not fight."

I nodded for he had watched us practise, "You think we are not good enough and we might not be but if we cannot fight for our home then we do not deserve it. If we are marked to die, then so be it. The Norns spin, Sámr Ship Killer, and we are helpless for their threads have bound us."

He beamed, "A good answer, Fótr the Wolf."

I nodded, "I will leave your great grandfather's wolf cloak here."

His face became serious, "No, for I have dreamed and Ylva has spoken to me. Until the Norse are driven hence then we need the illusion which terrified the Danes. When this is over you and I will return to the cave and we will both say goodbye to the Dragonheart and to Ylva."

After he had left us Æimundr Loud Voice said, "That was well spoke, Fótr, but you realise that the Norse will try to get to you. Their heroes will try to defeat the one they think is the spirit of the Dragonheart."

"I know and that means I place all of you in danger too. For that I am sorry."

"No, Fótr, you are the jarl and when we return to the clan, the Thing we hold will confirm that. I confess that I was not sure you were anything more than a good sailor, but I can see now that I was wrong. When you went into that cave you changed and were transformed. I will follow you wherever you lead!"

The others all banged their shields in agreement, and I felt humbled and a little afraid of the responsibility. I held their lives in my hands!

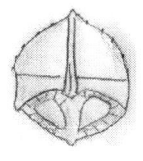

Chapter 11 Fótr

As we marched, in the thin light of dawn, down the water with the craggy features of Old Olaf looking down on us, Sámr confided in me that he did not think we had enough men. There were less than two hundred warriors. Forty boys and youths accompanied us, and they would be the ones whose stones and arrows would weaken the Norse before we clashed but Sámr knew that the best warriors had died.

"I have much rebuilding to do." He smiled, "As do you and yet you are far younger than I. Perhaps you will succeed where I will fail. I have three tasks: defeat the Norse, make my land strong again and find my family." He shook his head, "I put the task last which I should do first but that is because I lead the people. You are the leader of your clan, Fótr the Wolf, and there will come a time when you will have to choose."

He was right and as we headed towards the forest path I thought of Arne. He had not put the clan first. He had put himself first and the clan had paid the price. My father had always put the clan before all else and we had prospered. If I were chosen to lead the clan then that must come first; my family and I would be secondary.

Bear Tooth was beaming as we walked along the rough road through the forest, "I like this land, it feels like my home in the west."

Ebbe asked, "Do you miss your land and your people?"

I saw that he was thinking about it and he finally said, "Yes and no. My old family is dead, and I miss their spirits but my

The Bear and the Wolf

new family, the Clan of the Fox, Anya and you two make up for that. When I die, I will be with them all."

"Do you have to die with a weapon in your hand for that to happen?"

"No, Fótr, but when you are reborn it is with the body you had here in this world. A cruel enemy will take your eyes so that you cannot see in the next world."

Their heaven was different from ours. We could look forward to Odin's mead hall. Which was right?

Sámr had scouts out ahead of us; they were men who had lived close to Whale Island before the Norse had come. Sámr had wondered why the enemy had not sent warriors to scout us out and he had concluded that they knew that we had retaken our two burghs and were waiting for us. I also suggested that they were not as strong as Sámr had believed. Egge had told us that Finehair's men had ravaged the land after they had captured Sámr. Perhaps the Norwegian King believed that three warbands and his mercenaries could control the land for him. It was not long after the sun had reached its zenith that the scouts returned. Whale Island was closed. The gates were barred, and men stood on the walls. I thought that did not bode well but Sámr appeared happy.

I joined him and his senior warriors as we neared the edge of the forest. "Sámr, if they are locked within their walls then how will we take it?"

"We will not. They will come out to fight us. They, like us, do not know our numbers and their leader is being cautious. When they see how few we are they will bring us to battle."

"But if they have more men than we then they will defeat us."

"They will think that they defeat us. Riders headed to the south and east when you freed me. Men will join us from the east. My great grandfather fought battles here and I remember the stories. We will fight them with the forest behind us and we will leave them space to the east. Our men who come from the east may be few in numbers, perhaps only twenty or so but if you fight in a shield wall then the last thing you want is to be attacked in your rear. We fight to hold them. Men will arrive in Cyninges-tūn even as we speak and our people there will send them down to reinforce us. This battle might last all day, perhaps even into the night. The Norwegians will not be reinforced but we will."

Bjorn Asbjornson asked, "But, lord, you are still weak. How will you be able to fight all day and all night?"

"I am the last of Dragonheart's blood in the Land of the Wolf. The land will feed me, and the spirits of the dead will come to our aid."

When we left the security of the forest, we found ourselves in farmland and pasture. Sámr had told me that there were people who lived here who had occupied the land before the clan had arrived. They were friends and allies. It was they who had cleared the land. Sámr marched us obliquely to the south-west. We could see, in the distance, the wooden towers of Whale Island and, further east, the smoke from the houses of Úlfarrston. We stayed in column as we marched but Bjorn Asbjornson sent the boys as skirmishers ahead of us. They would warn us of any attack from the warriors who had taken the stronghold. I saw sunlight glinting from the helmets and the mail of those who were within the walls. I knew that they would see us as a long metal snake winding its way towards them. If Sámr was right, then the jarl who led them would be making his decision as we marched.

When we were half a mile from the walls Sámr had one of his men blow his horn three times. It was the signal for us to form a line. My clan warriors all wore mail and so we were in the front line. Sámr was twenty men from us and there were another twenty to our left. Those who formed up behind us had spears and shields but no mail. The boys advanced to stand forty paces in front of us. I saw the slingers picking up stones from the ground around them to add to their stock. We stood and waited. Eventually, Sámr began to sing and the Clan of the Wolf joined in. We did not know the words, at first, and did not join in immediately.

The Danes they came in dark of night
They slew Harland without a fight
Babies children all were slain
Mothers and daughters split in twain
Viking enemy, taking heads
Viking warriors fighting back

The Bear and the Wolf

Viking enemy, taking heads
Viking warriors fighting back
Across the land the Ulfheonar trekked
Finding a land by Danes' hands wrecked
Ready to die to kill this Dane
Dragonheart was Eggles' bane
Viking enemy, taking heads
Viking warriors fighting back
Viking enemy, taking heads
Viking warriors fighting back
With boys as men the ships were fired
Warriors had these heroes sired
Then Ulfheonar fought their foe
Slaying all in the drekar's glow
Viking enemy, taking heads
Viking warriors fighting back
Viking enemy, taking heads
Viking warriors fighting back
When the Danes were broke their leader fled
Leaving his army lying dead
He sailed away to hide and plot
Dragonheart's fury was red hot
Viking enemy, taking heads
Viking warriors fighting back
Viking enemy, taking heads
Viking warriors fighting back
Then sailed the men of Cyninges-tūn
Sailing from the setting sun
And now the blood of the Dragonheart
Will make the Norse fear and start
Their blood will flow from cowardly veins
Their bodies leaving base black stains.
Finehair will find that the wolf can bite
And even a cub knows how to fight
Viking enemy, taking heads
Viking warriors fighting back
Viking enemy, taking heads
Viking warriors fighting back

The Bear and the Wolf

We joined in with the chorus and I felt power surge through my body as we sang with the Clan of the Wolf. We were now part of the clan.

Either the words carried to the defenders, or the jarl decided that he had enough men to defeat us for the gates opened and disgorged Norse warriors. It soon became obvious that they outnumbered us, and I began to fear that our time fighting with the Clan of the Wolf would be brief. They formed a shield wall.

Bear Tooth was observant and said, "They have no bows. That is a mistake!"

Bear Tooth was a warrior and he had not seen the beaker as half empty but half full. We were outnumbered but they had no missiles. Our slingers and archers would weaken them before they could bring us to battle. As we had seen at Hawk's Roost that could make all the difference. The shield I had taken had belonged to Harald Haraldsson and had his dragon still on the front. I had not had time to change it. I knew that, along with my mail and helmet, it would make me a target and I felt guilty for I was bringing danger to Ebbe and Bear Tooth, not to mention the others of my clan. It was the Norns and I could do little about it now. I would have to kill as many as I could before I fell.

I saw that their line would overlap ours and I saw Sámr speak to two warriors. One came towards the men behind us and I heard the order given to echelon back. As I looked, I saw how clever Sámr had been. He had chosen to anchor our line by a wood and there was forest just half a mile further back. The echeloned line now touched the small wood and would give us some protection.

The Norse began to bang their shields and then I saw my first berserker. He began to chew on his shield and then threw it away. He took a long Danish axe and started to run at us. I had heard that the convention was for one of our warriors to go and fight him but Sámr was having none of it. He shouted, "Archers and slingers, kill him!"

The man was brave, and he was tough but the arrows and stones which battered him ended his life within twenty steps. That enraged the Norse and the whole line raced at us. The slingers and archers barely managed to loose a few arrows and stones before they had to run for the safety of our line. It was only later that I realised just how cunning Sámr had been. He had precipitated the attack and a line of Norwegians racing at a shield wall is not as effective as a solid line of men striking as one. I was relieved to see all the slingers and archers make our line and then, as Bjorn Asbjornson shouted, "Brace!" I squeezed tightly on the two spells held in my left hand.

I said, quietly, "Ylva and Ada protect me!"

The enemy came at us piecemeal and a large warrior with an axe ran at me. I saw him begin to swing his axe over his head when he was five paces from me. He was an experienced warrior who had done this before. I was almost mesmerized by the axe head, but I had enough of my senses to thrust with my spear. Ebbe and Bear Tooth struck at the same time. My spear hit his shield and his chest but Ebbe hit his shoulder and Bear Tooth's spear punched through the Norwegian's screaming mouth and emerged from the back of his skull. The axe fell from his lifeless hands and I punched his body away with my shield.

Bear Tooth's Skraeling scream chilled even my blood. And then the rest of the Vikings hit us. I felt a shield being pushed into my back as four Vikings struck at us with their spears. Æimundr Loud Voice had been correct. It was hard to strike while watching for the spear which was coming at you however the spirit of the Dragonheart must have been with me. Perhaps it was the wolf cloak or the helmet but, as I thrust, I swayed to the side. My spear hit the Norse shield and then slid up to tear into the Viking's eye. His spear scraped off the side of the Dragonheart's helmet. I punched again with my spear as the Viking screamed in pain and then the screaming stopped as my spearhead entered his brain. I feared I might be knocked off my feet but the shields in my back held me there. The dead man was held before me and it became not a battle of weapons but of bodies as the two armies pushed against each other. Then I heard the whoosh of arrows as our bows loosed their missiles into the sky to descend on those pushing against us. More than half would do no harm for they would hit helmets and mail but enough struck flesh to make warriors behind the front line lift their shields and suddenly we were pushing them from their feet.

Æimundr Loud Voice shouted, "Sword foot, move!" I stamped forward and the dead Viking began to slide down.

I said, "Watch your feet!" If any of us fell, then we would be skewered in an instant. I saw the dead Viking's body and used it to stand upon. The height it afforded me allowed me to strike down at the nearest warrior who was now below me. My spearhead struck his shoulder. He had mail but the head of my spear popped open a link and entered his flesh. Æimundr Loud Voice had told me to twist the head once it was in flesh as this would cause a bigger wound and make it easier to withdraw it. The Viking screamed in pain and was forced back. His movement allowed me to step forward and push his body to the ground. As I withdrew my spear, I stamped hard on his head with my sealskin boot. His skull crunched as he died.

It was at that moment that the enemy shield wall disintegrated. We had made inroads in places while, in others, our men had fallen. My shield was no longer locked with those of Ebbe and Bear Tooth. I saw a warrior run at me. It was obvious that he had sought me out on the battlefield.

"You have taken my kinsman's shield and I will have that wolf skin as weregeld! The Clan of the Wolf is a spent force!" He chopped at my shield with his sword.

I thrust at his shoulder as I shouted, "I am Clan of the Fox and I fear no faithless follower of Finehair!" Although my spear caught his shoulder, he had quick hands and he chopped the head from my spear. I rammed the broken stump at his head, and I caught his cheek. The shards and splinters of wood ripped into his skin. I dropped the ruined spear and drew my sword from the scabbard over my back. I squeezed the two spells as I did so. Now I would need all the power of every witch I had ever known.

Spitting out a tooth I had dislodged, he snarled, "You are a trickster! Wearing blackened mail like the Dragonheart will not help you for I am Leif the Mighty, and I have killed many men in single combat." He twirled his sword above his head and then suddenly lunged at me. I think he thought I would step back, but I did not. The sword came dangerously close to my head, but, as I swayed, it slid over my shoulder and I swung my sword hard below his shield. I hit his knee which was not protected by his byrnie and my hand jarred against the bone. He screamed again and I knew that I had hurt him. I sawed back with the sword and this time he had to step back on to his good leg to avoid falling. As I stepped forward, on my left leg, I punched with my shield into his already mangled face. He tried to step back again but his injured leg would not hold him, and he tumbled to the ground. I knew that I was lucky and as he fell, I put my sword to his throat and pushed my whole body down. He died instantly and I withdrew my sword and then looked around for my next enemy.

I saw that despite our lack of experience the Clan of the Fox had held, and my small band of warriors were all alive and together. Sámr, on the other hand, was surrounded. I shouted, "Clan of the Fox, on me! We must save Sámr!" They obeyed as one.

Æimundr Loud Voice was in his element and he bellowed, "Wedge!" Mikel and I stood behind him and the rest behind us. Æimundr Loud Voice shouted, "Get in step and sing!" We began to march towards the beleaguered Sámr.

> *Clan of the Fox*
> *March to war*
> *Clan of the Fox*
> *Hear us roar*
> *Clan of the Fox*
> *We fight this day*
> *Clan of the Fox*
> *The Viking way!*

I was on the left and a Norse warrior ran at us to stop us going to Sámr's aid. His spear hit my shield and, behind me, Bear Tooth's sword hacked into his neck. Æimundr Loud Voice was a force to be reckoned with as he sliced and slashed into the backs of the warriors trying to get at Sámr and his warriors. More of the Norse ran into the side of us but we were moving quickly, and we protected each other. I had never fought in a wedge before, but it was a formidable formation and their attacks were met by our shields, helmets and mail. Our swords and shields despatched those who came at us. Had they joined together then they might have succeeded but we had broken their attack and now our slingers and archers wreaked havoc as they picked off the isolated warriors who could use their shields to defend against one missile but against five or six they were helpless and stones cracked into helmets, broke arms and shattered kneecaps. Then arrows and seaxes ended the warriors' pain.

Those trying to get at Sámr turned as Æimundr Loud Voice used his sword to slice through the backs of two warriors. He had not gone berserk but Æimundr Loud Voice killed with such efficiency and immunity from the Norse weapons that he seemed unbeatable. Then Mikel and I were called into action. Mikel defended Æimundr's right side with his sword while my shield protected his left. I brought my sword over my shield and chopped into the shoulder of a Viking who was using his sword two-handed. I sliced through flesh to the bone and the sword dropped. As it did I skewered him. We were relentless and kept the same rhythm. To have stopped would have been fatal, certainly for Sámr. We hacked through three more of Finehair's men and watched the Clan of the Wolf as they bled for Sámr Ship Killer.

I saw Bjorn Asbjornson as he was felled by an axe and then Æimundr Loud Voice shouted, "Turn and protect Lord Sámr!"

For me, this was easy as my shield was to my left and I stood before Æimundr and Sámr. Sámr was wounded and I saw blood dripping to the ground. We had broken the Norse attack, but we were surrounded, and a ring of bodies marked where the brave warriors of the Clan of the Wolf had died protecting Sámr. Now that we were no longer moving, we had to endure sustained attacks. Had this been before I had been in the cave then I think I might have given up, but I was alive and had killed two handfuls of men. As a spear shattered on my shield and a second clanged off my helmet, I realised that I was encased in mail and the men we fought were not. We had a chance and I felt a new energy. Raising my sword, I launched myself at the nearest Norse and swung it down to hit his shield. He lifted his arm, but my blow was so powerful that I drove him to the ground. I swung my shield which had a metal rim and smashed him in the side of the head. I should have stepped back, but I saw another Norse warrior whom I thought I could defeat, and I stepped forward.

I heard a voice from close by shout, "No!" but I ignored it.

The warrior ran at me with his axe held high and he brought it down with the intention of splitting open my helmet and skull. I did not sway but I pivoted on my right leg so that the axe struck the earth and, as I spun around him, I brought my sword across his back, shattering his spine. I was unbeatable. I think that had the battle continued then I might have become a true berserker but, fortunately, there was a wail from ahead and I heard Æimundr Loud Voice shout, "They are being attacked in the rear! Help has come!"

Sámr, his voice a little weaker than it had been, shouted, "Clan of the Wolf, charge!"

The battle had been on a knife's edge but the sudden attack by, as we later found out, thirty fresh men, added to our attack, broke the spirits of the Norse. They began to fall back and the people of Whale Island, seeing victory in our grasp, poured forth and used every conceivable weapon to wreak vengeance on their oppressors. I joined the rest of our band as we ran after the fleeing Norse. They were trying to get to their ships, but it was too late. The townsfolk had blocked their escape and we were too close to them. They would have been better to form a shield wall and make us bleed. They did not. It was not a battle it was butchery and not a single Viking made it to their drekar, bobbing in the water.

Sámr fell and I feared he had succumbed to his wounds. I ran to him while the Clan of the Fox stood guard. "Where is the wound?"

He nodded towards his leg, "It was a spear."

I saw the body of a Norse warrior nearby and I took his belt and fastened it around Sámr's upper leg to slow the bleeding. I shouted, "I need a healer!" Then I smiled at him, "I am no healer, but it is not fatal."

"And, once again, the Clan of the Wolf is in your debt. Who would have thought, all those years ago that coming to your aid would save my land? *Wyrd*."

It was getting on to dark when we carried Sámr into the stronghold on a litter. We had, against the odds, won but Sámr had lost many of his best warriors. As his leg was stitched by a volva I said, "Have you enough men to rid your land of the last of Finehair's men?"

He smiled, "We shall have to try but we have their fleet and, if we sail north then we may find a way to defeat them without a battle. My great grandfather was a great believer in using your mind rather than a sword. We shall see but this wound means I shall not be stirring for a little while. Bring your people here. They will be safer. I will furnish a guide who can take you to the coast."

I was relieved for I had fretted and worried about my family. "Thank you, Sámr Ship Killer, I will do so."

Bersi Bjornson was from Cyninges-tūn, but his father had been the headman of the village which we had occupied. He was happy to take us and, as we headed north and west, he told me how he had avoided the slaughter. "I was on a drekar, *'Dragon's Breath'*, and we were raiding Hibernia. Bjorn Asbjornson was the captain. I think he was unlucky and may have been cursed." He shrugged. "Who knows? The Norns were spinning, Fótr the Wolf, for we ran aground in a storm. We almost wrecked the drekar and it took a month to repair it. We did not know of the treacherous trick which drew Sámr, Ragnar and Gruffyd from our home. We knew nothing of the attacks on Whale Island, my father's home and the stad of the clan. We spent a month collecting slaves and then returned. We were almost trapped on Whale Island, but we escaped. We planned on going to my father's home but when we headed up the coast, we saw that it had been destroyed. We found the same on the Eden. We held a Thing and decided that we should head for Cyninges-tūn. That is the heart of the Land of the Wolf. The repaired drekar was still leaking and so we let the slaves go and sank the ship. We headed south with the intention of fighting the Norwegians."

Ebbe said, "I could not sink a ship!"

"It was hard, but she was old and weary. It was kindness."

"You said you would have fought the Norwegians; what stopped you?"

"Úlfarrberg."

"Úlfarrberg?"

"Wolf mountain; it overlooks the Grassy Mere, the Water at Rye Dale and Ulla's Water. The mountain is alive. It is said that the Dragonheart found there the wolf which saved his family. It was as we camped nestled at its foot that the spirit of the wolf came into our camp and spoke with us. It told us to bury our weapons and to wait for the return of Sámr and the fox."

"Us?" Mikel's voice was filled with incredulity.

I knew that this was the work of Ylva for she had spoken to me. I said, "The Norns spin and their threads trap all of us. So, you pretended to be defeated?"

"Aye, it was hard for all of us wished to destroy the Norse, but the wolf had a powerful effect. I think it was the spirit of Ylva in the form of a wolf. That was how we were able to come to the aid of Sámr for as soon as Harald Haraldsson led the warriors from Cyninges-tūn we found our weapons and mail, slew the ones they left and then headed for Hawk's Roost."

Bersi was a good warrior and excellent company. We enjoyed our march, all the more so because it meant we would be seeing our families soon. We approached the beach from the south and I was relieved to see the drekar, snekke and pirate ship still there. I saw that *'Jötnar'* now had a mast. Aed and Padraig had been busy. The sun shone on our mail and we were welcomed like heroes. My heart sank when I realised that although I could see Erik, my son, my wife was not to be seen.

As the others greeted their families Ada took Ebbe and I and said, "Fear not, Fótr, for your wife is well and you have a daughter. She is not named yet for Reginleif said that she dreamed you and you would name her."

I nodded and, as we entered the hut and I saw the golden bundle that was my daughter, I said, "Aye, she is Ylva and here is her first gift from the great witch herself." I took the golden wolf and put it around the baby's neck. She smiled. I kissed Reginleif.

Ada nodded, "And that explains the power I felt from the babe when she was delivered. This will be the new matriarch of the clan." Her eyes went upwards, "I see Gytha's hand in all this." Turning to me she stroked the wolf cloak which I still wore. "And I can see that there is another tale to be told here, Fótr Land Finder!"

It was Ebbe's turn to laugh, "No, mother, for he entered the cave with the witch and was reborn and renamed. This is Fótr the Wolf and as great a warrior as any in the Clan of the Fox."

As I took in the looks of surprise on Ada and Reginleif's faces I was certain that I could hear the sound of the cheers from the dead. Perhaps it was just the waves on the beach but I knew that I had come home and would never cross the Great Sea again.

Chapter 12 Erik

I could not show the disappointment I felt, and I smiled as I climbed on to the quay at the deserted Bear Island and I forced a brave face, "We have a roof tonight and we can build a big fire. There is plenty of kindling." I pointed to Gytha's Hall. It was the best-built hall and, somehow, I knew that Gytha would wish us to sleep there. "We will sleep in there." As they carried their belongings into the hall, I lifted mine on to the quay and began to dismantle the sail. "You are not the biggest vessel I have ever sailed but you saved our lives and I will heal you so that you can sail again!"

I saw Stands Alone peering, fearfully, through the open door and I shouted, "Fear not. This is a good place."

"Come, sister. There is a sleeping chamber just for you!" Stands Alone took her sister's hand and entered.

Although the clan had taken all that they could, inevitably there were still valuable items to be found. I used my flint to light the bowl of oil in which a wick had been dropped. I saw the look of wonder on the faces of Laughing Deer and her sister. "Welcome to my world! I will fetch kindling and get a fire going. There is water at the rear of the hall."

I knew that the largest barrel would not have been moved. Kept filled with water it had no top and was impossible to move. I found the dried wood and soon the fire was roaring and made the hall seem homely. I had emptied the boat and brought in the last of the large fish and the dried meat. What else could I scavenge? I reasoned that the women whose husbands had died in the battle would have been shocked and more likely to leave hidden treasures behind. Palni's wife was young and I went to her hut first. I was immediately rewarded. She had left one cooking pot and four beakers. When I reached up to the roof, I found a forgotten jar with dried deer meat. In the corner, I found some pickled fish. The fish was a treasure but the vinegar even more so. On my way back I passed the vegetable plot and found that some winter beans were still in the ground. I picked them and some of the cabbage. We would eat well. I had, as yet, no plan but we had a roof, we had water and we had some food. With luck, I could repair the boat and, perhaps, improve it. Sailing up the coast had given me many ideas.

Laughing Deer said, "You must be a rich people. You left a bed which is filled with feathers! Was this the hall of a chief?"

I shook my head, "A witch, but do not worry, she was a kind lady and her spirit will make this place the safest home on the island. Here we have dried meat, cabbage and beans. I will seek out some ale for that would make the repast complete." I left the two of them to prepare the food and went to my hall, Ada's home. I almost wept when I entered. Ada had left all that belonged to me. Dreng's old mail was there along with my bear cloak. A sheaf of arrows in an arrow bag hung behind the door. There was my wood axe along with my spare daggers. I saw my shield and spare helmet. When I went to the cooking area, I saw clay jars lined up. She had expected me to return or, perhaps, hoped that I would. She was a volva. Had she seen me? I opened the jars and found seal oil, more pickled fish, dried pig meat, sausages and, best of all a small barrel of ale. I picked up the barrel and then saw, next to it, my drinking horn and a jar of mead. This was even better for Ada's mead was the best on Bear Island.

"Thank you, my love, and may the Allfather watch over you, your children and our children!"

Laughing Deer had never tasted mead and her first sip showed just how much she liked it. It was then that Stands Alone spoke her first words, "Can I taste?"

Laughing Deer just burst into tears and I smiled, "Of course, but just a little. This is a powerful drink but tonight we celebrate

The Bear and the Wolf

for we are now a family and a clan." I looked over to the corner where I had dumped my bear cloak, shield and weapons. "Perhaps we will be the Clan of the Bear!"

I am not sure they heard us for Stands Alone took a drink and laughed with joy and Laughing Deer hugged her little sister. For myself, I was content.

There were two sleeping areas in the hall which had belonged to Gytha and Snorri. While Snorri and his wife had shared one Tostig had had the other. I knew that if they had returned to the east then they would not have had the space for the beds. Stands Alone was content to have Tostig's. In truth, she was more than a little sleepy. Your first mead will do that to you. Laughing Deer was also a little giggly. While they prepared to sleep indoors for the first time since the rescue, I went outside to make certain that all was well. The boat was still tied to the quay but the empty village felt lonely and deserted. I was glad to return indoors and extinguish the seal oil. I put another log on the fire. It was warm enough, but I liked the comfortable glow it gave to the room. I could see that Laughing Deer lay naked beneath the blanket. I stripped too and slipped next to her.

Her breath was sweet with honey and she smelled of some flower I could not identify but the combination was intoxicating, and I found myself becoming aroused. "I have dreamed of this, Erik, since you first slipped into my thoughts and my dreams. Even though I was at first afraid, I desired you. Each night when we lay in our shelters, I wished to hold you like this."

I kissed her, "Enough words!" It seemed to be over too soon, but she sighed and fell asleep in my arms. I was now set on a new course and all that I knew was gone from my life. I hoped that Gytha would come to me and offer advice for I knew not what to do.

The spirit of the volva was powerful in the place she had died. As I slipped into a deep sleep, she came to me.

This is meant to be, Erik. Ada and the clan are not yet safe, and they face many dangers, but they are strong and Fótr will lead them. There are forces of which you are unaware and the Norns have spun. Spirits in the east have summoned the clan and they have a task to perform. You are no longer Clan of the Fox, they are gone. This is your world now and, while I am able, I will come to you. This maiden is meant to be at your side but the web which has been spun is a complicated one and I cannot yet see its shape. Trust to your instincts for they are good. They led you to the New World and there are other worlds that you will discover. While you live in this hall then I can speak with you but once you are on the mainland then it will be hard. One day you will have to make that journey. Be strong.

And then her voice left me, and I felt desperately empty. My world had been the Clan of the Fox and now it was gone. I took comfort in Gytha's words and knew that I would have to make this world, my world.

Now that Stands Alone had found her voice she could not stop speaking. She was like a chattering magpie. She was desperate to explore the other huts and halls on the island. That was no bad thing for I knew there would be much left which we could use. Nothing would be wasted. The three of us searched all of the huts close to the bay and we found many things which had been discarded. Some because they were broken and others because they had been forgotten. There were one or two things which were simply too big to take. One was a cart and Laughing Deer and her sister were in awe of the wheel. Stands Alone was still enough of a child to squeal with delight when I pushed her along the trail. We also found crops which had been sown but not harvested and the winter barley and oats were a boon. We could make bread and I could brew beer.

The second day we moved further from the bay and Stands Alone was delighted when I took the cart. Here we passed the graves of those who had died, and we passed homes which had been emptied long before our people had left. Already some of them were crumbling. Unless a turf hall was maintained then it would revert to whence it came, the earth. Laughing Deer and her sister repaired some of the kyrtles, tunics and breeks which had been discarded while I repaired Gytha's hall. There were not many repairs needed but I made the hall sound once more.

After a week the weather improved, and we felt the warmth from the land and the sun. We sat watching the sunset over the bay and I asked the two of them what they wished. Laughing

The Bear and the Wolf

Deer was surprised at the question, "You are a man and our leader. We do not decide such things, you do."

I shook my head, "The head of our clan was a woman. Arne, my brother, was the warrior but when Gytha spoke then all men listened. I would know what it is that you wish. I think of Stands Alone. You and I are content here and the island has all that we need. Does Stands Alone?"

Laughing Deer looked at her sister who smiled and said, "I am content here and I trust Erik. I still fear that the Penobscot will come to find us!"

Laughing Deer nodded, "And that is my fear too. We are safe here. Let us live on this island for there is peace and we both have much to forget."

"Then I am happy too!"

The next day I took my axe and headed into the forest while Laughing Deer and her sister made bread. The bread oven was a revelation to them! I hewed a tree which was as long as the birch bark boat. I intended to make it more stable. I would attach it a pace and a half from the side of the birch bark boat and then I could make a proper mast and sail. I would make a steering board. In my mind, I was planning for the day when we would visit Chief Wandering Moos and reaffirm our friendship.

This would be the fourth vessel I had built, and it was the smallest. Despite its small size I needed to be careful for the birch bark was fragile and I needed to use the original vessel as the base of the boat. I stripped the bark from the log and then shaped and attached bracing arms which, eventually, I would fit to the boat. I cut a cross piece which would be parallel to the new log and the boat. That would be the most crucial part of the design for that would house the mast.

That first day my work was cut short when a storm came from the south and west. We were lucky, for we were on the edge of it, but it was a terrible storm and we retreated inside the hall and barred the door while the wild wind tore branches from trees and wrecked some of the houses. The rain pounded down and Stands Alone was so afraid that she slept in our bed that night. The next day the storm had done its worst although I could still see it to the east and I feared for the clan. Perhaps they had avoided it. I prayed that they had. It took a day to repair all the damage which had been done. I was lucky that I had not yet begun to assemble the boat which I had decided would be my own invention, a Mi'kmaq snekke! Gradually, over the next few days, the winds abated and the weather became clement.

Each day, as I worked, Laughing Deer and her sister explored the island and foraged. They would be there when I needed food and rest and they would both talk, excitedly, of something which they had found from the time of the clan. They were excited about things I took for granted like the quern stone which had been left. It made grinding the grain much easier. Although we had made our mark on the land as I walked with them I saw the damage done by the storm. Some of the farms had crumbled as the rain had weakened the turf walls and they had fallen in on themselves. There were only two in such a bad way but over the years there would be more. Some of the trails we had first used when we arrived and explored were now overgrown. Nature was reclaiming Bear Island.

They came with me when I went to cut the mast and the crosspiece. These had to be strong and straight lengths of timber. I found a tree which was perfect. It looked like an ash tree from home but it was subtly different. I had learned that the Mi'kmaq just called them trees apart from the birch bark. To them, that tree was almost sacred. I could see why; it allowed them to build the boats they used and as I had learned, the land was riven with waterways. The boats could be carried easily, and they were the horses of their land.

One evening, as we ate another satisfying meal, I asked Laughing Deer about horses. I used the Moos to help me to describe an animal which looked similar to a Moos but without the antlers. When I described men riding them then they laughed. The Mi'kmaq did not domesticate animals except for dogs. Without our sheep, cattle and fowl, I could not show them how we did so. Our life was almost idyllic. The days were getting warmer. I found a pouch of seeds which Laughing Deer and her sister planted, and each night Laughing Deer and I lay together as happy as any pair of people anywhere.

It took a month to finish my Mi'kmaq snekke and then I had to find a sail. Once again, we scavenged. The old sails from the knarr and *'Jötnar'* had not been discarded. The clan had used them to make their homes watertight. We found enough pieces for Laughing Deer and her sister to sew together to make a sail. The honeysuckle climbers we had used before would not be good enough for the new sail and so we had to make rope. The unexpectedly early departure of the clan aided us for they had left the hair we had collected from the Moos and I showed them how to make rope. That tedious task was so new to the two of them that they found it enjoyable. As Skerpla came and the sun's rays grew hotter I was almost ready to sail. The night before I was due to sail her, I had a bad dream. This was not a Gytha inspired one, it was an old fashioned one. A storm raged and I could barely control the ship I sailed. I thought I was going to drown. I watched people I recognised being swept overboard and I could do nothing about it. When I woke, with a start, the hall was quiet and Laughing Deer and Stands Alone were asleep. Did this bode badly for the boat?

As I spoke to Laughing Deer, I tried to keep the nervousness out of my voice but inside I wondered if the dream was a premonition of disaster. "I will take her out into the bay and around the headland. When I come back, I will take you around the island to show you my new boat. I will call her *'Ada'*."

Laughing Deer was amused that we named our ships. I knew that one day I would have to tell her about Ada and my children. *'Ada'* was much stronger than the simple birch bark boat had been and it was much easier to climb aboard. The wooden framework I had made gave her strength. I fitted the steering board. I had found some small, discarded pieces of metal and I had made them into cleats to allow me to operate the sails from the steering board. The sail was not as big as the snekke's, but it was bigger than my cloak had been. Waving to the two of them I headed out into the bay. The bay itself was sheltered and the wind did not catch me. When I left it, however, a freak gust almost capsized me. I had to lean over the larboard side of the birch bark boat to stop it from doing so. The birch bark part was too light. The log was heavier! I needed another log on the larboard side to counterbalance the other log. I turned, lowered the sail and returned to the quay.

Laughing Deer looked terrified, "I thought you were going to fly! Did you mean to do that?"

The Bear and the Wolf

I shook my head, "The Allfather was telling me that I am not as clever as I think I am. I will need to work on the boat a little more."

"Do you have to? If you just wish to go to the mainland and see the tribe who live there, then we can use the birch bark boat."

I shook my head, "I need to finish this. I am Erik the Navigator and I need to sail. Besides, when I am finished this will be a very safe vessel."

I had learned my lesson and after another week I had a boat which I hoped would be better balanced. The second log was not as thick as the first, but I hoped it would counterbalance the other. I also added thwarts so that we could carry more. The Mi'kmaq snekke was heavier and might not be as swift but she was strong. When I took her out on the second attempt, I saw Laughing Deer and Stands Alone clinging to each other. If I drowned, then they would be trapped on the island. It was a sobering thought. I knew that I would have to make contact with Chief Wandering Moos before his tribe headed back to their winter camp.

The wind, once again, caught me as I left the bay but this time it was only the new log which rose slightly out of the water. When I had passengers or cargo that would not be a problem. I took *'Ada'* to the east where the waves were slightly bigger. I never left sight of the island and I knew that I could swim back if I needed to. I had been wrong about *'Ada'*; she was even faster than the birch bark boat. The original hull was supported by the two logs and the fact that I had taken the bark from them made them slip easily through the sea. I headed back to the bay where I saw Laughing Deer and her sister smiling.

"Come aboard!" They both looked nervous. "Trust me, she will not capsize, and we can fish for the larger fish." We had caught fish in the fish traps my people had used but they were only small. I had carved more bone hooks so that, as we circumnavigated the island, we could try to catch something bigger.

"Come, Stands Alone, we must trust Erik for we owe him our lives." They clambered aboard and Laughing Deer smiled, "This is easier, and we do not get wet."

"Nor do you need to use a paddle."

Once we hit the sea, I heard a squeal of delight from Stands Alone as *'Ada'* flew across the waves. If we were going to fish then I would have to sail more slowly but, for the moment, it was good to let *'Ada'* have her freedom. I remembered where the good fishing grounds were from Aed and Padraig. I sailed to the northern end of the island where there was a channel between Bear Island and the smaller one to the north-west. I adjusted the sail so that we sailed slowly and threw out the lines.

Laughing Deer turned to me and said, "We could be at the mainland quickly in this boat."

I nodded, "And we will make the voyage in the next moon or so. This is the time we need to plant for when winter comes and the tribe leaves, we will be alone."

She nodded, "And the Penobscot will not come in winter."

Stands Alone was fascinated by the fish below the boat and I spoke quietly, "You still fear them?"

"Angry Voice lost his warriors and he lost me. His reputation was damaged when you took us. He will seek us. He will know that we sailed away and that we went in this direction. He will come but, each morning when I walk to make water, I look to the land of the Penobscot and I pray to the gods that he will not find us."

I nodded, "If he does then I will end his life for I am a Viking, and no one harms my family while I live and breathe!" It was a bold statement, but I meant it. I would not lose another member of my family!

We caught two large fish and they would feed us for a few days. I was pleased with my new boat and, as we neared the bay, I looked over to the mainland. I could see the smoke from the fires of the Mi'kmaq, and I knew that they would see ours. If Laughing Deer was correct then, by now, the Penobscot scouts could also be watching from the mainland.

I let the two of them land at the quay and then sailed the boat up the river. I saw storm clouds and I wanted the boat secured not to the quay, where waves could batter her against the pilings, but tied to three trees where she would be safer. She was also protected by overhanging bushes. If the Penobscot came I did not want them to find the boat easily.

As the other two carried the fish to the hall and after I had I secured the boat to the trees, I looked at the hall. We had some defences, but not enough. Walking to my hall I saw puddles which remained from the storm we had endured. We had thought of a ditch around the settlement, but Arne had deemed it too much work when there was no danger. I could not dig a ditch all the way around the settlement, but I could around Gytha's hall. I had been told how the Romans sowed stakes and spikes in their ditches to trap the unwary and they would be easy to manufacture. As I looked at the ground, I realised that, if I made the ditch, it would keep the hall drier. The turf walls still looked firm enough but the ones which had crumbled on the other side of the island were a warning. If I hewed more logs or, even better, re-used the ones from the wrecked homes then I could make the walls of the hall stronger, more resistant to attack and they would keep us warmer in winter. Leaving Laughing Deer and her sister to their work I went to scavenge logs. It was easier than I had expected. We had logs I had hewn to make **'Gytha'** and not used because they were not straight enough. After splitting them I placed those around the base and found that I had one course. By the end of the afternoon, my muscles burned but I had two courses of half logs and timber in place. The food, that night, tasted even better for all the hard work I had put in.

It was as we ate, I thought about the small deer which lived on our island. We had not taken them all and if I left them for a year then the herd would build up and we could cull them. They would not be domesticated as such, but I would be providing a source of food for my small family. The island had more than enough for the three of us.

That night Laughing Deer nuzzled into me, "We do not need to go to the mainland. We are happy here."

"Is that fair on Stands Alone?"

"For the moment it is. She was hurt by the Penobscot and I do not just mean her loss of voice. She bled and was close to death. When you first found my mother and me, we were collecting herbs to heal her. We did but then my mother died. Let us wait until the new season when the tribe return. Then this will be a secure home and Stands Alone may need to see others. For now, she has all that she needs."

I was content for my world was in balance. I missed the clan, Fótr, Ada, my children, but Gytha had not come to me to tell me that they were hurt. Until she did then I would believe that they were safe and happy. For the next four days, life was idyllic and then on the fourth night, as Laughing Deer fell asleep in my arms, I saw Gytha and she was with a woman I did not recognise. I heard no words, but I saw smiles and the woman, who was older than Gytha, looked to be both beautiful and terrifying. They parted and I saw a warrior wearing a wolf cloak. He bowed and then they faded and disappeared. I sat bolt upright in bed. What had happened? I knew it had something to do with the clan and the warrior with the wolf cloak could have been Sámr. I was speculating. Wherever my clan was they were an ocean away or at the bottom of the sea!

For the next four days, we worked hard for the days were becoming longer but I had the same dream or a variation of it for the next nights.

Laughing Deer confronted me for she knew that something had upset me. "You have had more than one night where you have not slept well. It is time this stopped for you disturb me and… it is not good for you. We will build a sweat hut."

"Sweat hut?"

"My people use them. You build a hot fire in a dwelling and close the entrance. The smoke and the heat purify you."

I had vaguely heard of their use by the Clan of the Wolf. How did the Mi'kmaq know of them? "I will be fine."

For the first time since I had known her, she did not accept my words. She argued with me and it marked a change in our relationship; it was a change for the better! "No, we will build a sweat hut. You have lost your clan, and this will bring you a little peace."

It was quite easy to make. There were many willow-like trees on the island and we bent them to make a sort of wooden structure which looked like an inverted helmet but much bigger. Leaving a hole in the top she wove more willows into it and then plastered leaves on the outside with river mud. She had me light a small fire inside to dry it off. "It will be ready tomorrow. Stands Alone and I will collect some fragrant herbs. We will light the fire and, after we have eaten, then you can sit in the hut and reflect. I guarantee that you will sleep easier."

I nodded but I knew that what would help me sleep even easier was the batch of ale I was brewing. I had toasted some barley for I liked the darkened ale it produced. The winter must have killed off the bees for I could not find any wild honey and we would not be able to make mead. Despite Laughing Deer's words, I knew that the fermented ale would do me more good.

The ale was not ready, and we had drunk that which Ada had left. The steam hut would have to do. When we had eaten our food Laughing Deer had cooked some mushrooms. At the time I had not noticed that neither she nor Stands Alone had eaten them. They were delicious but made me feel sleepy. I had lit the fire before eating and after stripping off in the hall I covered myself in the bearskin and went to the hut. Already it felt hot. Once inside I dropped my bearskin and sat upon it. Laughing Deer had placed a ladle and a bowl of water in the hut. I was given clear instructions. *'Sprinkle water on the fire. You do not wish to douse it, but you need to make steam. Breathe in the smoke through your nose and out through your mouth. I will come for you when the time is right.'*

She kissed me and then dropped a large handful of dried herbs on the fire. I did not recognise them. Some were green and some were brown. The smell of the herbs as they began to rise was something I had never experienced. I followed my orders and sprinkled water. I did not cough, as I thought I would. Instead, the smoke seemed to clear my thoughts. I breathed regularly as she had suggested and found that I seemed to be floating. I was not aware of the ground. And then I was no longer in the hut. I was in the dark night and I was flying.

I was not flying over the sea for I could hear nothing and below me was blackness. It was all around me and I felt as though I might be dead. I heard a voice called softly to me and I saw a dim glow in the distance. I did not seem to need to move anything, it was as if I was being drawn towards whoever it was. It was then I realised that I was in a cave and I saw the beautiful and terrifying woman who had been with Gytha. There was a fire burning before her which lit up her face and I saw that she looked not only at me but into me. I seemed to

float gently to the ground and landed on a large flat rock. It was a cave and there was a pool of water, but I felt no cold. I could still feel the heat from the sweat hut. Even as I looked at the woman, I knew that this was just my spirit and my body was still on Bear Island. Wherever this was it was not Bear Island. She smiled, 'You are clever, Erik the Bear. You have understood that I have summoned your spirit.'

'Did you ask Laughing Deer to suggest the steam hut?'

'Gytha planted the idea but she was compliant; your new woman has skills and you should cherish her. We do not have much time and I will speak quickly for what little power you have will soon be used up. My name is Ylva and I am in Myrddyn's cave in the Land of the Wolf. Your brother, Fótr, is safe and lives. He is to become a great hero soon. I have summoned you so that you can know that all is well. Ada and your children accept their new life and sad though they are, they are also proud of you. You will never see them again and after this night you will see neither Gytha nor me. Our threads and those of the Clan of the Wolf are woven tightly. You and the Skraeling are also woven. Your future is in the land in which you now live but you have a purpose. Your seed will spread across the land and the blood of the Clan of the Fox will make the tribes you meet stronger. Your name nor you will ever be forgotten. Your son and daughter will have their own children and they will tell your tale for you were the first to sail the Great Sea. Be content.'

'But....' The light in the cave faded and I found myself flying once more. I felt cold and I had not felt cold in the cave. I opened my eyes and I was in the steam hut. It was dark and the fire was now just embers.

I wept. I had not wept before, but I did then. Ylva had not meant it unkindly but her words were like a death sentence. The life I had known was ended and a new one had begun. No matter how good my new life was I would regret the goodbyes I had not made. My life seemed to be filled with such unsatisfactory ends. I stood and wrapped my bear cloak around me. When I entered the hall I saw that Laughing Deer was not asleep. She sat by the fire and I saw that beneath the deerskin she was naked. She put her arms around me and held me tightly. Without speaking I knew that she had realised I was sad and had been weeping.

She said huskily in my ear, "I am sorry that you are sad. I did not mean it to be but a voice in my head told me that you needed the steam hut."

I kissed her, "I am not angry, and the sadness will pass. It was right what you did for I am now resolved. We make a new life, but we need to find it in the west. I dreamed on the birch bark boat and saw a thundering waterfall which was as big as a sea."

She stepped back with wide eyes, "I have heard of this place but how have you?"

I shrugged, "I dreamed it. We will speak more of this at another time. I am guessing it is many miles from here."

"It is not in the land of the Mi'kmaq and I believe that the tribes there are fierce. They call it, Onguiaahra."

I smiled, "My life, it seems, is not destined to be an easy one."

Chapter 13 Erik

We did not speak of the dream again for some time. I had much to do. The first thing we would need to do would be to visit the mainland and speak to Chief Wandering Moos. As events turned out we should have done so sooner rather than later.

As it was the time of plenty Laughing Deer and Stands Alone worked on the vegetable garden as well as collecting the fruit which was gradually ripening. Poor Laughing Deer bemoaned the fact that there was no corn for her to grind. At first oats and barely had been considered a novelty but now she yearned for the food she knew. It was another reason to go to the mainland. I worked on the ditch. I used the spade made from the shoulder of a cow and the spears we had taken from Yellow Feather. I broke up the soil with the spears and then moved it with the spade. I mixed it with water and used it to pack behind the wood I had attached to the walls. The wood was now half-way up the hall. I wanted the ditch as deep as my leg and I knew I was making a great deal of work for myself. The safety of Laughing Deer and her sister was paramount. It took almost half a month to dig the ditch all the way around. I left a connecting bridge until I could manufacture a moveable one.

We celebrated the completion of the first part of the defences by eating our first lobsters. Laughing Deer knew how to make lobster traps and we captured our first ones just as I finished the ditch. We had four and they were delicious. My black beer was ready and that went down well too. Stands Alone still yearned for the sweet mead she had tasted. "We will need to find a hive and the bees who make the honey. I fear that there are none on the island. It is another reason to go to the mainland."

Laughing Deer shook her head, "Not yet for it will soon be the time of the long sun and I would like to be here when that day comes."

And so, we put off the voyage. I had intended to go in the next few days for it would not take me long to finish the ditch. The next day I made the bridge and the day after broke through the narrow piece of earth to complete the ditch. We were able to bring the bridge in to the hall or even have it as extra protection for the door. I saw no sign of danger and so I left the bridge in place while I prepared stakes and spikes. I intended to fill the ditch with seawater. When the clan had built the halls, we had dug a channel and it would not take much to resurrect it. To celebrate the completion of my task I lit the fire in the steam hut and indulged myself. I knew, from Ylva's words, that I would not see her or Gytha but the smell from the leaves Laughing Deer had used had been soothing. Once again, I sat naked on my bearskin and I had the same floating experience. My thoughts were random, and I saw pictures in my head. It was like a dream rather than a nightmare and then suddenly a Penobscot warrior leapt at me. It was so real that I reeled, and my eyes opened. There was nothing there but what had made me start? The fire was not yet dying but I left and went indoors.

"What is wrong, my love, you look troubled."

I forced a smile, "It is nothing; I just had a bad dream. I think, tonight, we will sleep with the bridge on the inside of the door."

"Why?" I heard the fear in her voice.

"It is not finished yet and I want to try it to see how it can be improved." She was not satisfied with my answer, but I began to kiss and caress her and soon she forgot my words.

That night I sent myself to sleep working out how to use ropes to pull the bridge up from inside the hall. The bridge was easy to build and then I dug the old channel out. Stands Alone loved it when I broke through and seawater cascaded along the ditch.

"I must warn you to stay away from the water. There are stakes and spikes in there. You could hurt yourself." Once the water settled and the rush of water ceased, she became bored and wandered down to the river to search out shellfish.

Laughing Deer walked over to me and said, quietly, "Do we need this?"

I decided to tell her the truth, "You said you fear that Angry Voice had not forgotten you and that he might come to hurt you. It is a hard journey here in a birch bark boat but if he is determined…" she nodded, "and I dreamed we were attacked. It may be nothing but for a few days' work then I have given us a warning."

"The Penobscot are fierce warriors!"

I smiled, wryly, "I know, they killed my brother, nephew and cousin but I am a warrior, and this is now my home. It will not be as easy as they think."

"You are a good man."

"But I wish us to travel to speak with Chief Wandering Moos as soon as we can. Firstly, so that word can be sent to your family that you are alive and also to make an alliance with them. We are a small clan and cannot live alone."

"We need weapons."

I had expected that "Come inside and I will let you choose."

There was a chest of weapons. They were not ones the rest of the clan wanted which was why they were left behind but each of them was superior to the bone weapons of the Penobscot and Mi'kmaq. She chose two seaxes for her and her sister. One was smaller than the other. They both had a scabbard.

"I will sharpen them for you. This weapon is not a stabbing one. It is a slashing weapon." She did not understand the word and so I went to one of the fish we had caught in a net. It was hanging close to the front door. I took my seax and slashed it quickly. Even though it was a big fish with thick skin the razor-sharp blade ripped through it and the guts fell into my ditch. "That is how you use it!"

She nodded, "Stands Alone and I will practise. If they get in here, they will pay."

"Hopefully, that will not happen, and my dream will just prove to be a piece of bad meat!"

She laughed, "I believe I am coming to know you and I hear when you lie."

I flushed and said, "I am just protecting you."

"You need not. Living with Penobscot men has made me, what is the word you use, tougher than you think."

I hugged her, "And I will try to remember that."

For the next few days, we both walked around the hall and tended to our tasks with one eye on the sea and one ear cocked for the scream of a Penobscot. Each night I walked to the spit of land which afforded the best view of the south and the west. I spied nothing except for the smoke from the Mi'kmaq fires. Crossing to the mainland was vital and yet neither Laughing Deer nor I wished to leave the island for our life was perfect. Stands Alone had grown to be an inquisitive and lively child. Her traumas were behind us and we both knew that the longer she stayed on the island then the better she would become. If she saw Mi'kmaq warriors, then she might revert to her silent world. I returned each night to the hall as the sun set over the mainland. I did not think that they would come at night. I was wrong.

It was two nights later when our world changed irrevocably. I had managed to hunt an old deer on the far side of the island. I had gone there because I wanted to look at Horse Deer Island in case the Penobscot had gone there. It would have given them the shortest journey to our island. I knew that the deer had prospered for we had seen their dung. I had trailed them and seen that they were growing in numbers. One old female was limping. The herd would be better off without her and I used a bone arrow to wound her and then ran after her with the Penobscot spear. I caught her and finished her. Stands Alone was delighted when I returned to fetch the cart and she came with me. There was much we could take from the deer and after I had skinned it, I chopped off the hooves to melt them down for glue. We pulled the cart back to the village where Laughing Deer pegged out the hide and the two of them began to scrape it before we made water upon it. I butchered the animal and we hung the haunches in the larder and put the offal to be cooked. The head was put on to boil. We had salt in abundance, and we would brine and salt most of the meat. The choice cuts we would have when they had hung for a few days. I knew the meat of such an old animal would be tough and we would cook it slowly.

The Bear and the Wolf

I had explained to Laughing Deer that soaking the tough meat in ale for a few hours before we cooked it would help to make it tender. She was looking forward to it. That night we were exhausted but we ate well, and I finished off the last of the black beer. I had a golden ale which was almost ready and as I drained my horn I said, "That beer was good. I think I will just taste the new batch."

Laughing Deer laughed, I loved her laugh, "Let us hope you can find your way back to our bed then!"

We had not raised the bridge for that was the last task each night. Usually, I would go outside to make water and when I returned, I would raise the bridge. The brewery was just forty paces into the forest. Our alewives had chosen that as the best place. I took my horn and scooped a frothy golden hornful. It was as I was leaving, I realised that I needed to make water. My horn had a flat stand and so I went to the estuary mouth and laid it on the quay. By then I was desperate to pass water and I barely opened my breeks in time. When the splashing stopped, I pulled up my breeks and it was as I was washing my hands that I heard a regular splash. Waves might seem regular, but they are not, and this splashing was very regular. I stood and I sniffed. As usual, the wind was coming from the south-west and the mouth of the bay. As I sniffed, I listened; the sound was not one regular splash but a number. When I smelled humans, I knew that the sound I could hear was the sound of birch bark boats' paddles. It was night-time and the Penobscot had come for Laughing Deer! I ran straight back to the hall and pulled up the bridge before dropping the bar into place.

One look at my face was enough for Laughing Deer who simply said, "The Penobscot." Stands Alone opened her mouth to scream and Laughing Deer placed her hand over her sister's mouth, "You must be strong. Get your weapon."

I went to don my mail. I had no idea how many were coming but the mail would stop them from hurting me too quickly. The hall had a half-floor above the sleeping chambers. We used it for storage but as the only access was by a ladder the sisters would be safer there. "Take hatchets and my bow and get into the store above our bed. Pull up the ladder."

"What will you do?"

"What I have to! Keep silent no matter what happens. Let uncertainty be our ally."

I had my mail donned and my helmet was on my head when I heard the first splash and then scream which told me that the Skraeling had found the traps in the ditch. More shouts and cries followed. I strapped on my shield and donned my bearskin. I put the head over my helmet and fastened the clasp around my neck. Putting my seax into my left hand, I drew my sword and waited just three steps behind the door. I heard a noise from halfway up the wall. They were trying to climb onto the roof. There was little to grip there, and I heard a rumbling above me and then a splash and a scream as the warrior fell into the ditch. The others might just be injured or wounded; falling from the roof onto the spikes meant that at least one was dead. And then there was silence. I knew what they were doing. They were looking for another entrance. They could search all that they liked there was none. Viking halls had one way in and out. Another splash and a shout told me that they had discovered the ditch and traps behind the hall.

This time the silence seemed to go on forever. Were they trying to make me think they had gone? I would not fall for that trick. I heard whimpering from the half-floor and then Laughing Deer as she whispered to Stands Alone.

What they were doing became obvious when there was a crash from the bridge. They had made a ram and were trying to break down the door. It would take time, but they would break it down eventually. The longer it took then the more exhausted they would be. They had already paddled across the bay and the longer this went on the more chance I had of surviving. The ones who had been wounded would be bleeding and, as I knew, bleeding weakened a warrior. I just hoped to kill enough of them to allow Laughing Deer and Stands Alone to survive. Bear Tooth had told me that when a leader died then the rest lost heart. Angry Voice would be the one with feathers in his hair and the one who would come for me first. Then I heard hammering at the sides of the door. They were using their stone clubs and knives to smash the hinges. A splash and a scream told me that they had paid the price for such an attack. A voice shouted something, but I could not understand it. The noise stopped and was replaced by a sawing sound. They were cutting through the ropes which bound the bridge to the inner door. The moon must have shone and illuminated the knots. After some time I heard a crash and knew that they had succeeded. Now they had just the main door to breach.

The ram began again and now I saw the effect. Dust and splinters flew from the inside of the door and its hinges creaked. They were made of leather and were the weak point. If they realised that and used hatchets and tomahawks instead of clubs then they could cut them. The bar on the door would brace it, for a while at least. After many strikes, there was a crack and a shard of wood fell from the centre of the door. Voices outside screeched with delight. I said nothing but I could hear Laughing Deer's soothing voice as she calmed her sister. Would the tale of our clan in this New World end with the three of us being butchered? Had my brother's martial ambitions brought us to this? In my heart, I could not believe it. Gytha had not spoken to me but I felt her presence and that of Snorri. There were other spirits too. I was a Viking, I was Clan of the Fox and I would fight!

Through the ever-growing crack in the door, I saw in the moonlight the three Penobscot warriors who held the ram. It came to me that if they held the ram, which was a roof support torn from one of the huts, then they could not hold a weapon at the same time. If I could strike quickly when they broke through, then I might be able to hurt all three of them. I realised that if I stood directly in line with the door then they would hit me when they broke through. I stepped to my right. The centre panel shattered, and the bar cracked telling me that I had but moments. I wanted to shout to Laughing Deer to warn her but that would tell the warriors where I was. I had to remain hidden for the hall was dark and the moonlight outside would affect their ability to see well. I had to use every chance the Allfather gave me. I prayed that the Norns' threads were stronger than the Penobscot's will to kill us. The voice outside, I assumed it was Angry Voice, screamed out an order. It was that order which gave the three warriors extra strength and the ram smashed through the door, the bar and they hurtled in.

I had to be quick. The Penobscot were both smaller and shorter than I was. I had the advantage of height. My change of position also helped me as I brought my sword down on the back of the neck of the first one as he tumbled forward and even as bright blood spurted, I backhanded my sword across the throat of the second. As the first two died the third began to stumble and I stabbed him in the back, my sword sliding next to his spine. Outside I saw two more warriors as they began to cross the bridge and I stepped over the three bodies and the ram to fill the door. The first warrior had been watching his feet and as he looked up, he saw a huge bear, my helmet and bear head making me even bigger than I really was. His spear struck my shield but without any force for the terror on his face told me he was too shocked to fight. I pushed him back with my shield as I lunged at his shoulder. My sword went into soft, yielding flesh and muscle and, tearing it out sideways, he fell into the ditch.

I stepped into the doorway for that way I was protected by the hall and it meant none could get by me. In the bright moonlight which made the night almost seem like day, I saw that there were eight warriors left but at least half were wounded, and they were standing further from the hall. That meant there were three or four I had to fight. When I looked, I saw that one had feathers hanging down from his half-shaven head and when he shouted orders then I knew this was Angry Voice. They did not rush me, instead, they each threw their spears. I raised my shield to block them, but one hit the bear head. I heard a cry of joy and then a wail as the spear fell to the ground.

I spread my arms wide and shouted, "I am Erik the Navigator! I was Clan of the Fox but now I am the Bear! Flee while you can!" I spoke in Norse for I wished to terrify them, and it worked. Three recoiled but Angry Voice picked up a spear one of his wounded warriors had dropped and he ran to hurl it at me. He was just four paces from me when he released it and it struck my chest. The blow hurt but the bone head, sharp though it was, did not penetrate and shattered on my mail. I was not the warrior my brother and father had been but I knew, at that moment, that I had to take the offensive before they realised that they had weight of numbers on their side and that despite my defences they could overcome me. I ran towards Angry Voice.

The warrior was no coward and he drew his club and his knife. Two of his companions also drew their weapons. I took the blow from the club on my shield and the knife thrust was blocked with my sword. Pulling back my head I butted Angry Voice who tumbled backwards. I did not slow and stepped forward to punch at one Penobscot with my shield while I swung my sword at the second warrior. A knife grated off my mail, but my sword sliced through the warrior to his spine. The warrior I had punched was dazed and I lunged at him with my sword. It entered his stomach and I twisted as I withdrew it. The wounded warriors were trying to get away and back to their boats but Angry Voice, his head bleeding from my head butt stood and advanced.

This time, when I spoke, I spoke in Mi'kmaq, and I spoke slowly, "I am Erik and Laughing Deer is my woman. You will die here, and I will take your hands so your spirit will never touch in the Otherworld."

He understood enough of my words to scream some Penobscot curse and race at me. I was ready and I pivoted on my left leg so that my shield protected me from his wild blow, and I was bringing around my sword to sever his body in two. He was dead before his torso hit the ground. The survivors had halted close to their boats for their leader was dead. I heard one say something, it was the one who had fled without wounds, and they began to advance. Suddenly an arrow flew past me and smacked into the warrior's chest. It was too much for the four already wounded warriors and they stumbled to one of the birch bark boats and began to paddle west. I turned and saw Laughing Deer behind me with the bow. Stands Alone no longer looked afraid and she held her seax purposefully. They would have come to my aid if I had been attacked! I watched the warriors take two of the boats and paddle away as quickly as their wounded limbs would allow them.

By the time dawn arrived, I had placed the bodies in the cart, and we had pushed it to the spit of land at the end of the river mouth. In the distance, I could see the Penobscot as they struggled to paddle back to safety. They were finding it hard for the wind was fresh and in their face. If I had wished I could have taken my own boat, hoisted the sail and caught them. Perhaps I should have but hindsight is always perfect. Instead, we gathered kindling and made a funeral pyre for the dead warriors. There were eight of them. My traps had not only wounded some of them, but they had also killed. Laughing Deer took Angry Voice's feathers as a trophy. She told me they would give me more power next time we fought the Penobscot.

As I lit the kindling I said, "They will not return."

She shook her head, "I fear they will for this is now a blood feud. We killed Yellow Feather and so Angry Voice made this impossible journey to end our lives and when the warriors reach their home, they will tell the chief and he will want vengeance for his son. It will not be this year for soon they will return to their winter camp but come the new buds they will wish to make war."

She seemed remarkably calm about the whole thing. As we walked back to the hall where we would have to clean up the blood and I would have to repair the door, I said, "And that does not worry you?"

She laughed, "I have watched you slay many warriors here and at the river, yet you have not a scratch. My people spoke of battles with tribes like the Penobscot, the Odawa and the Mohican. None ever slew as many. We are not afraid. Your hall slowed them down and we were ready to fight."

Stands Alone smiled and took my hand, "I am afraid no longer, Erik the Bear. They could not harm you and I saw that they were weak men. You are strong and we will survive."

The burning bodies sent a huge column of smoke into the sky. The fleeing Penobscot would see it as would the Mi'kmaq. Now we had no choice. I would need to sail to the mainland as soon as possible.

Chapter 14 Erik

We set sail three days after the fight. I repaired the door, bridge and added stakes to replace the ones which had been damaged. It was harder to leave our home than I had expected. On Laughing Deer's advice, I took my bearskin and the wapapyaki, but I left my mail on the island. Laughing Deer also suggested that I take a gift. We had found a small hatchet close to one of the deserted farms. The handle had been broken. I had repaired and cleaned it. We both thought that it would make a suitable gift. The voyage across the bay did not take long for the wind was from the south and west. We had to tack a couple of times, but *'Ada'* was a fine vessel and she flew. The Mi'kmaq were still at the coast and as we neared the beach, I saw a youth run inland. The fact that there were two Mi'kmaqs with me made my arrival less intimidating than had I been alone. A couple of boys even helped me to drag my boat on to the beach and two warriors approached us.

"I am here to speak with Chief Wandering Moos."

One of the warriors who was guarding the shellfish gatherers nodded to me, "We have sent word, Shaman of the Bear." He looked curiously at Laughing Deer. "What tribe are you? I see you are of our people, but I do not know you."

"My sister and I live far from here and we were captured by a Penobscot raiding party. This warrior killed many Penobscot and rescued us."

"I am Black Bird and I am impressed that you are a shaman and a warrior. Few are granted both skills." He suddenly looked to the sea. "We saw some Penobscot birch bark boats, it is why our Chief sent guards. Did they come to your island?"

Before I could answer Laughing Deer said, proudly, "Aye, but Erik the Bear slew seven Penobscot with his own hands, including the son of the chief!"

I saw the respect on Black Bird's face, "That is a tale I would hear."

The youth arrived back. He was out of breath, "Chief Wandering Moos has asked me to take them to the camp."

Black Bird said, "When we return to the camp, I will leave boys to watch this boat and it will be safe."

I followed the boy who hurried ahead. He was obviously nervous about being so close to the Shaman of the Bear. The whole of the tribe had gathered to meet us and they formed a funnel at the head of which stood Chief Wandering Moos, his shaman and his chief warriors. I recognised the one who had been friendly to us, Long Sight. I saw that they were not painted for war and that was a good thing although the Wapapyaki should have ensured our safety in any case. They waited until we were close and then the Chief held his hands for the Wapapyaki. In the time we had been back on Bear Island I had added the pictograms which told of the battle with the Penobscot at the falls and the departure of the clan. The Chief studied it and then handed it to the shaman.

"Sit Shaman of the Bear and your two companions." He was polite for I could see that he was intrigued by their presence. Like Bear Tooth he recognised them as Mi'kmaq but the fact that he did not know them made him curious. He clapped his hands and two women brought us food and drink. I knew that we had to partake and to refuse would be an insult. Stands Alone was shaking in the presence of warriors. I knew then that she might never overcome this terrible fear she had. We ate and I wiped my hands on my breeks as I had seen the Mi'kmaq do the last time I had been in their camp.

The Chief smiled, "I can see that there is a tale to tell here but I do not wish to rush it. We would be honoured if you would eat with us and spend the night in our camp."

We had already eaten but I understood the protocol and ritual of such matters. I glanced at Laughing Deer who smiled at the chief and then nodded at me. "We would be happy to, but I hope that you are not insulted if I ask for a sleeping chamber for the three of us." He gave me a questioning look and I added, "When you hear the tale then I hope you will understand. And you are right, the tale is long and is complicated."

"Then while we wait for Black Bird and the other warriors to return from guarding the gatherers and hunting, for they will wish to hear the tale, Long Sight will show you and…"

"I am sorry, I have been rude. This is Laughing Deer and Stands Alone."

"Welcome Laughing Deer and Stands Alone, know that you will be perfectly safe here in my camp!"

Long Sight was grinning as he led me around the camp and explained who everyone was. I could not possibly remember all of the names, but I nodded and smiled when he spoke to them.

He stopped by one of the larger dwellings, "And this is my home. White Doe, we have guests."

His wife came out. She was a short and squat woman, but she had a smile as big as a billowing sail. "This is Laughing Deer and Stands Alone; take them inside away from the eyes of the tribe."

When they were inside, he said, "I can see that the little one is much troubled; her eyes show too much pain for one so young."

"And their tale is bound up in mine. I beg your patience for I would not spoil the tale I will tell."

He laughed, "And your language has improved. That is the work of Laughing Deer?" I nodded. "She is your woman?"

"She is and we are happy."

"I can see that." I glanced at the door to the dwelling. "Fear not, my wife is kind and she will be seeing to their needs. Women have different needs from men. We can sit here in the open and enjoy the air. They like to have their heads together." He glanced at my bearskin. "I see you do not wear the magic coat you wore last time."

"Last time I did not know what reception I could expect."

"Aye, Eyes of Fire and his friends were foolish. Chief Wandering Moos has other sons and they do not have the wild streak of war which infected Eyes of Fire."

The Bear and the Wolf

I spent a pleasant hour or so speaking with him about the tribe and their winter camp. I was interested in when they left for that would mean we would be alone and the Penobscot attack had worried me a little. The fact that they had attacked at night and over a dangerous stretch of water showed me how much they wanted Laughing Deer. He told me that their winter camp lay three days to the north-west. When the tribe left for their winter home, after the harvest, we would be alone on our island.

As the sun began to set, Black Bird led the fisherfolk from the beach and the hunters returned from the woods. Long Sight stood and said, "White Doe, it is time,"

I noticed that when Stands Alone emerged she looked happier than when she had entered. Laughing Deer was beaming. We made our way across to the open space before the chief's home. Women were fetching food and drink and I saw that I had a place of honour between the chief and Long Sight. Laughing Deer and Stands Alone were with the women. That would please Laughing Deer's sister. Eating was obviously a serious business for the Mi'kmaq, and they ate with purpose. When the meal had finished, I was offered a splinter of wood to clean my teeth. It was fortunate that I had been offered one by Laughing Deer before or else I would have looked foolish wondering if I should eat it!

Chief Wandering Moos gestured to the open space before us, "The tribe awaits your words, Shaman of the Bear."

It felt like standing before a Thing, except that it was worse. I did not know these people, and, despite my improvements, I would still be butchering their language. I decided to keep it simple. I stood and began to speak. I told of our coming from across the seas and I mentioned my dream. Everyone looked at Laughing Deer when I did so and some of the younger women giggled. I realised why. I was bigger than almost all of the Mi'kmaq and Laughing Deer had already told me that I would be attractive to the women. I spoke of Gytha, her prophecies and her death. The Shaman looked intently at me and I could almost hear the questions in his head. When I spoke of finding Laughing Deer and the horrors inflicted upon the two sisters, I heard a murmur of anger and I stopped so that it could subside. The Chief glared at the ones who had spoken. When I spoke of the battle at the falls, I saw that each and every man and boy was listening carefully. They were the ones who had fought the Penobscot. I went into detail about what I could remember for I wanted them on my side. When I spoke of our flight, the death of Yellow Feathers and the capture of the boat some of the younger ones could not contain themselves and they gave a delighted war cry. Once again, the chief silenced them. I was careful to explain in detail about the flight of my people for Laughing Deer did not understand how my family could abandon me despite the fact that her family had, apparently, abandoned her. The building of my new boat caused the most interest. I saw Long Sight look at the Chief for he wished to interrupt but knew he could not. I paused in my tale, "When I have spoken then I will happily answer any questions which the tribe has." That brought relieved nods. When I spoke of how I had improved the defences of the hall and then the details of the attack you could have heard a pin drop. After I had finished I said, simply, "And as you are our neighbours and our friends I thought to bring you this news for Laughing Deer is convinced that the Penobscot will come for her again and I would not have our neighbours suffer because of our actions. That is all I have to say."

I was going to sit but the Chief stood and walked over to me, "I have a question. Will you be sailing to your people in the land of the rising sun?"

Shaking my head, I said, "The journey would need a bigger ship than the one I have now."

"And yet you built one of these after the peace." He was an astute man. "If the tribe helped you, could you make one?"

"I could but a spirit has come from across the Great Sea to tell me that my future lies here in the west."

Seemingly satisfied he nodded, "And will your people return from across the water?"

I smiled, "That is a good question. I do not expect my brother and my clan to return but others may come. The journey, however, is not easy."

"Those are honest answers," He sat down and waved a hand. It was the signal for questions, and I noticed a hierarchy in the clan. Long Sight and the senior warriors, the ones with scars, asked theirs first and then the shaman, Finally, the younger warriors asked theirs. I answered them all honestly although I had to struggle to find some of the words. Finally, Chief Wandering Moos said, "Our guest has done enough. Come Erik, Shaman of the Bear, and sit by me. We will smoke a pipe."

I was introduced to the ritual of smoking leaves in a wooden bowl. I confess I never particularly enjoyed it but the Mi'kmaq, like many other tribes, seemed to find it rewarding. "We have watched your island since we returned to the summer camps and we expected you to come to hear the words of our council. When we saw the ships with the fierce faces gone, we wondered and when you returned there was much talk of how the spirits had devoured your ships and eaten your people." He smiled. "I did not believe those tales and yours makes more sense."

I spoke to him for it gave me the opportunity to drink some water and rid my mouth of the taste of the burned leaves, "And what did the council decide?"

"That you Erik, Shaman of the Bear, should present yourselves to them at our winter feast."

"I missed that feast?"

"Aye, you did, and I will have to return this winter to do the same. You could come with me."

I could tell from his voice that he did not wish me to come and I filled in the gaps in his words. Their council sounded like a Thing and at our meetings there were always dissenting voices. Some of those would be angry that Wandering Moos had not done as he had promised. It was understandable. I made it easier for him, "Stands Alone is better now than she was but a winter with Laughing Deer and me will help to heal her more."

Long Sight had been listening and he nodded, "You are wise, and I believe it is a good thing that you have come to our land."

I nodded, "And Chief Wandering Moos, I am also forgetful for we brought a gift for you, a hatchet!" I took the hatchet and a seax with a simple scabbard and handed it to him. He withdrew the blade and I counselled, "Be careful, it is very sharp."

I thought he would have been more excited, but he frowned, "And have these magic within them which will ensnare me?"

Shaking my head, I pointed to Laughing Deer and her sister, "They both have a blade like yours and they are unchanged."

He sheathed the weapon and smiled, "And there you are wrong. I do not think you speak an untruth, but they are under your spell. I will accept these gifts and I will think if I will use them or not."

I nodded although I did not understand. "If you do use it then you must slash with it and not stab." I mimed the action.

He placed the seax and scabbard reverently on the ground along with the hatchet. "And when you have gone, tomorrow, my warriors and the elders will speak of these matters for you have given us much to think about. The Penobscot are our enemies. Laughing Deer and Stands Alone are not of our tribe but they are of our people and if our enemies return, we will fight them for their land is south of the Peace River. We should have challenged them when they sailed north."

I had wondered about that.

Long Sight gave me the answer, "They were clever, Wandering Moos. They came up the coast and camped on the islands. In that way, there were able to disguise their presence until young Hawk's Feather spied them."

"Aye, that was the way we sailed north. There are many islands. They do not have much game, but they give shelter."

"It seems to me, Erik, that you know parts of our land better than we do."

I spent a short time explaining how I used maps. They were confused until I likened them to the wapapyaki and then realisation set in. "So you use these," Long Sight paused as he made his mouth say the Norse word for map, "maps, to find the places you have been. Interesting."

I could tell that he did not see the value in them, "The sea is vast. We sailed for more than twenty days out of sight of land. I had just the sun and the stars to tell me where I was, and the chart helped me."

The Mi'kmaq were not that much different from the Clan of the Fox. They each had an amulet or a bracelet which they thought protected them and my words made all but the chief hold them. He smiled, "It is late, and you will wish to sleep. White Doe will take you to where you will sleep. For myself, I will sit here and smoke a pipe. You are like the stone which begins its journey from the top of the mountain. You cannot be stopped but a man does not know if you will make the journey alone or will you set other pebbles and rocks cascading down. One pebble cannot hurt us but a whole mountain can be shifted."

Stands Alone was exhausted for a variety of reasons and she fell asleep almost immediately. The Mi'kmaq are a very hospitable people and the furs were comfortable. Laughing Deer and I spoke in whispers. "White Doe is a wise woman. She reminds me of our grandmother. She gave Stands Alone good advice. When she saw the seax you had given Stands Alone she laughed and said that no Penobscot would ever hurt her again." She kissed me, "She says that we are perfect together."

I chuckled, "As the spirits were the ones responsible for our union, I would expect nothing less."

"We could live with these people for they like us and that is important."

I sighed, "We will have to have a winter on our own but that may well hasten the time when we find your tribe. You and Stands Alone were quite happy to remain on the island."

"I know and it is unreasonable of me but Stands Alone and I enjoyed the company of the women. The Penobscot women treated us as badly as their men did for they blamed us for their men using us."

"That is ridiculous!"

"I know but it made our isolation worse. I think my mother gave up because of that. She was a strong woman and might have survived the beating but the attitude of the Penobscot women broke her spirit." I was silent as I had not thought of that. "A winter alone will not be so bad and the winter seas will make it hard for the Penobscot to return. The tribe will leave at the end of the month, Erik. They will return to their winter camp and harvest the summer bounty. They will hunt; we should prepare for the winter."

I kissed her and was alone with my thoughts. She was right but that meant travelling to one of the other islands. Horse Deer Island no longer had Moos but it did have plenty of white-tailed deer. We could sail there and hunt. However, I would need to make more arrows and spears. The next month would be hard work for me.

The next morning, we were greeted by all in the tribe as old friends. The fear of the Shaman of the Bear had gone and many of the young warriors came to ask me about my weapons. They were keen to see my sword and seax. I could tell that they wished to touch them but feared their power. Long Sight scattered them, "Go, you chattering birds, leave the warrior alone! I would not have him add Mi'kmaq to the warriors he has slain!" He laughed when they fled, "They are all impressed at the number of warriors you slew. Until you came, I had slain more men in battle and that was two!"

"I am sorry, I did not wish to take away from your reputation."

"I do not mind but I confess that I am interested in your people. Would you be offended if I came to your island and looked at your homes? We have looked at them from afar and wonder how you live."

"Of course, and you can bring others for there is nought to hide."

He nodded, "I know what women are like and Laughing Deer will wish to make your home look as good as she can. I will come in seven days!"

Chief Wandering Moos, the shaman and the elders all came with Long Sight and Black Bird to see us off. I think they were curious about the new boat and how I sailed it. Stands Alone and Laughing Deer were now happy sailors and they climbed in while I held the boat against the tide. I jumped in and, in one motion, lowered the sail so that we leapt away. I heard the collective gasp from the beach. Turning I waved. I think the sight of my improvised boat flying across the waves impressed them more than anything and that included my sword. Long Sight was a wise man and he was right. When Laughing Deer heard of the impending visit it was like a gale at sea. She and Stands Alone cleaned not only our hall but my old one for she was sure that Long Sight would wish to stay.

"And you will need to make certain that you have your ale and plenty of food! Wandering Moos' people were generous when they entertained us. We must be as generous."

I was kept busy and all the tasks I had planned, such as making arrows, was forgotten as I hunted and fished to have

The Bear and the Wolf

food for them. One advantage I had was that I could sail a little way out to sea and catch the bigger fish. The Mi'kmaq fished each day, but they caught the smaller fish which came to the shallows. I was able to catch fish which were as long as my leg. After seven days I watched and saw a birch bark boat coming across. I had not expected Long Sight to come alone but, as I spied the boat, I recognised White Doe sitting in the middle along with Black Bird and Long Sight's two sons.

Laughing Deer and Stands Alone were approaching and I shouted, "There will be five guests."

She nodded, "And we prepared ten places to sleep. You have found enough food. It is well."

As they edged in towards the quay, I saw them looking with wonder at all that they saw. I held the prow of the boat as Laughing Deer helped White Doe to the wooden quay. I handed a rope to Long Sight. "Tie this to the boat and it will stop it moving."

When they stood on the quay Black Bird shook his head, "This is so simple and yet so clever. You do not get wet when you board your boat and it must be easier to land your catches."

I nodded, "If you wish I can take three of you with me, there," I pointed to the east and the open ocean."

Black Bird nodded, "I would like that."

Long Sight said, "And I can do no less although those waves look big enough to destroy us. I will trust you, Shaman of the Bear."

"And your sons?"

"They will stay ashore. Their mother will need someone to protect her if the sea devours me!"

I did not laugh for I had superstitions too. White Doe was being entertained and so I took them first to see the fish and lobster traps and then to examine where I grew vegetables. They were most interested in our bread oven and my brewery. Only Long Sight had tasted my ale and that had been just a mouthful. I poured them a beaker and I used my horn. I saw the young warriors' eyes widen as they tasted the beer but Long Sight was more interested in the horn. "Where did that come from?"

"We have animals called cattle. They give us milk and they have horns like this. They also pull our wagons and ploughs. When they are old, we eat their meat."

"And they have horns and do not try to kill you?"

"No, Black Bird, for we have tamed them. We tame pigs too." They all looked puzzled. "An animal smaller than a small deer but much fatter and heavier. It has good meat."

"You have much that we do not. Your world is as different as the sea is from the land."

Long Sight was right. I showed them the hall where they would be sleeping. We had lit a fire and that amazed them too. "Then you are never cold in winter?"

"No, for we keep the fire burning and it saves us having to relight it." When I took them into the forest to show them the abandoned farms and fields, I explained how we built our homes. That fascinated them. When I showed them the handful of arrows with the metal tips that, too, impressed them. "My people believe that you must have this iron beneath your ground. It is hard to find but if you find the rocks which melt then I can show you how to make such weapons as arrowheads, swords and seaxes."

"You truly are a Shaman for what you do is magic." Black Bird was younger than Long Sight who was not as easily impressed.

"Come, Laughing Deer has food ready." Before we entered my hall, I showed them the ditch, traps and bridge."

Long Sight smiled, "Now I see how you managed to defeat the Penobscot. You protect your family and that is good."

The ability to cook inside solid walls had almost mesmerized White Doe and immediately demanded that Long Sight build her a hall."

He sighed and shook his head, "We have two homes, White Doe. That means we would need two such halls!"

She shook her head, "Warriors! See how the flames do not blow out and the food does not cool before it can be eaten!"

Laughing Deer was keen to impress, and she had cooked them oat bread. We had found, in Ada's hall, an old cheese, so along with some dried beef I had found we had a veritable feast.

Laughing Deer pointed to the pot bubbling on the fire. Before you leave, we will serve you a stew."

We ate and drank some of the beer. I counselled the sons of Long Sight not to drink too much. Long Sight asked, "Why not?"

"It takes away a man's senses. He falls over and not only can he not defend himself, it is as though he does not know how to be a man."

I had found one of Ada's distaff's and I had demonstrated how to weave. A couple of old sheepskins still remained, and Laughing Deer had been fascinated by the art of spinning. As I left with Black Bird and Long Sight to go to *'Ada'*, Laughing Deer demonstrated the art of weaving. Long Sight's two sons seemed happy to explore my island.

That the two Mi'kmaq were nervous was obvious, but they could not and would not show fear before Long Sight's sons. "You will not need the paddles, so you sit flat in the boat. Their nervousness was shown when they just nodded. I paddled us out to the sea and then I raised the sail. I already knew whence came the wind and the boat took off. It was fortunate that I had three men aboard for the boat lifted a little and I heard the sharp intake of breath from the Mi'kmaq. I tugged on the sheets and we landed on the water and then flew. I knew how exhilarating it was, and I wished I could see the expressions on their faces. We rounded the island and then went even faster. I headed due east. Black Bird fingered his amulet and I smiled. Their world had intimidated me, but this was my domain. I took us east until Bear Island was just a speck to the west. I turned the boat until we were barely making way and began to head back slowly.

Long Sight risked turning around, albeit gingerly, "I see how you can sail with the wind behind you but how do you sail into the wind?"

"You cannot but you can sail close to the wind. We have finished sailing quickly and you can move if you wish. The wood which holds the boat together is strong and you can sit there." I pointed to the cross pieces." We can fish."

Black Bird shook his head, but Long Sight said, "I will trust you."

"Just make your movements slow."

He did so and he sat close to me. I handed him a strong line with a well-carved bone hook. I placed some of the fish guts from the fish I had caught a couple of days' earlier. They were pungent and would attract fish. He tossed the line over the stern and said, "Black Bird, are you a woman? Sit here and fish."

Black Bird did so reluctantly, and I gave him a second line. I just sailed the boat. I did not wish to risk losing either Mi'kmaq over the side and so I made slow and gentle movements. When we had caught fish then we would fly home. The Norns were spinning or, perhaps it was just meant to be but after we had caught one fish similar to the one I had caught we snagged a shark. It was not one of the monsters which had attacked the carcass of the whale, but it was as long as Laughing Deer. Long Sight had never seen such an animal close up.

"Black Bird help him. This is a monster. Do not go near to its teeth or you will lose an arm! Hold on and we will drag him." I regretted taking the spear from the boat for if we had had that weapon we could have speared him. I turned to the north so that the wind was with us and we used the power of the boat to weaken him as he thrashed to escape. The two of them were strong warriors and they pulled hard on the line. Each time we crested a wave they were able to pull him closer. I had warned them of the danger of the teeth, but I saw the dead eye and the teeth approaching me and knew that we were in trouble. I had not brought my sword, but I had brought my long dagger, King Rædwulf's blade. When I had told Wandering Moos and Laughing Deer to slash with the seax I had been speaking the truth but there was a point on this dagger, and I used it now to ram it into the eye of the shark. I would have struggled to break the tough skin of the shark, but the eye was another matter. I pushed until my hand struck the rough flesh of the shark and it died. As soon as it did, I turned into the wind to bring us to a dead stop. Black Bird almost tumbled over the side, but Long Sight caught him. Despite the danger, both were grinning. That single moment bonded us into warriors, brothers of the blade. We had not done as I had done with Arne and Siggi all those years ago, but we had fought the beast and defeated it with the dagger, King Rædwulf's blade.

The Bear and the Wolf

Long Sight said, "That is a powerful blade." I tossed it to him, and he caught it. "Turning it over he said, "There are markings on the blade."

"Aye, for it belonged to a king, a Great Chief and I won it."

He nodded and looked at the dead shark. "We have seen these from the shore and their fins. Once we saw a boy taken by one from the rocks. It was bigger and had more white patches. You hunt them?"

"We do and, with our drekar, we also hunt the whale." I used Bear Tooth's word and I saw that they were impressed.

"Is the meat good to eat?"

"It is and the skin can be used to smooth wood. We have done well."

Black Bird had now forgotten his fear of the boat and he grinned, "Aye, we have."

"Secure the shark and then sit once more in the boat for we shall fly!" This time there was no fear and with the shark tied to the larger log, I turned the boat to head south and east. The wind helped us and when I turned to sail north and east then we flew. I could see that they were confused by my route and so I explained it to them. "This is not like sailing one of your boats. I use the wind. It sometimes means sailing in the wrong direction but when we pick up the wind then we can move more quickly."

It was late in the afternoon when we pulled in and the others were all waiting for us.

White Doe hugged her husband, "You disappeared beyond the seas! Did you fall from the edge?"

He laughed and kissed her, "There is no end to the sea and see what we have caught." They had all been so relieved to see us safely returned that they had not noticed the shark.

I kissed Laughing Deer. "We will butcher and skin it now so that when they return to their own camp they can take most of it."

I confess that as much as I loved my family, that feast in my hall when the Mi'kmaq ate with us was one of the most enjoyable evenings I ever spent on Bear Island. None of us knew it but the Norns had spun and our threads were tied. All of us felt like family. It was *wyrd*.

Chapter 15 Erik

It was sad to see Long Sight and the others depart for all of us. Within days they would begin to pack up their camp and head to their winter home and we would be alone again. Two days after they went Laughing Deer was ill. I blamed the shark for she vomited and brought up most of the food she had eaten the night before. When she recovered, she smiled and I thought that was strange, "It is not the shark, Erik, I am with child. White Doe sensed it and she told me what to expect." I suddenly remembered Ada when she had been carrying Lars. She had endured the same symptoms. Then my heart sank. When Ada had given birth the women of the clan had been on hand. There was just Stands Alone. Laughing Deer seemed to read my thoughts. "Fear not for we know what to do and we have the whole winter and, perhaps, into the new grass before our child will be born."

My world changed then as I realised the danger we were in. The Mi'kmaq were leaving and if the Penobscot returned then we could all die. I hoped that the Mi'kmaq council would allow us to live on the mainland and be part of their tribe. The Clan of the Bear was growing, and I wanted all of us to survive. It was then that Stands Alone also changed. As her sister bloomed and grew so she matured. It was as if she put her terrible childhood behind her and began to become an adult and she became invaluable to Laughing Deer. When there were tears then it was Stands Alone who comforted her sister for often I would be

The Bear and the Wolf

working on the island or fishing. Our routine changed but all was well for we were together.

I knew that I would need one more hunt on Horse Deer Island, but I kept putting it off for I feared for my wife. Laughing Deer seemed to know my moods better than I did for, as we lay together in our sleeping chamber she asked, "You are not worried about me or our unborn child, are you?"

I had learned not to lie to her, "In truth, I am for in our clan it is the women who deliver babies and birth is not the domain of a warrior. It is a strange country."

"And in our tribe, I am a woman and I can deliver the child, with the help of Stands Alone of course."

"But I cannot leave you alone."

"Of course you can, for I am fit and healthy. This is about the deer hunt, is it not? You need to hunt the deer on the neighbouring island." I nodded, "Then do it."

"I may need to spend the night on the island. I do not wish to make numerous journeys."

"And we know how to bar the bridge. We will be safe for one night."

And so it was decided. I had succeeded in making twenty arrows. Two of the arrows I had made bore metal tips and the rest were bone and stone. The deer I would hunt were red in colour. When he had visited with me Long Sight had told me of them and where they lived on the island. He had said that the Mi'kmaq often hunted them. They had realised that slaughtering the moos on the island had been a mistake and that had resulted in the death of Eyes of Fire. The shaman had said the punishment was that the clan should not hunt on the island for five seasons. When he had told me, I realised that they did not blame me for the death of the Chief's son. He had committed the sin against nature by slaughtering all of the moos. Long Sight told me that the deer were bigger and harder to find but that they provided a great deal of meat. I would have to kill fewer than the smaller white-tailed deer. I tied one of our older and smaller barrels on the cross pieces of the boat; in it was salt. It was hard saying farewell and made all the harder by the first bad weather since the storm. It was cold sleety rain which made Laughing Deer and Stands Alone race back inside the hall as I pushed off from the quay. I wore my sealskin cape, but I knew that I would soon be soaked. At least the rain would make animal tracks easier to see and the wind was from my stern which meant that I flew across but that swift journey meant a slow one home.

I knew from both the clan's hunting and Long Sight's words, that there were few predators on the island. Accordingly, I had left my sword at home. I wondered as the wind took me under stormy black clouds if Fótr and Ebbe had needed their swords. By now they would have made landfall. I did not believe that they were lost for Gytha or Ylva would have come to me and I had had no premonitions for quite a while. Ylva's presence in my dreams meant that the clan had made contact. Was the clan happy? I could no longer take care of my foster son and brother. The spirits would have to watch over my son. The low cloud obscured the mainland, but the island could be clearly seen. I lowered the sail and let the wind blow me gently on to the beach. I lifted the steering board and then pulled *'Ada'* up the shingle and sand beach. I tied her to a tree and proceeded to build myself a Mi'kmaq shelter. I had hoped to sleep under the trees, but the rain meant I would need a shelter. I used the same technique that Laughing Deer had done, and I soon had a dry shelter. I laid my bearskin on the ground and put up an improvised door to keep it dry. I carried a spear and my bow. The rain meant that I would not string my bow until I had to even so the feathers on my arrows were already sad and bedraggled.

Had Long Sight not advised me then I might have had to search for a longer time to find the deer I sought. As it was, I knew roughly where their herds lived and within a short time I had found their tracks. I was concerned, at first, that there appeared to be fewer tracks than I was expecting but, when I heard the cracks from ahead and smelled the musky smell of deer then it all became clear. Two stags were fighting and the Allfather had sent me to dispatch the loser of the battle. The rain actually helped me and I moved from tree to tree knowing that they would not smell me and their attention would be on each other. I saw them in a clearing. Of the herd, there was no sign. The does and hinds were not stupid; they knew that two fighting deer could accidentally hurt one of them. Whichever emerged as the winner would lead the herd. I strung my bow and rammed my two metal arrows in the ground. Bone arrows would do for a smaller female, but a stag was a different matter.

One of the stags was older. I could see that from the old scars on his head and body. The younger stag also had an advantage for one of his antlers was not uniform and being at a strange angle could inflict a terrible wound. At first, the older stag appeared to be winning. He was using all of his guile and experience to defeat the young usurper. He chose the better ground and the advantage of high ground. As I watched I observed that the younger one was fitter and more agile. He evaded some of the wild charges and, as the older one tired, so the young stag gained the higher ground. The rain had stopped and so I risked nocking an arrow. When the battle ended I did not want the loser to escape. The end, when it came, was a surprise to all three of us. I had envisaged another hour of battle when the rogue antler, coming from the side, speared the older stag in the shoulder. The shoulder muscles, along with the muscles of the hindquarter were the ones that decided a battle. The old stag was game but when the young stag not only avoided the older stag's wild charge but raked an antler across the old stag's side then it was over.

Fortune favoured me for, as it fled, knowing it was defeated, the old stag came towards me. I raised my bow and sent an arrow at him. All of his cunning came into play and he lowered his head when he sensed me. My arrow struck an antler and the old stag came directly for me. I had no time to think and I just grabbed my spear and braced the end against the tree behind me. The stag ran into the spear with such force that he drove the spear through his body and out of his back. He snorted blood at me and then died at my feet.

"You died well old one and there will be a place in deer Valhalla for you." I did not know if there was such a place, but I hoped that there was. I carefully pulled out my spear and my arrow. I did so without damaging them too much although the feathers on the arrow suffered a little. Long Sight had said that the only predators on the island were foxes. I gutted the deer and, picking up the entrails, threw them into the clearing. Then I took the rope I had brought and hauled the carcass into the tree.

Crows and carrion might pick at it, but it would be minor damage that they did.

    I hurried after the younger stag. I would not hunt him, but he would lead me to the herd. As I had expected, the herd was not far away and they were at a small stream, grazing and drinking. The young stag had a few scars and was licking them. They could not smell me, and it gave me the chance to look at them. I identified the second deer that I would hunt. It was an old hind. It may even have been a former consort of the old deer. She limped which would make her slower. More importantly, she could not bear more fawns and so I would not harm the herd if I took her. I reached into my arrow bag and pulled out an arrow. I was careless and I did not look at the arrow. After nocking the missile, I aimed at her and drew back. I must have made a slight sound for the heads of the herd came up as one and I released, aiming at her body. The herd fled. I saw from the flight of the arrow that I had used the slightly damaged one from the dead stag. Instead of hitting her side it spiralled and struck her in the head, the weakened arrow shattering as it did so. The herd thundered up the watercourse before I could draw another arrow. Cursing my own carelessness, I picked up my spear and slung my bow over my body. I ran up the stream. I found the dying deer just twenty paces from where I had hit her. I had been lucky.

    She was smaller than the stag and I decided that I could carry her. I hefted her carcass across my shoulders and began to trudge back to the dead stag. A sudden scurrying and the sound of leaves and branches being disturbed, told me that foxes and birds had already been at the guts and the stag. I shouted and ran; they fled. It would keep them from the dead animal for a little while and I hurried back to my boat. The rain began again and this time there were icy drops in the rain. The seasons were changing. I was tired and my back was aching when I reached the camp. I dumped the deer on my boat. It would be safer there than on the ground. Leaving my bow and arrows there I went back to the dead stag. The birds had pecked out the eyes and the foxes had tried to jump up to get at the cut I had made in the body. I lowered it to the ground. There was no chance for me to carry it back as it was far too heavy. I had little choice but to fasten the

The Bear and the Wolf

legs together, tie the rope around his neck and drag the stag back. I had to use a route between the trees, and it took me some time. The thick clouds and rain meant I could not determine the time of day, but I knew that it had to be after noon.

I was chilled to the bone when I reached my camp which looked miserable and mean. Although I had camped so that the wind did not directly blow across the camp, the proximity of the white flecked waves meant it felt exposed. I placed the stag on the boat. I had much to do and little time before dark. Laying down my spear I gathered rocks from the beach to make a fire pit. I needed warmth and I needed fire. Then I went back into the forest to find dead wood, pinecones and timber to burn. I do not think that anyone had gathered wood since the Mi'kmaq had hunted the moos! Once I had the fire going, in the lee of my boat, the camp looked cheerier. I put a pot of seawater on to boil. The pot kept the fire a little drier.

I went to the boat and gutted the hind. She was smaller and would be easier to butcher. Working quickly and efficiently I skinned the deer and then took out some of the choice pieces: heart, kidneys and liver. I placed them on the rocks to cook. The guts I would reserve as bait on the journey back. Then I began to butcher the animal. The hooves were put in the bottom of the boat along with the guts. That done I cut the legs off and hung them from the crosspiece of my boat. it would soon be night time and the sea birds which were flocking above me would begin to roost. Already the sun was setting in the west. I cut the body into four equal pieces. I took them to the barrel and salted them before laying them on the boat's cross pieces. The skull I dropped into the water. I would cook it and extract the precious metal arrowhead. I looked at the stag. I was not as cold as it was hard work and made me sweat but I wished that I was back in my hall for I had to do the same for the stag and the beast was bigger and would take more work. It would be dark before I finished. As I began to drag it to the fire I looked over to my hall. I could not see it but the smoke which rose from its fire told me how close I was to Laughing Deer and a warm bed.

The skinning took longer and when I had finished, I weighted the two skins in the shallows under rocks. The smaller fishes would clean them a little and the salt in the sea would help to

The Bear and the Wolf

cure it. I tied the four legs over the creaking crosspiece. I would have to salt all eight legs before I could eat my food and enjoy some of my ale! I tossed the seared heart, liver and kidneys into the pot with the heads and trimmings of meat. I was weary and wet beyond words when I had finally salted the last of the deer meat. The preservation would continue but only once I had reached Bear Island. I ladled the heart, liver and kidney on to my wooden platter and poured some ale from my ale skin into my horn.

After shedding my cape, I slipped into the den I had made. It was dry and it was cosy. The Mi'kmaq technique of building sleeping shelters was a good one. I pondered if Bear Tooth would be teaching it to Fótr and the others. As I ate the most welcome food and washed it down with delicious ale my thoughts turned to the clan. I wondered if they had a new home yet and if the Clan of the Wolf had welcomed them. There would be some, like Eidel Eidelsson, who might regret our adventure which had cost almost half of the men from the clan. I knew that you could never go back and undo what you perceived were mistakes. If we had not come to this land, while it was true that there might have been more of the clan alive, others would not have been born. Lars for one. My brother might not have married Reginleif and Bear Tooth would not be in our lives. Would the Mi'kmaq cope with life in our world? No, you could not go back but, as I finished the last of my food and poured my last horn of ale I knew that the only contact with Fótr and Ada would be in the dream world and so I emptied my horn and went outside to make water. The rain had stopped. Taking the pot from the fire I built it up so that the flames would frighten away the animals of the night and I went to my bed to sleep.

The next morning, the storm had passed but there was a damp and cold feel to the air as I headed back beneath grey skies to my home. The journey was slower for I had not only loaded the boat with the deer meat but also the roots of a pine tree I had felled. I towed the tree. The roots would be made into pine tar. If the Mi'kmaq council accept us then, when we left the island, I would have to take many things from our island. My boat needed work. I still had the birch bark boats abandoned by the Penobscot and I intended to make them stronger and watertight.

Stands Alone must have been watching for me from the headland for Laughing Deer and she greeted me as I landed. I had been away but one night and yet it felt like a lifetime. Laughing Deer and I rushed into each other's arms. I had been meant to be with Laughing Deer. As fond as I was of Ada it was Laughing Deer whom the Norns had selected to be with me and all the doubts from the previous night evaporated. I was meant to be here, and I could not change it. I found myself almost saying goodbye to the Clan of the Fox as we unloaded my boat and took the meat to our hall where we would complete the preservation.

Winter shrank our world to the hall and the empty buildings which surrounded it. I stripped the sail and mast from my boat and dragged it and the other birch bark boats above the high-water mark. I weighed them down with rocks and covered them with pine branches to protect them. Then I left them until the new grass began to grow. We had sown barley and oats in the two small fields close to the hall and buildings. We had harvested them and sown one of the fields with winter barley and oats. It was as we brought the last of the cereal for winnowing that I saw the deterioration in another hall. It was Arne's and the turf had given way on one side; the side exposed to the worst of the rains. The roof had collapsed, and I knew that within a year or so the land would have reclaimed it. When I had taken the Mi'kmaq through the woods, trees had already begun to grow in what had been Benni's Stad. He must have used trees which had not been seasoned and they had grown, fed by the rotting turf. If I had not known there had been a farm there, then I would not have been able to point it out to Long Sight. The clearing which Benni and his family had made for their hall encouraged trees and plants to grow. When we left, if we left, then the sea and the forest would reclaim it and there would be little sign that we had ever been here. I wondered if there had been other Skraeling who had lived here long before the Mi'kmaq and Penobscot. Their mark would also have been eradicated.

As winter shrank our world so Laughing Deer grew. We had never been married but I regarded her as my wife. To me Stands Alone was my foster daughter. Since our return from the Mi'kmaq village, she had begun to turn into a young woman, and we got on really well. She laughed when I joked and was a great help to Laughing Deer. Our measurement of time was twofold, Laughing Deer's growing belly and the shortening of the days. When we reached the winter solstice we feasted. It was strange that both of our people celebrated on the same day. We were an ocean apart, but we had similar customs. I also knew that the Mi'kmaq would be gathered and some time during that shortest of days they would be speaking of us and our place in their world. When Ada had been carrying Lars, I had not been at home as much, but I saw Laughing Deer each and every day. So it was that I saw my unborn child kick and I put my hands to feel the feet and to listen to the heartbeat. We had no wise women to discern the sex and the three of us had games where we each put forward theories. It passed the long nights.

For the first time since I had been on Bear Island, we had snow which fell and lay for many days. We had wood and we had food so that the snow did not harm us, but it made me think back to the Land of Ice and Fire. My mother lay there along with many of the clan. I knew that there were Vikings there. Would they have the courage of the Clan of the Fox and make the hazardous and uncertain journey south and west? Despite my words to Chief Wandering Moos that was a fear. We had been an almost peaceful clan compared with those we had left on the Land of Ice and Fire. Harald Finehair had driven us there and I wondered how many others had been driven west. Despite our defeat at the falls I knew from my own personal battle that, properly prepared, Vikings could not be defeated by Skraeling. If more came from the east then it might mean the end of the Mi'kmaq, Penobscot and all of the other tribes.

It was when the snow lay all around us and the island was as quiet as could be that my son was born. The waters broke in what would have been the early morning, had it been summer. As it was it was dark, and the fire was dying. I built up the fire and put on a pot of water and then did something which no Viking warrior had done before. I witnessed the birth of a child. Stands Alone came into her own that morning for it was she who delivered my son while Laughing Deer squeezed my hand. She gave birth in silence and, later, she told me that was the Mi'kmaq way for if there was danger around then cries would alert an enemy.

After cleansing his mouth Stands Alone said, "You should cut the cord, Erik, for that will bring the child luck."

I took Karl's knife, the blade of King Rædwulf, and sliced through the bloody cord. I was transported back to my youth when the three of us, Arne, Siggi and myself had sworn an oath on the bloody blade. I said, "My son, by this bloody blade I swear to protect you while I live and after I am gone for my spirit to watch over you."

Stands Alone wrapped him in the fur of a bjorr and handed him to Laughing Deer who kissed him and then, as he began to wail, offered him food. "What shall we name him, husband, Erik after you?"

I shook my head, "No for that is a Norse name and he is not Norse. He is Norse and Mi'kmaq. He shall be Bear for I will name him after this island and your people call me the Shaman of the Bear. It is *wyrd*."

And so my son became Bear. It became Bear son of Erik later on and so the Norse side was honoured but I cared not. I had lost one son, Lars, who was now back in the east but I would watch this one as he grew.

Chapter 16 Erik

By the time the snow had melted the days were increasing in length and the three of us ventured forth to repair the damage done by winter. We might be leaving the island but, then again, we might not. I knew that we would not be isolated. Long Sight, Black Bird and I were friends. They would visit. White Doe also had a connection with Laughing Deer and Stands Alone. While the winter crops were checked I went to the boats and removed the fir branches. They were undamaged. Before the winter I had made the pine tar and so I lit a fire outside and began to heat up the magical potion which would lengthen the life of a boat. The hard part was taking apart my boat for I could not invert the whole thing, I was not strong enough. In the end, it proved to be a useful activity for I found that one of the crosspieces which tied the logs to the birch bark boat was damaged. It needed replacing. Over the next few days, I sealed the boats and then began to rebuild *'Ada'*. The repair meant I had to start again when building her and I learned from my mistakes. This time I used two birch bark boats to make the hull. It would make her slightly slower, but she could carry more and would be far more stable. It also allowed me to place the mast so that it was more central. I replaced the steering board withy and I used the last of the pine tar on the two logs. With them out of the water I was able to scrape off all of the sea-life. Choosing a bright, albeit chilly day, I tested the new *'Ada'* and found her a joy to sail. Black Bird might be disappointed that it was no longer a wild ride, but it would be safer for Laughing Deer and Stands Alone. I

The Bear and the Wolf

took her all the way to the mainland. I knew that the Mi'kmaq would not have returned but I wished to explore the coast. My words and conversations with Long Sight had told me that the Mi'kmaq rarely ventured far from the beaches that they knew. I had charcoal and some of the doe's skin. I began to make a map. I discovered beaches which could not be reached from the land. The shellfish there would be a rich harvest and I saw driftwood there too. All could be used. By the time I returned to Bear Island I had a much better picture of the coast and, as I approached my island from a different direction, I saw how the Penobscot had reached us without being seen. There were islands every mile or so. It meant that they had approached hidden from view. If they had done it once, then they could do it again. It showed me the isolation which had not been a problem with the whole clan, but I was now the only warrior and with a son to protect I knew we would have to leave.

The end of winter was a time to prepare and with Laughing Deer spending increasing amounts of time with the baby then Stands Alone became the cook and also, when I needed her, my helper. She had changed beyond all recognition in the last year. She was on the cusp of womanhood. However, it was the changes in her mind which were the more obvious. She chattered and she smiled; she voiced opinions and offered suggestions. I prayed that some young warrior would heal her heart, but I was not sure. We were thrown together and she was invaluable not only to her sister but also to me. She was stronger and when we began to harvest the winter oats and barley, she was able to move sacks which were quite large. She could even pull the cart while I scythed the cereal. As the clan had done when they lived on the island, I kept back a tenth of the crop for seed. Would I be planting it on the mainland? She helped me collect the last of the greens and, after fertilising the soil, she helped me plant new crops. Our work lasted from sunrise to sunset. When she went to help Laughing Deer or cook the food then I emptied the lobster, crab and fish pots. The island was bountiful, but it was not safe.

The new shoots had just begun to appear when we spied the smoke from the land. The Mi'kmaq had returned. I had assumed that they would set up their camps and then come to speak with us after a week or so and I was surprised when, as I went to empty the fish traps, I saw a canoe powered by five warriors racing across the choppy waters. It was not good sailing weather and whatever the reason for the visit it was important. I began to fear the worst, but I did not alarm Laughing Deer. It took many hours for them to paddle across and I had Stands Alone prepare hot food. We had just brewed some black beer and I put out five beakers. I waited on the wooden quay and saw that it was Long Sight, Black Bird and three other warriors I did not recognise.

Long Sight shook his head as I helped him from the boat, "That is hard! I wish we had a boat like yours."

I smiled, "I have improved it and I can tow you back if you like."

He shook his head, "I fear you will be returning with us. I have dire news."

"Then tell us all at the same time for I have no secrets from my wife." He nodded. "By the way, I now have a son, Bear!"

He was genuinely pleased and hugged me, "This is good Erik, Shaman of the Bear."

Stands Alone stood close to Laughing Deer when the five warriors entered for there was no White Doe with them. "Sit, eat and drink and then tell me the news that blackens your faces." I glanced at Laughing Deer. She was clever and, like Ada and Gytha, could read people. She was prepared for the worst.

Long Sight ate a little and quaffed a whole beaker of ale which I refilled before he spoke. "We went to the council with our news and we found your clan, Laughing Deer and Stands Alone. I have bad news for you. After you were taken your clan tried to take you back, but they were ambushed. Your father and your brothers along with most of the warriors of the clan died. Your Chief, Grey Otter, also died and his son, Talking Beaver took the few men of the clan and they joined with the Clan of the Hawk. When Wandering Moos told the other clans of the attack on your island and your request, there was much debate. Some tribes fear the Penobscot. However, it was decided that the tribe owed it to the dead to welcome you to our lands."

I smiled, "Then that is good news!"

"I have not given you the bad news yet. The Mohawks sent a messenger to us for they are our allies. The Penobscot asked them to join them in a war against the Mi'kmaq. They have renounced the treaty of the River of Peace. The Mohawks said that they had no grievance against us and refused to join. There is now bad blood between the Penobscot and the Mohawks, but they will not fight, not yet. When we heard that the council sent emissaries to the other, smaller tribes who live close to the Penobscot the news they brought was not good. The whole of the Penobscot tribe is ready to fight, and they are a mighty tribe. His father, Chief Red Hand and Angry Voice's younger brother, Runs at Night, have roused the tribes and sworn vengeance on the pale-haired shaman of the bear and the Mi'kmaq. Now that the ground is warm, they will come, and they will number more than our tribe."

I emptied my horn of ale. We had fled from Larswick to avoid a war and it had followed us. It was *wyrd* and no matter what we men did the Norns would decide our future. I nodded and when I spoke every eye but Bear's was on me. "We have too much to pack to leave today. It is good that you have come. Stay this night and tomorrow we will begin to take our home to the mainland."

Black Bird shook his head, "They may be on their way already! What if they are heading for this island in their boats?"

I smiled, "Then they are doomed before they begin. When you came, Long Sight, was it easy?"

He shook his head, "The waves threatened to swamp us."

I nodded, "I am the only one here who has sailed from the south. Your journey was easy compared with the one the Penobscot will have to make. I do not doubt that they will come and that they will come armed with the knowledge of those who fled but it will not be for a moon at least for they will wait until these storms and wild winds have passed. We have time. Tomorrow we take my family and as much as we can load then I will make daily trips in my boat until there is nothing left on Bear Island but the ghosts of the dead and they, I believe, will make life hard for the Penobscot. Now eat, Long Sight, and enjoy the food and the ale!"

He smiled, "You are as wise as a chief, Erik, and you have great courage. It will be an honour to fight alongside you."

"And while I do not have many weapons to bring, I have skills in making weapons which are better than yours."

I saw that they doubted me and so I brought out my shield and my bow. I handed the shield to Black Bird. He said, "This is heavy!"

"And can your arrows penetrate the wood?" He shook his head. I took my yew bow which was as long as I was. "If you could use a bow like this then it might but even if you cannot draw such a bow, we can make ones which are still better than yours. You can send arrows from a greater distance." I went to my chest and took out my mail. "Wearing this then the only weapons the Penobscot have which can hurt me are their clubs and for that, they have to get close." I dropped it on the table and saw the three warriors I did not know examine it. "However," I knelt down to take something else from the chest, "you can all make these." I took out my metal-studded hide jerkin. "You may not have the metal, but bone attached to the hide will help to deflect Penobscot arrows."

Long Sight said, "We do not have long and these would take time."

I handed the leather jerkin to Long Sight. "Here is one you do not have to make! It is my gift to you." I went to the corner and found my wood axe. "And here, Black Bird, is my gift to you. Now two of your warriors will be stronger and if they do not come for a month then anything that we do will help us. Do not look, Long Sight, as though that beaker of ale is half empty." I topped it up. "It is half full!"

My words filled them with hope. I sat and ate while they examined my gifts. Laughing Deer placed the sleeping Bear in the crib and came to me. She kissed me on the cheek and said, "You are wise, my husband, and I believe that we will overcome the Penobscot, but I fear that many of Wandering Moos' people will suffer."

"And you can do nothing about that for the Penobscot have set this in motion. Tomorrow you take that which is most precious, and I will come back each day to remove everything. All that was left for us we will take, and we will share it with our new clan." I waved over Stands Alone who had been quiet since the five warriors had entered the hall. "And you, Stands Alone, will you be happy?"

She smiled at me, "Erik, you are thoughtful and if all men were like you then my heart and my mind would be settled but I have seen the worst of men. I know that Long Sight is a good man for White Doe told me and I believe that Black Bird is also honourable for you told me so but the others? I look at them all as though they will hurt me, even these three."

Laughing Deer said, "Then, sister, you shall continue to stay with me, and we will ask for a home which is close to White Doe. We cannot stay here for that would mean a return to..."

"I know."

Long Sight and I sat up long into the night for he wished to talk, and the ale flowed well. He wanted to know how we fought. When he and his clan had fought us, they had been so shocked that they had not learned anything from us. I told him how we used a shield wall and fought together. I told him how we used younger warriors with slings and bows to harass the enemy.

He nodded and then said, "We were doomed to failure because of your superior weapons."

I had had long nights to reflect on the disastrous battle of the falls and I thought I understood the reason. "And yet the Penobscot killed my brother and many other warriors."

"And how did they do that?"

"My brother made the mistake of assuming he would win and did not fight as he should have done. He tried to attack the Penobscot. When we waited for our foes we won; when we used defences, we won. We need to make your camp stronger."

He beamed, "Use nature to help us win the war?"

"Now you have it. The enemy will come for vengeance and will assume that they will win. They will fight you the way they always have and expect you to do the same. If your warriors will listen to me then no matter how many men they bring we have a good chance of winning." By the time we had talked things through he was happier.

We loaded *'Ada'* at dawn. Black Bird and the three warriors would stay at the island and continue to bring our belongings to the quay. My new enlarged boat meant we could take more cargo. We had our bedding as well as all that Bear needed. Long Sight would take them to the camp, and I would continue to ferry the rest of our belongings.

As we sped across the water Long Sight shook his head, "You will be back at the island in the same time it took us to cover half the distance. This is a wondrous boat."

"You should have sailed on *'Gytha'* now there was a vessel!"

There were many hands to help us unload and I quickly turned around. The voyage back was quicker as I had the wind and when I reached the island Black Bird and the others had managed to bring the most important things to the quay. I looked at the sky, despite the swift journey, the loading and unloading, allied to the shorter days meant this would be our last crossing of the day.

"Tie your boat to the stern and you can cross with me."

Black Bird saw the fearful look on the faces of the three young warriors and, winking at me, he said, "Are you women? Laughing Deer and Stands Alone sailed without fear and they had a baby with them."

They climbed reluctantly on board and I smiled as I saw them gripping the sides. When the sail snapped and billowed, they each grabbed their amulets. They had a relatively quiet voyage, but I knew they were praying all the way! When we had unloaded, I stepped the mast and the warriors helped me to drag the boat onto the beach. There was little likelihood of her slipping off as she was well above the high-water mark. We then carried what we had brought up to the main camp. The Mi'kmaq were creatures of habit and the dwellings were in exactly the same place as when I had last visited. As we entered Black Bird pointed and said, "Your home will be next to Long Sight. My wife and I wished for you to be our neighbour, but Long Sight is the senior warrior."

I smiled, "Thank you for your help and we shall see each other often for I will be living here."

"Do you need to return to the island?"

"There is still much that we can bring. There is the salt for a start."

"Your people are industrious, and I can see the result of that work. Our men like to hunt and that is all. Few make things. That is the work of women."

I said nothing for there were men like that in Norse villages. I was not one of them.

The Bear and the Wolf

White Doe and Stands Alone were in the Mi'kmaq shelter. I saw that it was efficiently made but I could make it better. I smiled, "Are you all well?"

"Aye, husband, they have made us more than welcome."

I saw that Stands Alone looked happier and put that down to the presence of White Doe.

White Doe smiled at me, "Tonight you eat with the tribe for Wandering Moos wishes to speak with you. The women will eat apart." She looked pointedly at Stands Alone, "That will make it easier for all of us."

I decided not to wear my bearskin but, instead, to wear a simple kyrtle. I could tell, as I headed for the fire, that there was disappointment. Long Sight chuckled when he joined me, "They prefer the Shaman of the Bear as they think the cloak makes you more powerful."

"I am sorry; should I return and don it?"

"No, my friend, for I have seen that the magic comes from within and you need no bear cloak to show it. Wandering Moos has clear eyes and he can see it too."

Wandering Moos gestured for me to sit next to him, "Our tribe is united against the Penobscot but, I fear, our neighbours may arrive too late for many of my warriors."

"I have spoken with Long Sight and I believe that we can give the Penobscot a surprise when they come. They think they know us because of the battle of the waterfall but that was my brother. He was like your son, Eyes of Fire, and he was hasty and reckless. Like your son he was brave but sometimes you must temper courage with caution. There is a time to be wild and a time to be patient. If they give us fourteen nights, then we can prepare defences which will make them pay heavily for their arrogance!"

Wandering Moos looked relieved, "That is good for I do not wish to lose all of my warriors. Your people took some of the best of my warriors."

I felt guilty even though it was we who had been attacked.

There was a different mood that night compared with the previous feasts I had enjoyed. I sensed a hunger in the younger warriors for war and Wandering Moos' words had told me why. Long Sight and Black Bird were now two of the more experienced warriors and the young ones had yet to be blooded. They saw this battle with a more traditional enemy as their opportunity. In addition, I knew from Black Bird that there was a sense of outrage that Mi'kmaq women had been taken and abused by their hated enemies. Younger warriors came to me to ask for me to recount, in detail, how I had slain the Penobscot when they had attacked my island. When Long Sight asked then to leave me alone, I noticed that Wandering Moos was now seated alone. Despite being the chief, he was isolated. There was just Long Sight who was what I would call a veteran warrior. Wandering Moos had his sons but all those who were of an age with him were dead and he looked sad. All around him was the excited chatter of much younger warriors but he was like a rock in a bubbling mountain stream, it all went on around him and did not seem to touch him.

"Do you have grandchildren, Wandering Moos?"

His eyes brightened and he nodded, "I have six of them and they brighten my days. I hope I will live long enough to see them grow."

I had learned much from my time, first with Bear Tooth, then Laughing Deer and now the tribe. "You are not the war chief?"

He shook his head, "I have always counselled the path of peace. This life we live is difficult enough without trying to kill each other but I know that war is necessary. My son would have been war chief had he lived." He leaned in, conspiratorially, "He asked me many times to let him be chief. Sometimes you cannot give your children what they want. I hope that his children have not inherited their father's love of war." He began to pack his pipe with the dried leaves. "I shall not be here then. I will be with the spirits and my influence will have gone."

As he lit the pipe, I saw a change in him. He became more relaxed. Laughing Deer had told me that some of the leaves they smoked had that effect, they calmed the smoker. He opened his eyes and said, "Despite the number of warriors you have killed I do not think that you like war."

I shook my head, "That was my brother. If the Penobscot had not come to my home I would not have sought their deaths. I am here in your camp because they seek to harm me and my family and I will fight. Some people assume that any man who does not shout about war is not a warrior. That is not true. I have killed many men, but I never sought a man's death. I killed to defend that which I held dear."

"It is good talking to you, Shaman of the Bear and is like talking to those warriors with whom I grew up. You are wise beyond your years, but you have passed across the water and that must change a man. If I went east, would I like what I found?"

I shook my head, "It is a wondrous place, Wandering Moos, but I do not think that you would enjoy it."

"Wondrous?"

"I have told Long Sight and the others of the buildings that great men have. They are built of stone and they have stairs to climb to the other floors." I had to try to explain what a floor was. "In the north of our land is a wall which stretches from sea to sea across the whole land and it is as tall as one man standing on the top of another."

His eyes widened, "A wall made of stone?"

"Aye, and it is as wide as it is tall. My clan who sailed east hope to live close to it."

"Because it is magical?"

"No, Wandering Moos, because the chief who lives there keeps the land peaceful and none attack him. The wall was built in ancient times, but it helps to protect them."

He nodded and laid the pipe on the ground. "Your people are strange. They keep their homes in one place, but they are happy to sail across the sea."

I laughed, "To me, the sea is not an enemy, but you are right, we are a strange people."

"And you have been sent here to spread your seed in this land. Your son, Bear, is the first and he will have all that is good in your people and all that is good in ours. I think I would like to see the kind of person that comes from such a union."

When we all retired, I felt that Wandering Moos was, somehow, happier.

It took me six days to fetch all that I wished from the island and, as Black Bird and I packed up the last barrel I felt sad. Already the halls had a deserted look to them, but I saw, as we headed west, Gytha and the women spinning, I heard the sound of squealing children, I saw Aed and Padraig taking the snekke to fish. I was silent and Black Bird said, "When we leave our winter home, we are not sad for we know that we will return but you know that you will never come back here."

I nodded for it was hard to speak. The island had been part of the clan. The clan were gone but while I had lived on the island it had been as though they had not truly gone, and the spirits of the dead had been within the village. Would they follow me?

This time when we landed, I took the boat around the headland to a small river which lay to the north. I was loath to lose *'Ada'* and when the Penobscot came I did not wish their vengeance wreaked upon her. Black Bird and I sailed her half a mile up the river to a sheltered bend where I moored her to a tree. I knew that the river's source was close to the winter camp of the Mi'kmaq. When the tribe moved, I would sail her. Black Bird led me through the forest to the camp.

Despite my words and my advice, the tribe had still to prepare defences against the Penobscot. I knew that they were waiting for me to organize them. Laughing Deer told me so when Black Bird returned me to the camp. I was loath to take on the responsibility and my talks with Wandering Moos had made me hope that the Penobscot would not come and the Mi'kmaq could live in peace.

It was Laughing Deer who dashed those hopes for me. "Husband, you are a kind man, but you cannot conceive of the cruelty of the Penobscot. I know, for we lived amongst them, that they have a bad seed in them and wish to rule all of this land. You and I are an excuse for war, that is all. They would try to destroy us, that you can believe. My people need you, not as a war chief but a shaman of war for your people know how to fight. You were sent to us for a purpose and this is it. You need to save the Mi'kmaq."

Chapter 17 Erik

And with that sobering thought in my head, I set about the defence of the camp. First, I took Black Bird and his brother, Runs Far, to the forest and showed them how to use the axe to hew the right sized trees to make shields and defences. Black Bird did not like the idea of using the axe for anything as mundane as tree felling for he thought it would destroy the blade. I took the axe and with just a few swings, for it was a good axe and I knew what I was doing, I had a good tree felled. I then took one of the stone axes they used and, reversing the axe hammered the stone axe head into the log to split it. I repeated it until there were four rough planks.

"There. That is what you do!"

He shook his head and looked at the axe, "But the magical blade is damaged. It is not sharp!"

I took out my whetstone and quickly sharpened it. I let him feel the edge and when blood dripped from the cut he grinned. "There, and now it is sharp again, but you do not need to sharpen it with each tree that you fell."

He beamed, "You are truly a shaman."

"When you have done that cut down bow staves from that." I pointed to a tree which looked like a variety of yew. It was not exactly the same, but I had cut one suitably sized branch and knew that it had similar qualities to yew. I took the bow stave back to the camp with me.

As I left him, I realised that we needed some way to cut the planks into the right lengths. Then I remembered the shark we had taken. We could use the teeth to make a rough saw. It would not be as good as the ones Fótr had taken home with him, but it would do. When I returned to the camp, I sought out Long Sight and asked him for the teeth.

He looked confused as he fetched them from his dwelling, "You would do magic with them?"

"Sort of. We will embed them into a piece of wood and used them to cut planks in two." We spent some time discussing how to do this, but the Mi'kmaq were an ingenious people who knew how to bend natural objects into tools.

Leaving him to do that I wandered the camp. I think the tribe thought I wished to socialise for I was accosted on my walk but what I was doing was assessing the potential for defence. It was while they spoke that my eyes wandered. I saw that they had chosen the site because it was on a slightly higher piece of ground which meant they could not be flooded. They had protection from the winds due to the trees and that was a weakness. The path which led from the sea was the main approach, but the trees had enough space between them for men to move easily. There was a stream which ran along the northeast side and that would give a little protection. By the time I returned to Laughing Deer I had seen the potential. I made the assumption that the Penobscot would expect to find a Mi'kmaq village which was like their own. When they attacked, they would try to use their superior numbers to overwhelm the warriors and then destroy them. I had to devise a plan to funnel them towards the path and then make their progress into the village hard.

While I was thinking I was shaping the bow stave with my seax. In a perfect world, I would have seasoned the wood. The bow I was making with unseasoned wood would not be as effective, but I had little choice. Long Sight was convinced that the Penobscot's arrival was imminent and I had to work on that assumption. I enjoyed working with wood and it helped me think. By the time the bow was finished, I had my plan.

That night I sat with Wandering Moos, Black Bird and Long Sight. I showed them the bow stave and then explained my plan. "Tomorrow I will show the young warriors how to make a bow stave and how to make a shield. The shield does not need to be as polished as mine. We need as many of them so that we can present a wall of them when the Penobscot attack. My aim is to make them approach along the path. While the shields hold them your youngest warriors and women will attack them with rocks and arrows to thin their numbers."

"How will you channel them?"

"We put the spiky bushes and climbers between the trees. They could cut their way through, but their weapons would be weakened, and it would slow them down. We have trees hewn and placed next to the trees along the trail as a barrier and to channel them so that when we know they are coming we make it hard for them to climb up the path."

They nodded their agreement. Wandering Moos, however, looked me in the eyes, "And all of this will weaken them and thin their numbers, but they will still outnumber us, and the plan will not defeat them. Tell me, Erik, Shaman of the Bear, what is your plan to defeat them?"

"Me. I am the plan to defeat them. We put me in the centre of the line and I will draw them to me. They will see the bear; the ones who escaped my island will have told their chiefs that it was I who slew Angry Voice and they will wish vengeance on me. If they are attacking me then warriors like Long Sight and Black Bird will be able to slay great numbers of them. Long Sight has a seax and Black Bird an axe. If they wear the hide vests, then they will reduce the risk of wounding."

Wandering Moos nodded but Long Sight said, "Is that honourable? We fight without protection to show our courage."

I shook my head, "You are the only veteran warrior left Long Sight. When you fought my clan, your men died. Was there honour there? If you and the men of the tribe are killed and your women enslaved, like Laughing Deer and her sister, is that honourable? Fight in a hide vest or die and the tribe will cease to exist. I do not honey my words. I speak the truth." I looked him in the eye, "And you know it."

His shoulders slumped, "You are right. The tribe is more important than honour."

That single moment decided our course of action for Long Sight told the other warriors what they must do. Over the next days, while boys kept watch for the Penobscot, the rest of the clan toiled as one. Hunting and gathering were forgotten as shields and hide vests were made. Bows were made as were arrows. Stones of all sizes were gathered. I showed them how to tie honeysuckle vines around larger stones so that they could be thrown. When night came, we crept exhausted to our beds and I had my few moments of the day with Laughing Deer and Bear. The work went on from dusk until dawn but each day saw us stronger and better prepared.

The arrival of the Penobscot, although anticipated took us all by surprise for when the boys raced into the camp to say that they had seen the birch bark boats, they told us they came not for the beach but Bear Island. Long Sight, Black Bird and I all went to the headland to spy them. I counted more than thirty boats. They struggled across the choppy waters, but they purposefully paddled to the island.

Long Sight looked at me, "They call me Long Sight, but it is you deserve the name. They will come for you. The Penobscot risk the sea just to get at you!" He pointed as a boat was swamped and just two warriors were saved. Despite what we could see I knew that not all of the warriors and boats had been committed. There would be others who would come but I also knew that they had put their greatest effort into getting at me.

I smiled, "They are in for a surprise. I managed to raise the bridge to the hall and fix it closed. They will gain entry, but they will blunt and break weapons while they do so. Warriors will fall into the ditch and, in addition, there is nothing of value left for them."

We watched for a while and after some time saw a spiral of smoke rising, first on one part of the island and then another. They were destroying the houses. They could not harm the spirits of the dead and nature would reclaim the island. The only memory of the time of the clan on Bear Island would be in our heads and when we died it would be in our stories. We waited until the birch bark boats headed back and we saw more of them coming from the south.

I knew how long it would take them to reach us and that after paddling so far they would be in no condition to fight. I said, "They will not be here before dark. We can make life even more difficult for them. They will send scouts up to spy out the village

The Bear and the Wolf

in the dark. If we make traps and lay vines across the path they will be hurt."

Long Sight nodded, "I will organise that. Black Bird, find ten good warriors to wait in the woods and to slay any who escape them. War has come and we will show them that we are ready!"

Already the young warriors were geared up for war. Long Sight addressed them all. "The enemy will not be here before dark and we have time to prepare. Black Bird!"

Black Bird quickly chose his warriors and they put on their war faces and, those who had them donned their hide jerkins.

Long Sight turned to me, "Go to your family for tomorrow you will be vital to our victory. Black Bird and I can see to the rest. Your decision about the traps was a good one and I should have thought of it. You were sent here to save us."

I did not point out, as I headed to Laughing Deer that our arrival had also precipitated this disaster. It was the Norns. Stands Alone, my wife and son were seated outside our home and they had food ready for us to eat. They chatted as though this was a normal day, but I saw the nervous look Stands Alone gave to the trail.

"The tribe is prepared, Stands Alone."

She nodded and patted the sheath of her seax, "As am I. I was a child when they took me. If they defeat our men, then they shall see what a woman can do." She stood, "Give me Bear and I will wind him."

Laughing Deer had told me that she feared Stands Alone would never have her own children and I saw that Bear was lucky. He had two mothers. When we were alone Laughing Deer said, "She is not the only one who is afraid. Can we win? There look to be too few men in the tribe."

"When they come then the women will aid the men. The stones we will use to throw at them can be thrown by women and children. When the morrow comes it will be the tribe which fights and not just the men and the Penobscot will not expect that."

After I had eaten, I lay down to rest. I knew that I would not be able to sleep but I would rest while I could. When I rose, I would don my mail. I had decided to use some of the ash from the fire. I did not want them to see the metal of my byrnie beneath the bear cloak and I would blacken it with soot. My weapons were sharpened, and I had given one of the Penobscot spears to Long Sight. When we had been to Benni's farm on the island I had found, half-buried, a broken ploughshare. It had split, somehow, and Benni must have discarded it or, perhaps he had always intended to repair it but been killed before he could do so. On the other hand, it could have been the Norns. Whatever the reason I had two pieces of metal and I used the flat side of the axe head to beat them into shape before I sharpened them. Now the two spears were a pair of formidable weapons. The spearhead was narrow and pointed. Thrust hard it could hurt an enemy.

As darkness fell, I rose and donned my mail. I used the soot and ash to darken not only my mail but also my face and hands. That would be my war face. When I put the bear's head over my helmet, I appeared even taller than before. Long Sight nodded approvingly, "Black Bird and his killers are in the forest. When the scouts find the trail is full of traps, they will head into the trees and there they will die."

"And if the Penobscot come in numbers?"

"They will race back and tell us. Our warriors rest with weapons and their hide vests. They will be ready to fight and if I were to have to face you, Erik, Shaman of the Bear I would fear you and expect to die."

"Then let us hope that they do too!"

We waited at the head of the path and we listened. The night passed and we heard nothing, not even the animals of the night and that was because our men were there, and they would remain silent. Then, as the moon peered out from behind a cloud a scream pierced the night. I have no doubt that some of those in our camp were afraid, but none made a sound. Then I heard other noises, but I could not identify them. The night passed and we all listened. It was not long before dawn when Black Bird and his men reappeared. One or two had bloody scars to show that they had battled but, in their hands, they carried ten heads.

"We have made the logs into deadly traps and they will suffer injuries as they come." Black Bird grinned, "I will need to use the whetstone, but this axe hews heads as easily as a tree."

The Bear and the Wolf

Long Sight looked pleased, "Put the heads on spears here across the path. It will enrage them, and we all know that a warrior who does not fight with his head has lost the battle already. I will rouse the warriors for soon they will be here. They will come with the rising sun.

I was left alone, and I hefted my shield on to my arm. I wondered what Fótr was doing. Had he had to fight to claim his land? That, it seemed, was our lot in life. Neither Fótr nor I wished to fight, Arne had, but we had not and yet, it seemed, if something was worthwhile then we had to fight for it.

The Penobscot warrior who ghosted from the woods almost caught me by surprise, but I had not moved, and I was completely encased in black. He did not see me but I saw him for the white bone beads on his vest reflected light. I had my arm pulled back the moment I spied him. He was running towards our camp and did not see the spear which rammed into his middle, scraped off his spine and ended his life. I had just pushed his body from my spear when Long Sight and the warriors appeared.

Long Sight nodded approvingly, "Once again you impress me. You have finished that which Black Bird began. Come, we will form the wall."

We went back to the warriors who were shuffling into place. We had practised this once or twice, but I knew that it was not enough. However, imperfect though we might be, it was better than fighting the old Mi'kmaq way. All that I was attempting was to protect our warriors from the initial attack. Their best warriors would come first and if we could ride that storm and weaken them then we had a chance. The Mi'kmaq were uncomfortable with their crudely made shields. We had not smoothed and finished them and that was no bad thing. A splinter could hurt our enemies while the shields protected the warriors. Behind us, the women with the stones and the boys with the bows and stones lined up. As with the shields we had practised but it would not be enough. However, if one arrow or stone in four hurt the enemy then we would be better off.

Chief Wandering Moos appeared, and he wore feathers hanging in his hair. He had a bare chest and he carried a bone tomahawk and a stone club. Long Sight nodded to him. For this day it was Long Sight who would command, and he said, "Chief, stand behind the Shaman of the Bear. He wishes to draw the enemy to him, and your presence will encourage that." He did not mention that this was the best chance Wandering Moos had to survive the battle for the Penobscot would have to kill me to get at him.

When the sun began to appear, we heard the Penobscot war cry from the beach and then we heard them as they hurtled up the path. When we heard the war cries replaced by shouts and screams of pain we knew that they had found our traps. We saw faces appear at the edge of the trees, but our barriers stopped them simply striding through them.

Long Sight shouted, "Await my command!"

I had never witnessed a battle like this before. When we had fought the Penobscot it had been almost by accident. When Arne had pursued them into their trap he had not known how they would fight. Long Sight and Wandering Moos had told me that the Penobscot liked to charge and win by sheer weight of numbers. It was what had made me adopt this plan. Our traps had disrupted their attack but as soon as they reached the path and saw the skulls and the dead scout, they just hurtled towards us in a mad frenzy! That was their weakness for they had not formed up first and they ran at us, not in tens and twenties but in ones and twos.

I had taught the Mi'kmaq to brace with their right foot behind them and their spears held before them. The Penobscot had spears and some had deerskin shields, but we had a solid wall of wood. I knew how to time my blow the best and I thrust forward as the warrior who came at me was just two paces from me. His stone-headed spear shattered on my shield and my spear tore into his throat. The warriors on either side of him were splattered by it and that distracted them so that Long Sight and his son speared them easily. More Penobscot were now rushing and so Long Sight shouted, "Stones and arrows!"

The women had no skill with a bow, but they could hurl rocks and I saw one warrior whose head was smashed by a stone thrown by White Doe so that it resembled a ripe plum which had burst! Arrows hit other warriors and I knew that my plan was succeeding. What we now had to do was to hold them! As I had expected they came for me but there were so many of them that they spread around our sides. They expected the combat to break down so that they could fight two to one. Our wall confused them. I later heard that the ones who came around our flanks were given a rude shock when the women stopped throwing the stone missiles and swung them like clubs. The boys also drove their arrows at close range deep into bodies. I learned of that after the battle for I was busy using my spear and shield to fend off attacks. Some blows got through and the stone clubs hurt. I saw one warrior's eyes widen when he hit my head with his club, and it did not harm me. He struck the bear's head and the helmet beneath. I speared him and then roared like a bear at the younger warrior behind. He stopped and it was a fatal mistake. My spear drove deep within him but, in his death, his body broke the head from the spear, and I hurled the now useless wood in the direction of the Penobscot.

Even as it caught a glancing blow to the head of one warrior a second ran at me with his spear. I had my hand on my sword and when I was pulling it out his spear hit my bear cloak and the head shattered on my mail. I think he expected me to fall over for he carried on charging towards me and in drawing my sword I half severed his arm before ripping up and taking off the bottom half of his face. I blocked with my shield as my sword swept across the faces of two others. I was assailed on all sides by Penobscot. Their weapons hacked, slashed and chopped at me. I think they believed that they could overwhelm me by sheer weight of numbers. My shield blocked most of the attempts to hit me and their spearheads clattered off my helmet and mail. When a blow did strike me, my mail held. I slashed and stabbed with my sword and each time I found flesh. The Penobscot did not wear any protection.

The image came into my head of Siggi and Arne at the top of the falls when they were surrounded by Penobscot and had their bodies broken by stone clubs. I kept close to the Mi'kmaq and their shields for that way I had a chance to survive and I did not want to die. As the Penobscot fell back a little I glanced down the line and saw that Mi'kmaq warriors had fallen. I knew that when I tired and became weak then they would have the opportunity to finish me. I raised my sword and shouted in

Norse, "I am Erik the navigator of the Clan of the Fox. Hear my words and fear me. All of you will die unless you run!"

I saw the look of terror on the faces of those close to me and they recoiled. They had not understood a word of my cry, but I think they thought I had cursed them. Out of the corner of my eye, I saw an object flying towards me and, instinctively, I flicked up my shield; the club struck it and cracked in two when the stone weapon hit its boss. That proved too much for some of those who had thought about attacking me again. As the arrows and flying stones continued to wreak havoc, a Penobscot voice ordered them to fall back out of range. When they did the Mi'kmaq cheered although I noticed that Long Sight did not. The enemy were not yet beaten. Although thirty or forty bodies lay before us there were at least fifty warriors waiting to attack us.

I turned to Long Sight, "Have the dead moved and then close ranks. They will attack again!"

As he gave the order, I saw that his spear was broken and that Black Bird's axe was notched and he was covered in blood. He had the wild look of a berserker on his face for his weapon had slain as many as I had with my sword.

I watched as four Penobscot, all of whom had feathers hanging from their hair indicating that they were warriors of some renown, gathered behind the others. Wounded and bleeding warriors were making their way down the path and the numbers who were facing us lessened. They still outnumbered us but not by as many.

Long Sight came back and said, "We have them worried, but we have lost warriors."

"And when they attack again, we will lose more for the wooden wall of shields is no longer solid."

"Whatever happens we have hurt them and their dreams of conquering us are over. For that the whole of the Mi'kmaq people are grateful."

The debate amongst the Penobscot was long and heated. That suited us for it meant we were able to present a solid, albeit shorter, line of shields. Then some of the younger Penobscot were summoned and I saw them head down the trail. I wondered if the battle was over and yet more warriors remained than had gone. If this was a Viking warband we fought I would have understood their tactics better.

Next to me, Long Sight appeared equally confused, "I do not understand this. Where have those young warriors gone? Have they been sent to fetch reinforcements or have they been ordered to attack our sides?"

I shook my head, "I do not know how you people fight but I know the terrain and I have scouted out this land. The two deep valleys on either side of the camp means that if they do try to come that way, they will struggle to bring numbers of men. I think they are trying to confuse us. See one approaches."

"He is coming to speak. He holds no weapons." He turned to his son and said, "Hold my shield, I will speak to him."

Behind me, I heard Wandering Moos say, as he shouldered his way past me, "I have done little fighting and I have watched my young men die. Let me speak."

He walked forward to meet the Penobscot warrior. We still did not know who was the chief but that really mattered little. The battle hung in the balance and those words might bring either victory or defeat. The two men spoke for a while and then, while the Penobscot remained where he was, Chief Wandering Moos returned and faced me.

"This concerns you alone, Erik, Shaman of the Bear. They wish their champion to fight our champion or at least they wish their champion to fight you."

Long Sight shook his head, "I like not this, Wandering Moos. Erik will win. No matter who they send against him his metal shirt, his shield and his sword guarantee that whoever he fights cannot defeat him."

I put my hand on Long Sight's and smiled, "You are right, Long Sight, and for that reason, I will fight him for I can save the lives of your young men. I am of this tribe now and I will fight for them. Whom do I fight?"

Behind the Penobscot warrior, I saw another warrior being prepared. He was almost as tall as me and he was broader. He bore scars on his half-naked body and he held a tomahawk and a spear. In his belt were a knife and a club. "The warrior behind their war chief, Laughing Wolf, is his son, Wolf's Tooth."

I could almost hear the Norns spinning. My brother was trying to get the clan to the safety of the Land of the Wolf, and I was fighting a wolf. Long Sight was correct, this felt wrong, but I knew that I could do nothing about it. If I refused then my adopted tribe would lose heart, they would attack, and we would be defeated. "I am ready."

Our words had only been heard by the three of us and when I stepped forward the whole tribe cheered and shouted. The Penobscot remained ominously silent. When they saw that there would be a battle between champions the Penobscot warriors stepped back and Wolf's Tooth advanced. I felt overdressed as I approached. The warrior was about my age, but he would be able to dance around me. I had not seen the warrior fighting and that meant he would be fresh and his weapons sharp. I could see his plan; he would try to stay away from my sword and to get behind me and use the stone club to break bones and yet why was the club in his belt? He held a spear and a tomahawk. Neither could hurt me unless they were poisoned. I was no longer in command of my destiny; I had prepared as well as I could but there were other forces at work. I forced those thoughts from my head. If he was intending to dance around me then I would have to be alert.

I looked at his eyes. He could not see mine for I wore a helmet. His eyes showed no fear and that meant he thought he would win. The only way that would happen would be if he had allies who helped him and both tribes were a clear thirty paces from us. If he attempted to draw me closer to them then I would hold my ground. I was correct, he intended to use his speed and the length of his spear. He raced towards me and lunged with his spear. I saw it coming and flicked up my shield. He danced around my back and I felt a pain, as though I had been kicked; he had hit me with his tomahawk when he had passed. It was no consolation to me that I had been proved right. The Penobscot cheered.

I was unworried by the attack for my mail had held and I had a padded kyrtle beneath. I might be bruised, I might even suffer a broken bone but neither would impair my ability to fight. However, I was no fool and I determined to bring the fight to him. He placed himself before me and a thought came into my head. I know not whence it came except a voice said, *'Sway and plant your feet on the ground'*. It was not Gytha, but she had taught me to heed such words when they flowered in my head. When he launched himself at me, instead of blocking the blow with my shield, as his spear came at my head I swayed out of the way. The spearhead missed me completely and I was balanced so that, as he tried to get around my back, I turned the opposite way and my sword hacked through his spear and drew blood on his left forearm. This time the cheers were from the Mi'kmaq. The voice had aided me, and I now had a way to fight.

The eyes of Wolf's Tooth were still undefeated. I had drawn first blood, but he seemed not to care. He drew his stone club and advanced. Out of the corner of my eye, I caught movement in the trees. I thought nothing of it and, to be honest, my bear cloak and helmet made it hard to see but I should have heeded the movement. This time, as he approached me, the Penobscot warrior moved more quickly and danced from side to side. Once again, I swayed but he did not try to attack me, instead, he raced to the side and threw himself to the ground. Suddenly, from the trees, twenty arrows flew at me. I only knew they were arrows later. I was struck by all twenty. The stone and bone heads stuck in my bear cloak and mail, but some hit me below the mail byrnie and broke my flesh; one hit my right hand. More arrows came and I heard shouts of anger from behind me. This was treachery. Wolf's Tooth tried to rise and move away as a second shower flew. He tried to get away from the arrows but the Norns were spinning and he slipped. I brought my sword over and split not only the back of his skull but also his spine and then I turned to face the Penobscot.

I could feel the blood dripping down my leg, but I was angry. I shouted, in Mi'kmaq, "You have no honour and now you will face the wrath of the bear!" I ran at them and I watched them flee. They were not encumbered by mail and they would escape me and so I slowed. In addition, I began to feel weak. Those who had climbed the trees to shower me with arrows, however, were caught, not by me but by vengeful Mi'kmaq who hacked and chopped their bodies long after they were dead.

Even as a bloody but unbowed Black Bird came up to me, I felt the strength leaving me. I could not hold the shield and it fell from my hands as though I was lifeless. As my knees buckled and I fell to the ground I forced my fingers to hold on to the sword. If I was dying, then I would go to Valhalla and see my brother and my cousin. The brothers of the blade would be reunited. I saw Black Bird's mouth moving but I heard no words and then I fell into a black pit and I saw nothing.

I fell but I did not land, and faces flashed before my eyes. I was at sea and a terrible storm rocked and rolled 'Ada' and then I was tossed out into the sea. I sank to the bottom of the ocean and then, as I rose, I saw a tunnel and I headed along it. I even glimpsed an open doorway with a glow behind and the sound of wassailing warriors came to my ears. I knew that was Odin's mead hall and I was nearing Valhalla, from within I heard my name called and I recognised the voices of my father and Snorri. I tried to walk towards it, but it was as though my feet were stuck in mud; the door was closed as I saw two women approaching. I knew they were women from the shape of their bodies but I could not see their faces. That they were strong women became obvious for they lifted me easily and then I realised that I was as naked as Bear had been the day that he had been born. They took me to another dark place; it was as though we were journeying underground and then I felt the heat. Was this Hel? Had I committed some crime so that I was being punished before I could enter Valhalla? I would fight to get to Valhalla, or I would fight to live! I was a Viking and had been born into the Clan of the Fox. I had a new clan now and I owed it to my son and my wife to fight for life. I had been hurt but the pinpricks of the Penobscot arrows could not harm me. I tried to raise my arm and I could not and so I closed my eyes to will myself to move.

When I opened them then the source of the heat became clear. I was in a steam hut and then all went black and I knew nothing except that I seemed to be floating. Faces flashed at me and I saw Gytha and Ada. I saw the grey-haired woman I had not recognised before and then Laughing Deer's face flashed before me and then, as the door to Odin's mead hall opened, all went black and I saw nothing.

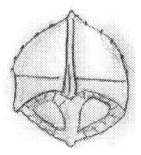

Fótr

It took many months to finally scour the Norwegians from the Land of the Wolf. When we did Sámr and I went alone to the cave. Sámr and his cousin greeted each other, and I waited without for they needed to be alone. Then they welcomed me within, and I placed the helmet and wolf cloak back where I had found them. Sámr and Ylva stood back as I addressed the Dragonheart's body. "Thank you for the loan of your helmet and cloak and for the skills you taught me. I will now live in your land and the Clan of the Fox will be a part of the Clan of the Wolf. I will kill a wolf, as you did, Dragonheart, and I will wear its skin. I can never be the Dragonheart, but I can be Fótr the Wolf."

Ylva hugged me as I left the cave. "Farewell, Fótr the Wolf. None shall see me again but you and Sámr here will always have me in your minds. Call to me when you need me, and my spirit will be here."

That goodbye was hard and, I think, was the goodbye I should have had with Erik if the Norns had allowed. There were tears in my eyes as I left the cave where I had become a warrior. I waited without as Sámr and Ylva said their farewells. When he came out, I saw that he, too, had wept. Nodding to each other, for we were too full for words, we headed down the trail towards the Rye Dale. We were both silent. We had just reached the Rye Dale when we heard a rumble and, looking back, we saw the rocks sliding down the Loughrigg to bury the entrance to the cave. I stared at Sámr who looked at me sadly, "You knew?"

He nodded, "She used her power to save the land and her body was weary. Now she and my great grandfather will use their spirits to watch the Land of the Wolf."

We walked in silence for I was lost in my thoughts. Already the Clan of the Fox was splintering. Aed and Padraig had decided to make their home where we had landed. I left them the snekke and the Hibernian pirate ship. They and their families would be fishermen once more. It was *wyrd*. Half of the clan chose to live at Cyninges-tūn while Ebbe, Bear Tooth and our families had made our home at Úlfarrston.

As we crested the col which overlooked the Water I said, "And you, Sámr Ship Killer, what now for you?"

"You are a clever man, Fótr the Wolf, and I think that you know what I will do. I will get a crew and sail to Norway. I have a family to find. You of all people know how important that is!"

I nodded, "Aye and I will come with you for our threads are tied. I believe that Bear Tooth and Ebbe will also choose to come."

He beamed, "Then there is hope for your return from the New World is a sign that anything is possible with a true heart and the courage of a wolf!"

Erik

When I opened my eyes, I saw Laughing Deer and White Doe peering at me. Behind them, I saw Stands Alone, and she was cradling Bear. Laughing Deer was weeping but White Doe had a joyous look upon her face. "He lives! He is a strong warrior and his gods have saved him."

I tried to speak but no words came. White Doe said, "Give him some of his ale, Laughing Deer, and I will go to fetch my husband. She went outside as Laughing Deer poured ale down my throat. I was parched and the ale tasted, to me, like honeyed mead. I heard a cheer from outside and Laughing Deer smiled, "She has told the tribe that you live. They have been anxious."

Wandering Moos, Black Bird and Long Sight came into the dwelling and Laughing Deer said, "Come, sister, let us give Bear some air."

I managed to croak, "What happened?"

Long Sight shook his head, "The Penobscot are treacherous. They used the venom of the snake to poison their arrows. Their young warriors sent more than sixty arrows at you and five of them found flesh. You should have died."

Wandering Moos nodded, "And you would have done had White Doe and Laughing Deer not spent two days and nights with you in the steam hut. Their potions and their love brought you back. You have lain here for seven days and each day you have come back a little more from the other side."

Black Bird asked, "What is it like there, on the other side?"

I shook my head, "It is dark, and it is frightening. Do not ask again." I shook my head for I knew how close I had come to death. "And the Penobscot?"

Long Sight smiled, "Those we found we butchered and when we reached the sea, we saw that the gods had punished them for their treachery. As they headed south a terrible storm came and every boat was swamped. None returned to their homes and the sharks feasted on their corpses. We are safe from them and it is thanks to you."

Wandering Moos said, "Come Black Bird, we need to celebrate with the tribe. This is a good day for the Mi'kmaq! We have a story to add to the wapapyaki!"

Left alone with Long Sight I asked, "Were many warriors lost?"

He shook his head, "You amaze me, Erik, Shaman of the Bear. You are near to death yourself and yet when you awake you think of the others. We lost eight warriors and that is sad but each of them has sons who will grow under the protection of the tribe. And you, what are your plans?"

I laughed and it hurt me, "To see the sky and the trees, to play with my son and to lie with my wife. When time allows, I will speak with Laughing Deer and decide but for now, I am content to stay with the tribe for this is my home."

He nodded, "For as long as you wish!"

The End

Norse Calendar

Gormánuður October 14th - November 13th
Ýlir November 14th - December 13th
Mörsugur December 14th - January 12th
Þorri - January 13th - February 11th
Gói - February 12th - March 13th
Einmánuður - March 14th - April 13th
Harpa April 14th - May 13th
Skerpla - May 14th - June 12th
Sólmánuður - June 13th - July 12th
Heyannir - July 13th - August 14th
Tvímánuður - August 15th - September 14th
Haustmánuður September 15th-October 13th

Glossary

Afen- River Avon
Afon Hafron- River Severn in Welsh
Àird Rosain – Ardrossan (On the Clyde Estuary)
Balley Chashtal -Castleton (Isle of Man)
Bebbanburgh- Bamburgh Castle, Northumbria is also known as Din Guardi in the ancient tongue
Beck- a stream
Beinn na bhFadhla- Benbecula in the Outer Hebrides
Blót – a blood sacrifice made by a jarl
Bondi- Viking farmers who fight
Bjarnarøy –Great Bernera (Bear Island)
Bjorr – Beaver
Byrnie- a mail or leather shirt reaching down to the knees
Càrdainn Ros -Cardross (Argyll)
Chape- the tip of a scabbard
Cyninges-tūn – Coniston. It means the estate of the king (Cumbria)
Dùn Èideann –Edinburgh (Gaelic)
Drekar- a Dragon ship (a Viking warship) pl. drekar
Duboglassio –Douglas, Isle of Man
Dun Holme- Durham
Dún Lethglaise - Downpatrick (Northern Ireland)
Dyrøy –Jura (Inner Hebrides)
Dyflin- Old Norse for Dublin
Eoforwic- Saxon for York
Føroyar- Faroe Islands
Fey- having second sight
Firkin- a barrel containing eight gallons (usually beer)
Fret-a sea mist
Fyrd-the Saxon levy
Gaill- Irish for foreigners
Galdramenn- wizard
Hersey- Isle of Arran
Hersir- a Viking landowner and minor noble. It ranks below a jarl
Hí- Iona (Gaelic)

Hjáp - Shap- Cumbria (Norse for stone circle)
Hoggs or Hogging- when the pressure of the wind causes the stern or the bow to droop
Hrams-a – Ramsey, Isle of Man
Hundred- Saxon military organization. (One hundred men from an area-led by a thegn or gesith)
Hwitebi- Norse for Whitby, North Yorkshire
Jarl- Norse earl or lord
Joro-goddess of the earth
kjerringa - Old Woman- the solid block in which the mast rested
Knarr- a merchant ship or a coastal vessel
Kyrtle-woven top
Ljoðhús- Lewis
Lochlannach – Irish for Northerners (Vikings)
Lough- Irish lake
Lundenburh/Lundenburgh- the walled burh built around the old Roman fort
Lundenwic - London
Mast fish- two large racks on a ship designed to store the mast when not required
Mockasin- Algonquin for moccasin
Midden- a place where they dumped human waste
Miklagård - Constantinople
Njörðr- God of the sea
Nithing- A man without honour (Saxon)
Odin- The "All Father" God of war, also associated with wisdom, poetry, and magic (The Ruler of the gods).
Onguiaahra- Niagara (It means the straits)
Orkneyjar-Orkney
Ran- Goddess of the sea
Roof rock- slate
Saami- the people who live in what is now Northern Norway/Sweden
Samhain- a Celtic festival of the dead between 31st October and 1st November (Halloween)
Scree- loose rocks in a glacial valley
Seax – short sword
Sennight- seven nights- a week

Sheerstrake- the uppermost strake in the hull
Sheet- a rope fastened to the lower corner of a sail
Shroud- a rope from the masthead to the hull amidships
Skræling -Barbarian
Skeggox – an axe with a shorter beard on one side of the blade
Skíð -the Isle of Skye
Skreið- stockfish (any fish which is preserved)
Smoky Bay- Reykjavik
Snekke- a small warship
Stad- Norse settlement
Stays- ropes running from the masthead to the bow
Strake- the wood on the side of a drekar
Suðreyjar – Southern Hebrides (Islay)
Syllingar Insula, Syllingar- Scilly Isles
Tarn- small lake (Norse)
The Norns- The three sisters who weave webs of intrigue for men
Thing-Norse for a parliament or a debate (Tynwald in the Isle of Man)
Thor's day- Thursday
Threttanessa- a drekar with 13 oars on each side.
Thrall- slave
Trenail- a round wooden peg used to secure strakes
Tynwald- the Parliament on the Isle of Man
Úlfarrberg- Helvellyn
Úlfarrland- Cumbria
Úlfarrston- Ulverston
Ullr-Norse God of Hunting
Ulfheonar-an elite Norse warrior who wore a wolf skin over his armour
Veisafjǫrðr – Wexford (Ireland)
Verðandi -the Norn who sees the future
Volva- a witch or healing woman in Norse culture
Waeclinga Straet- Watling Street (A5)
Walhaz -Norse for the Welsh (foreigners)
Waite- a Viking word for farm
Wapapyaki -Wampum

Withy- the mechanism connecting the steering board to the ship
Woden's day- Wednesday
Wulfhere-Old English for Wolf Army
Wyddfa-Snowdon
Wykinglo- Wicklow (Ireland)
Wyrd- Fate
Wyrme- Norse for Dragon
Yard- a timber from which the sail is suspended
Ynys Enlli- Bardsey Island
Ynys Môn-Anglesey

Historical Note

I use my vivid imagination to tell my stories. I am a writer and this book is very much a 'what if' sort of book. We now know that the Vikings reached further south in mainland America than we thought. Just how far is debatable. The evidence we have is from the sagas. Vinland was named after a fruit which could be brewed into wine was discovered. It does not necessarily mean grapes. King Harald Finehair did drive many Vikings west but I cannot believe that they would choose to live on a volcanic island if they thought there might be better lands to the south and west of them.

I have my clan reaching Newfoundland and sailing down the coast of Nova Scotia. The island I call Bear Island is Isle Au Haut off the Maine coast. Grey Fox island and (Horse) Deer Island can also be found there. The Indigenous people, the Mi'kmaq, inhabited the northeastern coast of America. In the summer they would migrate to the coast and in winter, when there were fewer flies, they would retreat back to the hinterland. The maps are how Erik might have mapped them. Butar's deer are caribou and the horse deer are moose. Both were native to the region.

For the voyage, I used the records of single-handed sailings and rowing of the Atlantic.

The Vikings were a complicated people. Forget movies where they wear horned helmets and spend all their time pillaging. They did pillage and they could be cruel but they were also traders and explorers. The discovery of Iceland and after that Greenland and America has been put down to the attempt by King Harald Finehair to create a Viking Empire. True Vikings never liked kings. Rather than be taxed they sought new lands. Iceland was empty and bare but they made it their home.

http://www.hurstwic.org/history/articles/daily_living/text/Demographics.htm is a good website with some interesting stats. In 1000 AD 75% of Vikings were under 50 and under 15s represented half! A boy was considered a fully-grown man by the time he was 16. A man could be a judge at the age of 12.

Helgi and Bergr were 10 and 12 when they avenged their father by killing his killer. We cannot imagine their world.

The compass I refer to was used in the Viking times. There is a Timewatch programme made by the BBC in which Robin Knox Johnston uses the compass to sail from Norway to Iceland. He was just half a mile out when he arrived.

On average, a Viking longship went about 5-10 knots (5.5 - 11 mph). Under very favourable conditions, they could reach 15 knots (17 mph). Therefore sailing during daylight they would cover between one hundred and one hundred and twenty miles. Sailing without stopping, under reefed sails, they would cover between one hundred and ten and one hundred and fifty miles.

A word about honey in the new world. One of my readers pointed out that the honeybee was not introduced into North America until the first Europeans came over. I found this hard to believe as honey is found on every other continent. I discovered that the Mayan's used honey from a stingless bee. I will continue, therefore, to allow Gytha to brew mead from honey and for my Vikings to use it for wounds. I am working on the principle that if the Mayans had it then another tribe might have been as resourceful!

I have had to use my imagination a great deal for I am writing about a time 600 years before the next Europeans visited the New World. The tribes who were found in North-eastern America would have evolved in that six hundred years. The landscape would, largely, be the same but the people would have different alliances, tribal areas and, perhaps, organization. I have used a dwarf deer in the story as there were such dwarf deer in the rest of the world. In south-east Asia, they continue to thrive but one species, Candiacervus, became extinct in Europe after the last Ice Age and when man was first colonising the northern lands. As I say, this is a what-if book- welcome to my mind!

I used the following books for research:

- Vikings- Life and Legends -British Museum
- Saxon, Norman and Viking by Terence Wise (Osprey)
- The Vikings (Osprey) -Ian Heath

- Byzantine Armies 668-1118 (Osprey)-Ian Heath
- Romano-Byzantine Armies 4th-9th Century (Osprey) -David Nicholle
- The Walls of Constantinople AD 324-1453 (Osprey) -Stephen Turnbull
- Viking Longship (Osprey) - Keith Durham
- The Vikings in England Anglo-Danish Project
- Anglo Saxon Thegn AD 449-1066- Mark Harrison (Osprey)
- Viking Hersir- 793-1066 AD - Mark Harrison (Osprey)
- Hadrian's Wall- David Breeze (English Heritage)
- National Geographic- March 2017
- Time Life Seafarers-The Vikings Robert Wernick

Griff Hosker
February 2020

Other books by Griff Hosker

If you enjoyed reading this book, then why not read another one by the author?

Ancient History

The Sword of Cartimandua Series
(Germania and Britannia 50 A.D. – 128 A.D.)
Ulpius Felix- Roman Warrior (prequel)
The Sword of Cartimandua
The Horse Warriors
Invasion Caledonia
Roman Retreat
Revolt of the Red Witch
Druid's Gold
Trajan's Hunters
The Last Frontier
Hero of Rome
Roman Hawk
Roman Treachery
Roman Wall
Roman Courage

The Wolf Warrior series
(Britain in the late 6th Century)
Saxon Dawn
Saxon Revenge
Saxon England
Saxon Blood
Saxon Slayer
Saxon Slaughter
Saxon Bane
Saxon Fall: Rise of the Warlord
Saxon Throne
Saxon Sword

The Bear and the Wolf

Medieval History

The Dragon Heart Series
Viking Slave
Viking Warrior
Viking Jarl
Viking Kingdom
Viking Wolf
Viking War
Viking Sword
Viking Wrath
Viking Raid
Viking Legend
Viking Vengeance
Viking Dragon
Viking Treasure
Viking Enemy
Viking Witch
Viking Blood
Viking Weregeld
Viking Storm
Viking Warband
Viking Shadow
Viking Legacy
Viking Clan
Viking Bravery

The Norman Genesis Series
Hrolf the Viking
Horseman
The Battle for a Home
Revenge of the Franks
The Land of the Northmen
Ragnvald Hrolfsson
Brothers in Blood
Lord of Rouen
Drekar in the Seine
Duke of Normandy
The Duke and the King

New World Series
Blood on the Blade
Across the Seas
The Savage Wilderness
The Bear and the Wolf

The Reconquista Chronicles
Castilian Knight

The Aelfraed Series
(Britain and Byzantium 1050 A.D. - 1085 A.D.)
Housecarl
Outlaw
Varangian

The Anarchy Series England 1120-1180
English Knight
Knight of the Empress
Northern Knight
Baron of the North
Earl
King Henry's Champion
The King is Dead
Warlord of the North
Enemy at the Gate
The Fallen Crown
Warlord's War
Kingmaker
Henry II
Crusader
The Welsh Marches
Irish War
Poisonous Plots
The Princes' Revolt
Earl Marshal

Border Knight

The Bear and the Wolf

1182-1300
Sword for Hire
Return of the Knight
Baron's War
Magna Carta
Welsh Wars
Henry III
The Bloody Border
Baron's Crusade
Sentinel of the North

Lord Edward's Archer
Lord Edward's Archer
King in Waiting

Struggle for a Crown
1360- 1485
Blood on the Crown
To Murder A King
The Throne
King Henry IV
The Road to Agincourt

Tales from the Sword

Modern History

The Napoleonic Horseman Series
Chasseur a Cheval
Napoleon's Guard
British Light Dragoon
Soldier Spy
1808: The Road to Coruña
Talavera
The Lines of Torres Vedras

The Lucky Jack American Civil War series
Rebel Raiders
Confederate Rangers

The Road to Gettysburg

The British Ace Series
1914
1915 Fokker Scourge
1916 Angels over the Somme
1917 Eagles Fall
1918 We will remember them
From Arctic Snow to Desert Sand
Wings over Persia

Combined Operations series
1940-1945
Commando
Raider
Behind Enemy Lines
Dieppe
Toehold in Europe
Sword Beach
Breakout
The Battle for Antwerp
King Tiger
Beyond the Rhine
Korea
Korean Winter

Other Books
Great Granny's Ghost (Aimed at 9-14-year-old young people)

For more information on all of the books then please visit the author's web site at www.griffhosker.com where there is a link to contact him or visit his Facebook page: GriffHosker at Sword Books